THE WITCHES
OF THE
CROSSWORLDS

BOOK II

HUNTER

The Witches of the Crossworlds
Book II
Hunter
Copyright © 2023 by Graham Anthony Davidson

ISBN: paperback 978-0-6459286-1-7
Second edition
First published 2019
Special thanks to all those who have contributed with their feedback
and support throughout the writing of these books.,

Published by Rack and Rune Publishing
rackandrune.com
email: info@rackandrune.com

For my children, Emily and Luke,
who taught me the meaning of fulfillment.

CHAPTER 1

Ferdinand raised his head when the kookaburras started laughing. Keen to know what the raucous was about, he leapt off Patsy's bed, raced out the door, down the stairs, then through the house until he reached the kitchen.

The aroma of crackling bacon made him almost forget his urgent mission to get outside. Then something extraordinary caught his attention. The cicadas were singing, now, at first light, during the cusp between autumn and winter. It took a while to make out their song, but the more he listened, the clearer it became: "She is here! She is here…"

Desperate to attract Cook's attention, he rubbed himself against her legs then looked up, letting out several short and insistent meows.

Maintaining focus on the eggs she was cracking into the cast iron frying pan, Cook told the cat, "You'll have to wait. I'll not let breakfast be ruined for your sake."

Ferdinand thought to himself, If only she would bother learning to listen like Patsy and her parents.

With the last of the eggs in the pan, the rosy-cheeked woman watched the ginger tomcat move toward the back door, each meow more urgent than the last.

"Okay, hold your horses." Wiping her hands on her apron, she made her way to the door, Ferdinand slipping through the gap as soon as it opened.

Cook stood in the open doorway, her breath turning to steam on contact with the crisp mountain air. She watched the cat race off toward the bushes at the bottom of the garden then stood still for a moment, puzzled as to why there were cicadas making such a racket when it was so cold outside.

·

Having worked his way through the bushes and down the bank to where the creek opened into a large pool, Ferdinand hid behind a small tea tree. A choir of fairies were circling a shimmering glow at the pool's centre. Like the cicadas, they were singing in harmony, "She is here! She is here…"

Then the singing stopped.

The fairies fled as the top of a woman's head broke the surface at the pool's centre. She had golden hair, crowned by a garland of daisies that appeared to look one way then another, as though searching for something. Her eyes were closed and she took measured strides toward the bank, rising further with each step.

Ferdinand backed away, concerned by something odd. No water dripped from her, nor were there any signs of moisture in her hair or on the loose white dress that rippled as though touched by a non-existent breeze.

She looked to be a few years older than Patsy, but not as old as the others in the household.

The young woman turned to him, then opened her eyes.

The cicadas called out, "Run, run, run..."

The cat turned to flee but found himself struggling, as though stuck in a sea of molasses.

A voice whispered in his head, *Do not run, Ferdinand. Stay by my side. Guide me. Tell me what I need to know.*

Ferdinand moved out from the bushes and sat on a sandstone step, part of the pathway Patsy's great-grandfather had laboured over when the family first immigrated from Ireland.

The cicadas screamed even louder, "Run, run, run..."

The young woman raised her arms to the side. Once they were level with her shoulders, she flicked her wrists downward.

The cicadas went silent.

The mist swirling above the pool and the rising sun created a backdrop of light beams as the young woman continued toward the bank. She was a vision of pre-Raphaelite splendour, dawn's warm light highlighting the simple gold-threaded girdle around the waist of her sleeveless white dress.

Her left foot emerged from the water and sank into the mud of the bank. Tiny violets sprang to life around it, blossoming in a multitude of colours, their rapid growth like a dance celebrating the essence of life.

She walked forward, flowers filling each of her footsteps, even as she walked along the solid surface of the sandstone path.

She reached where Ferdinand sat waiting and said, "Go now and bring them to me… but remember nothing of what you saw."

As the cat ran up the hill, the girl looked up at the trees, raised her arms and smiled. The cicadas renewed their song. "She is here! She is here…"

•

The roar of the cicadas jolted Patsy from her sleep.

Cicadas? At this time of year?

Fumbling in the dim light, her hands searched for the slippers she knew were under her bed. She crawled out of the cocoon created by her blankets and mattress, then lay on the floor, making sweeping motions with her arms to bring the slippers out of hiding. With the wayward slippers retrieved, she grabbed her dressing gown from the back of the door.

She ran into the corridor and headlong into her grandmother, Neridah, who grabbed her by the shoulders and whispered, "While we need to go see what's happening, can we do so without causing injury?"

"What do you think it is?"

"I suspect the portal has opened and something has come through. You, your mother and I need to go down together and see what's happening."

A male voice boomed over the top of Neridah's. "I'll be joining you on this reconnaissance, along with my flintlock and revolver." Patsy's father, Colin, was already dressed for riding, and his purposeful stride made each step reverberate like a hammer coming down on the floorboards. He was followed by Patsy's mother, Meredith. Like Patsy and Neridah, she wore her nightclothes and dressing gown.

Neridah grabbed Colin by the arm. Although many years his senior, circumstance had led to her appearing far younger. "If you take guns down there, you risk antagonising a delicate situation. The portal has realigned. We don't know anything about where and when it's aligned to."

Colin replied, "After what came through last time, I'm not taking chances, not until we know who the 'she' is that the cicadas are referring to."

Neridah rolled her eyes. "No, you need to let *us* see what's come through first." She turned and took Patsy's hand so they could go down the stairs together.

Meredith put a hand on her husband's arm. "Don't worry about my mother, you know what she's like."

"A stubborn old woman in a teenage body, that's all I see most days."

"Yes, I know what you mean, but I agree with her in this case. Please darling, just this once, listen to her and let us see what's there first. It's not like we can't look after ourselves."

Meredith let go of his arm and followed her mother and daughter, leaving Colin to contemplate whether he'd handled the situation in the best possible manner.

*

Cook looked up from her breakfast preparations as the three generations of Crossworld Witches entered the kitchen. "If you're looking for the cat, he's gone out and run down to the creek."

Meredith replied, "Thank you, Cook, we'll be back soon for breakfast."

Cook's cheeks glowed redder than usual and her breath became shorter. "Begging your pardon, ma'am, but shouldn't you have Master

Colin escort you down there… in case there's trouble afoot?"

Meredith frowned, turned away from Cook, and opened the door. She took a step back as Ferdinand raced inside.

The cat looked up at Patsy. "You need to hurry! You have to come meet her!"

Patsy squatted to give the cat a pat and asked, "Who is she?"

"She's here! You need to meet her!"

The cat ran back out the door, the witches following close behind. Cook called after them, "Breakfast will be ready in five minutes." After none of them acknowledged her she closed the door. A moment later, Colin entered the kitchen. "Will you be going after them, sir?"

He stared out the window. "Not just yet." He turned to Cook and asked, "Can you hear that?"

"The cicadas?"

"No, there's something else."

CHAPTER 2

The frost crunched underfoot as Patsy ran out the kitchen door and across the lawn with her mother and grandmother. After only a few strides her slippers were soaked through and her feet numbed with cold.

They were halfway to the bottom of the garden when the cicadas fell silent once more. Then the young woman emerged, climbing the steps leading up from the pool.

Patsy watched in awe at the trail of violets growing in her footsteps.

"Hello." The young woman's greeting startled Patsy. It was as though she'd somehow transported herself from being a good distance away to within a few feet of the three witches. "I'm Hunter."

Meredith stepped forward. "I'm Meredith." She gestured toward Patsy. "My daughter, Patricia, and my—"

"Why call her Patricia when she refers to herself as Patsy?"

Neridah stepped forward. "I'm Patricia's grandmother, and—"

"You look younger than your daughter. Why?"

"That's a long story that can wait till later."

"When can I meet Alfred?"

Neridah's eyes narrowed. "The Reverend Casey will be here when it's appropriate." She stood between Hunter and her family, putting her arms out slightly in a gesture to hold them back as though she were a kind of sentinel. "Where are you from?"

"Why does that matter?"

"If you want us to trust you, I need to know."

Hunter turned and looked toward the creek as she answered, "I'm from one of the other places. You call them 'crossworlds'."

"How do you know we call them that?"

"Your thoughts linger everywhere, speaking to me, especially near the door."

Neridah asked, "The door?"

"Yes, the one in the water. You call it a 'portal'? I believe that's what I heard in the memories floating above the pool's surface."

Neridah replied, "I'm very particular about cleaning up my memories, wherever they may be. And I was especially careful to ensure I'd removed them from around the portal."

Hunter tilted her head to one side. "Why?"

Meredith stepped forward and positioned herself close to her mother to create a barrier between Hunter and Patsy. She answered on her mother's behalf: "In case they attracted unwanted guests."

"Who?"

Neridah replied, "To begin with, there are the mind thieves. They take any piece of information they can find in their bid to control the wills of others. They already control many powerful people, but if they had access to *our* knowledge, this world would be in grave danger."

Meredith glared at her mother. Did she really need to share this information with a stranger?

"I know of these creatures you call 'mind thieves.' We call them 'Nasqa.' They are a nuisance. It's better to be rid of them altogether."

Patsy nudged her way through between her guardians. Knowing it would be futile to try to stop her, Neridah placed a protective hand on the girl's shoulder. Patsy asked, "What's your world like?"

Hunter looked at her and smiled. "It is much like this, except mine is ruled by those with the knowledge. My father is the leader of my world and many others." She cast her eyes across the three witches. "Why do you keep your powers hidden from those around you?"

Meredith replied on behalf of them all: "We seek not to rule, but to maintain order."

Hunter paused before responding. "So, you let the Nasqa do as they please?"

Patsy answered, "I don't, they're scared of me."

Hunter gave a gentle nod in acknowledgment and said, "I think they are wise to be scared of you."

Patsy blurted out, "I can see them better than anyone else." She cast a nervous glance toward her grandmother before looking down to avoid eye contact. *What a dumb thing to come out with,* she thought to herself.

"I can see you and I will be good friends, Patsy." Hunter turned her attention back to Neridah. Her words were cold and deadpan. "I want to meet Alfred."

"Why?"

"He fills your thoughts. He must be very special. Why aren't you together, when your thoughts are so entwined?"

Neridah frowned. "It's complicated."

Patsy couldn't help but tell Hunter what she knew of the Reverend's plans. "The Reverend will be coming to dinner tonight." She didn't notice the glare of disapproval from her grandmother. "Would you like to join us?"

Hunter smiled. "Yes, I would like that very much."

.

Colin said to Cook, "I could swear I heard Mrs Smith calling from outside."

Cook continued her preparations as she answered, "I'd rather not be talking of that woman."

"But did you hear her?"

Cook stopped and turned to face him. "Aye, or at least I thought so. I'd dismissed it as coming from my imagination… until knowing you'd heard it too."

"What did you hear?"

"It can't be her, sir. We've not seen her in almost a year."

Colin closed his eyes and took a deep breath. "Cook, just tell me what you heard."

"It sounded like a warning, sir." She looked to the ceiling as she tried to recall the words. "You cannot trust her."

"Hmm, I might have a look outside." Colin was halfway out the door when he stopped and added, "You may want to set an extra place at the table for breakfast. I suspect we'll be having a guest."

He pulled the door shut behind him and looked around the bushes. Sure enough, within two paces of the door, he found a large spider. "It's okay, Mrs Smith, you might as well reveal yourself."

Where the spider had been a moment ago, Colin now saw the aging fairy that was Mrs Smith.

Colin squatted and quietly asked her, "So, how about you tell me who it is that we shouldn't trust?"

"It feels wrong."

"But tell me, what is it that feels wrong, and why would I trust a warning that comes from the likes of you?"

"To be honest, I don't know who she is, but I know this: she's powerful. You shouldn't—"

She was gone.

Colin cursed her for disappearing mid-sentence, then stood up and made his way down the lawn to where the witches were talking to Hunter. On hearing her father's boots crunching on the frosty lawn, Patsy called out, "Father, Hunter said she can join us for dinner tonight when the Reverend Casey comes over."

He looked at Hunter's trail of violets as he replied, "I'm assuming your mother is happy with this?" He turned his gaze to Meredith for an answer. She, in turn, looked to Neridah, her mother's stern expression letting her know she'd need to find approval elsewhere.

Patsy asked, "Please, Mother, please say it's okay for her to join us."

Meredith placed a hand on Patsy's shoulder, then turned to face Hunter. As Hunter's smile grew, Meredith's indecision vanished. "Yes, of course she can." She turned to Hunter. "We'd love to know more about you." Then, she gestured toward Colin. "This is my husband, Colin."

Hunter took a step toward him. "I'm Hunter."

"Well, Hunter, I'm pleased to meet you. Tell me, the violets, are you able to stop them growing in your footsteps?"

"Why would I do that?"

Colin smiled, feeling disarmed by the innocence of her question. "To be discrete. If you're to join us for dinner, none of our servants or guests should know you have powers."

"You don't have the knowledge."

The bluntness of her comment made Colin bite his tongue and wait a moment to calm himself before replying. "No, I don't, but Meredith and I have long had an understanding about such things. Our servants might fear 'the knowledge' as you call it." By the time he'd finished his answer, any sense of irritation had not only passed but had been forgotten.

"I can make it stop for a time, but I will have to release the build-up later in the evening."

"How?"

A wide smile grew across Hunter's face. "I will come out here and dance."

Despite her charm, Colin was firm. "Perhaps you can go back to your own world and release it there? I don't know that it's fitting for you to stay beyond dinner."

"But I wish to stay for a few days. There's much that your family and I can learn from each other. When I go back, I'd like you all to come with me and meet my father."

"We'll discuss the possibility of that later. For now, I'll invite you to join us for breakfast. I've already told Cook to prepare another setting at the table." He turned to Patsy. "Patricia, can you escort Hunter up to the house? The rest of us will join you in a few minutes."

Patsy gave him a hug. "Thank you, Father."

As Patsy took Hunter's hand and started up the hill, Colin called after them, "It would be best not to arouse Cook's fears with the violets either. She's already on edge today."

Neridah grabbed Colin's arm and waited till she was sure Hunter was out of earshot before whispering, "I don't trust her."

Colin nodded. "Mrs Smith expressed misgivings as well, then vanished mid-sentence."

Meredith took his other arm, encouraging him to start slowly up the hill. "She deserves the benefit of the doubt for now. Patricia's already taken a shine to her."

Neridah retorted through clenched teeth, "We know nothing about this young woman, and you've already invited her into our home. If Mrs Smith warned you—"

Colin snapped, "I don't know that a warning from Mrs Smith is sufficient reason to distrust someone outright. However, I must concede, the nature of how she vanished while passing on her warning is disturbing to say the least. I will make a decision about the girl after we talk to her over breakfast."

Neridah released her son-in-law's arm, raising her hands in the air to free some of her frustration. "Am I the only one in this family who sees something wrong here? And since when was it up to you and you alone to make such decisions?"

Walking up the hill, arm in arm with Meredith, Colin replied without turning to face his mother-in-law. "It became my right to make such decisions the day Meredith and I took our vows. I will trust the girl until she gives me reason not to, as I do with everyone who comes to this property."

Neridah replied, uncaring as to whether or not her words were heard, "My daughter may have done so, but I never made a vow to honour and obey you. Mark my words, one day society's attitude will change, and marriage will be seen the way it should be... as an equal partnership. Who knows, men like yourself may one day even learn to respect their elders, whatever their gender." Neridah looked to the ground and lifted her gown slightly as she prepared to walk up the hill. How was the danger of taking the girl into their home not as obvious to the others as it was to her?

Then, something drew her attention.

Was that rotting vegetation she could smell?

She looked back at the path of violets and noticed something odd. As the violets grew, the nearby grass wilted. Determined to point this out to the others, she started after them.

As soon as she'd turned her back on the violets, all memory of what she'd just observed was gone. She headed up the hill, knowing there was something she'd wanted to say. By the time she was halfway there, all she could think of was her eagerness for breakfast.

.

Patsy laughed as she and Hunter burst through the kitchen door. They took Cook by surprise and almost knocked the tray with its plates of bacon and eggs out of her hands. "Oops! Sorry, Cook."

"Heaven forbid!" Cook put the tray down on a sideboard and made a show of placing a hand over her heart. "You know better than to come barging through like that, particularly with a guest... a guest you should rightly be bringing into the house through the front door rather than my kitchen."

"Oh, but Cook, you simply must meet Hunter."

Hunter looked at Cook and smiled. "Hello."

Cook made a subtle nodding gesture. "Hello, Miss Hunter, I'm pleased to make your acquaintance."

"Are you?" Hunter giggled, as though someone had told a joke. "Why?"

Cook ignored the question, picked up her tray, and headed toward the dining room. She glanced over her shoulder and said, "I'd be pleased if you can take your seats at the table. Breakfast is being served now."

Patsy turned to Hunter. "I like Cook ever so much. Do you like Cook?"

Hunter shrugged her shoulders. "She has no knowledge."

"Oh! No! That's not true! Cook knows lots of things, that's what I love about her."

As the two of them made their way to the dining room, Hunter asked, "What sort of things does she know?"

"Well, to begin with, she knows that sometimes, if you want the things that make you happy, you have to do other things that you don't want to." Patsy led Hunter to their seats at the highly polished red cedar table. She pulled back a chair for Hunter. "You can sit here."

Hunter ran a finger along the ornate carving on the chair before asking, "I don't understand, why would you do something you don't want to?"

Patsy laughed, then said, "Oh, come on." She sat down and patted the seat of Hunter's chair, encouraging her to sit as well. "We *all* do things we don't want to sometimes. I don't like taking a bath, but I like it when I feel warm and clean afterward."

Hunter took her seat and smiled. "You can feel that way without taking a bath... I can show you how."

Conscious of not wanting to be overheard by Cook, Patsy whispered in Hunter's ear. "I already know how to do that, but Mother says that it's best to do things without magic when you can. She says it gives your power more meaning when you use it."

The sound of Colin's boots on the floorboards in the kitchen heralded the others' arrival. He entered the room then turned to Cook and said, "Cook, you can spend the rest of the morning as you please. We'll take our own plates to the kitchen once we've finished."

"Very good, sir. I'll return and tend to the dishes before lunch."

Once Cook had left, Colin addressed the table. "Well, it's our great pleasure to host a visitor from another world! Welcome, Hunter, may your visit prove fruitful to us all."

Hunter's eyes stared in the direction of her plate, but she seemed oblivious to its contents. She spoke as though the two girls were the only ones in the room. "I don't understand. Why is it your father who speaks instead of the most powerful of you?"

Patsy's jaw dropped. She shook her head and said, "This is my father's property."

Hunter stared at her. "But he has so little knowledge, so little power."

"He has lots of power; it's just different to yours and mine. And he's very good at listening. He understands the cicadas and some of the animals too."

"He discourages your mother from using her knowledge."

Feeling the impolite nature of the girls' conversation had gone far enough, Meredith interrupted. "No, he doesn't. Patricia's father has always supported me doing as I wish, and I love him for that."

Glaring at their guest, Colin grabbed hold of Meredith's arm to keep her from continuing. "I must say, having overheard your commentary, I find your attitude rather, shall we say... confronting. But I understand that where you come from, the concept of what's normal is obviously different from ours." He released his wife's arm and put some bacon on his fork. "I'm curious to know more about where you come from."

Hunter smiled. "Would you like to visit my world? Then you and your family could meet my father."

Colin chewed his bacon, savouring the flavour before he swallowed. Everyone at the table watched in anticipation as he had a sip of his tea before answering. "I think such arrangements might be a little premature at this stage."

Hunter's smile grew broader, almost to the point of breaking out in laughter. "I think you'd like him." She paused for a moment then asked, "Can I let my violets grow now that the cook has gone?"

"Oh, no!" Meredith replied. She wiped the edge of her mouth with a serviette before explaining. "We try to keep all evidence of our magic to a minimum, especially indoors."

Hunter cast her eyes downward. "This is so hard for me to understand. In my world, if we can do what needs doing using the knowledge, then we do so. Magic then feeds on magic. Where I live, there is no physical labour. People think of what needs to be done, then those with the knowledge make it reality."

Neridah, seated directly across from Hunter, spoke for the first time since they'd sat at the table. "You do understand that using magic comes at a price, don't you? If you use magic in one place, its power comes from another. As a group, we're already deeply indebted to other worlds for the power we've used."

Hunter's eyes narrowed. "So, this bothers you?"

"Yes, it bothers me. It bothers me that I don't know which worlds my powers have been drawn from. It bothers me that by saving lives in this world, it may have cost lives in others." Neridah paused, waiting for support that never came. She picked up her knife and fork. "Perhaps I'm better off just concerning myself with breakfast."

Meredith asked, "How old are you, Hunter?"

"I lost track many years ago."

"Do you have memories of being a little girl?"

She laughed. "Yes, there was a time when I did little more than play. My father says you learn a great deal from play. Yet I enjoy life more since I've been older. The more you know, the more interesting it is talking to people."

As he cut another piece of bacon, Colin asked, "So, you like learning from the people you meet?"

"Sometimes people will tell me things I don't know, and I enjoy that. It doesn't happen often though."

Patsy grinned. "I think there's lots I can tell you that you don't know."

Hunter smiled. "I'm sure there is. Perhaps there are things I can tell you as well." She turned and looked at Neridah. "I look forward to listening to Alfred's stories too."

Neridah frowned. "Why are you so interested in the Reverend?"

"It's rare for men to acquire the knowledge. My father has it, but he is one of the few in my world."

Patsy touched Hunter's arm, seeking her attention. "My great-grandfather was a powerful druid priest." She turned to Neridah. "Wasn't he, Nana-Neri?"

"Yes, he certainly was." Neridah pushed away her plate, having eaten only a few mouthfuls. Everyone cringed at the sound of her chair scraping on the floorboards when she pushed it back and rose to her feet. She looked at Colin, wearing a cynical smile. "If you'll excuse me, I have matters to attend to." She turned and left the room.

Hunter turned to Patsy and said, "I like your grandmother."

Patsy struggled to hide a naughty giggle as she replied, "I don't think she likes you much though."

Hunter tilted her head slightly and looked up before bringing her eyes back to Patsy. "I don't understand. Why?"

Colin sipped on his tea then replied on his daughter's behalf. "Hunter, based on what you've told us, your life is considerably longer than ours. Because our lives are so short, compared to yours, emotion plays a greater role in our choices. While you may be able to dwell on decisions for years, like whether or not to trust someone, our time is somewhat more limited."

Meredith cut him off. "Darling, is it really wise to make such assumptions? Are Hunter's years the same duration as our own? Maybe her age isn't that different from a teenager in our own world. There's so much we need to learn before jumping to conclusions."

She could see by Colin's expression that he didn't agree. An uncomfortable silence hung over the table till he stood up. "I have preparations to attend to before the Magistrate arrives."

His passage toward the door came to a halt when Hunter asked, "Why are you so concerned about the Magistrate?"

He clenched his fists and almost began to reply, then thought better of it and left the room.

•

The Reverend Alfred Casey shivered at first as he strode into the icy-cold swimming hole and made his way to the waterfall that fed it.

There were many things in life that made him feel blessed, but few more so than having his home and church right next to such a majestic location.

Once he'd made his way far enough into the pool, he dived under, then pushed up from the bottom and let out a cry of joy as he broke the surface. He'd done this every morning since he'd discovered this spot within days of his arrival at the small church just out of Pulpit's Hill. He let himself drift under the falls and closed his eyes as he soaked up the sensation of the frigid water coming down on him.

A small voice snapped him back to reality. "Hey, shouldn't you make sure you're alone when you have your bath?"

"Bandah! Of all the times to stop by. We've not seen each other for months, and you choose now? You've known for years of my morning rituals."

The pixie laughed as he fluttered in the air just clear of the falling water. "Trust me, old friend, I would've much preferred to wait till you were through, but someone's come through the portal, and she's already throwing reality out of balance."

"I promised Neridah I'd be there for dinner this evening."

"You can't go earlier?"

"No, I've a funeral to perform this morning. And Colin has already informed me that he'll be receiving the Magistrate before lunch."

"In that case, I'll head over there on my own and keep a low profile while I learn what I can."

"Thank you, my friend." As the pixie flew off, the Reverend Casey let his head sink below the surface.

CHAPTER 3

With breakfast finished Patsy asked her mother, "Can I show Hunter the stables now?"

"As long as you make your bed first."

"Can't one of the servants do that for me? Just this once?"

"Patricia, you know my feelings on this matter. I'm sure Hunter will be happy to wait here for you, then you can show her the stables and find ways to keep yourselves entertained until lunchtime."

Patsy rolled her eyes then looked at Hunter. "I promise I'll just be a minute." She dragged her feet as she left the room, making the promise appear somewhat unrealistic.

Meredith turned to Hunter. "I hope you don't mind, I have matters I must attend to. Will you be fine on your own until Patricia returns?"

"Yes, I'm quite happy to sit and wait. I like Patsy. I like you too."

"I'm glad to hear it." Meredith's smile dissolved as she turned to leave the room. She was uncertain about leaving Hunter on her own, but there were matters she wanted to discuss with her husband before the Magistrate arrived. More importantly, she wanted to consult the Book of Wisdom regarding their new guest.

Within seconds of Meredith's departure, Hunter looked to where Bandah was peering through the window. She reached out with her hand then pulled back, dragging Bandah through the window and onto the table as if she'd lassoed him.

Although taken by surprise, the pixie felt no sense of fear. He wasted no time getting to the point. "Who are you, and why are you here?"

Hunter leaned forward and smiled. "A pixie! How cute." She flicked a finger in his direction and Bandah vanished, much the same as Mrs Smith had done earlier.

*

Meredith walked out the front door to join her mother and husband.

Neridah was in full flight. "I don't trust her."

Colin replied, "Don't you think you're being a little harsh?" He looked away momentarily before continuing. "Look, she may come across as rude and arrogant, but she's from a different world. We don't know what's considered polite where she comes from."

Meredith squinted as she walked out into the bright sunlight then took hold of Colin's arm. "Colin's right, Mother. She was quite sweet a moment ago, telling me she likes Patsy, and me as well."

Neridah turned to her daughter. "You left her alone in there? How could you be so naive? Colin should be firm and let her know she's not welcome. Then when she leaves, we need to do whatever it takes to realign the portal. The longer she stays, the harder it will be to be rid of her."

She tensed when Colin placed a reassuring hand on her shoulder. "Let's just try to stay calm for a while. No doubt Bandah will turn up later with Alfred. There's every chance the pixies may be familiar with her, and her world. I'll be very interested to hear what his thoughts are. Then, if collectively we have concerns, we can ask her to leave."

"It'll be too late by then. We need to make her leave as soon as possible."

"Any minute now we've got a magistrate arriving from Sydney with intentions to force us into parting with a good deal of the property. I'm not prepared to let this issue interfere with what will be a delicate situation. We'll consider our position on Hunter after dinner this evening. Until then, the matter is over."

Neridah brushed his hand off her shoulder. "Don't patronise me." She turned and stormed off into the house, leaving Colin shaking his head.

He glanced across at his wife and grumbled, "I swear, if we don't find alternative accommodation for your mother, I'll lose my temper with her one of these days."

"Oh really? So, you haven't already lost your temper with her on an almost daily basis?"

Colin stared at the empty space where his mother-in-law had been. "She just won't listen."

"Would it be different if she appeared as old as her years? She spent all of four decades deprived of her liberty, unable to move for all that time. Can you blame her for being apprehensive?"

As Meredith spoke, Colin nodded his head and closed his eyes. He'd heard this argument so many times that he expected it now whenever he raised objections to Neridah's behaviour. "That doesn't excuse her talking down to me in my own home."

"She grew up here, Colin. It's only your home now because you and I are married. She'd never even met you before she was taken captive."

Colin opened his mouth to respond but was distracted by the sound of a neighing horse heralding the approach of a sulky. "It seems the Magistrate's arrived early."

*

Bandah was flung out of this world and into the void between worlds with an ease that took him by surprise. He moved as close as he could to the boundary, allowing him to view a shimmering vestige of reality.

This was not a good place to be. Before fully leaving one world, it was important to have a foot firmly placed in another. While pixies were adept at jumping between the crossworlds without reliance on portals, they had little knowledge of how to escape from the void.

He was trying to focus on the hazy image of Hunter walking away when he heard a voice. "Of all the living creatures between Heaven and Hell, it has to be you that I'm stuck with."

He turned and asked, "Mrs Smith?"

"Wonderful, isn't it? Here we are, stuck in a state of limbo where we'll never age. We'll be getting to spend the rest of eternity trying to learn to get on with each other."

The pixie stared at her. "You have a knack for making things seem even worse than they are."

Mrs Smith approached the boundary, staring at the house as she replied, "Could it get much worse than this?"

"There is still a way out you know."

"Not one within our control."

Bandah nodded in acknowledgment. "I know that, but it's still possible."

Mrs Smith turned to him and asked, "What, you think someone's going to just wander up, knowing we're here, then reach in and grab us?"

"That's the basis of what I had in mind."

"They can't hear or see us!" Mrs Smith exclaimed. "I know of no being that can sense what lies in the void between worlds."

"Alfred will hear me."

"Oh?" She rolled her eyes and laughed. "And what makes him so special that he'll hear you?"

"We have a strong and unique connection."

"How can you believe such a thing when you've known the man for little more than a half-century?"

"I trust him like no one I've ever known. More than even my fellow pixies."

"Well then, won't you be disappointed when he ignores your cries for help."

．

Patsy broke into a run as she led Hunter to the stables. She looked over her shoulder. "I'll bet you can't keep up."

Hunter smiled, then lifted her dress and laughed as she tried to match Patsy's pace. Having been suppressed since she'd entered the homestead, a flurry of violets spread from each footfall. Hunter placed a hand over her lips. "Oops, sorry, I forgot to stifle the flowers." She came to a stop. "I've betrayed my word."

Patsy replied. "I don't think you have. It hasn't happened indoors, and they look beautiful."

Hunter giggled behind her hand and started running with Patsy once more. Patsy felt that, despite her age and powers, Hunter wasn't used to being able to be so carefree.

When they arrived at the stables, Patsy called out, "Darcy?" She looked around but couldn't see the young stablehand anywhere. "It doesn't matter, I know most of the horses well enough to introduce you." She walked up to the first stall. "This one's called Milly. She's the oldest and she's the mother of most of the other horses in the stables."

As Hunter approached the stall, Milly came forward and threw her head out, seeking attention. Hunter reached out to her saying, "Hello Milly, I've not met a creature of your kind before, although I've met countless others who are made beasts of burden." She placed her arms around Milly's neck in an embrace.

Patsy responded, "Oh, but Milly's not a beast of burden. She's quite happy."

"Then why isn't she set free, to roam as she would please?"

"If we did that, she might run off, or be stolen by a bushranger."

"I don't understand. You can hear all the creatures, but you don't always listen. Her thoughts tell me that's what she wants… to run free. Can't you hear them?"

"I hear her happiness when she whinnies with joy at being fed… or when I enter her stall to join Darcy as he rubs her down."

Hunter looked down at the ground, disappointed that Patsy didn't understand. "You talk to the cat, you listen to insects. But you don't bother to listen to their deepest thoughts-- they tell an altogether different story. Those with the knowledge are able to listen to each other's thoughts instinctively … that's why we understand each other despite growing up speaking different tongues. How can you believe you understand them when you don't delve deeper into their feelings?"

"Nana-Neri says that's a line we should never cross."

"Why?"

"Because that's what it says in the Book of Wisdom."

Hunter opened the door to Milly's stall as she asked, "Why would you do what a book tells you to do? I think it would be better to let Milly have control over whether she comes or goes."

Patsy drew in a deep breath. "I don't think that's a good idea."

"She won't leave. She likes it here. But she wants the door open."

"I don't think you under—"

Patsy was interrupted by Darcy calling out, "Hey! What are you doing?" The stablehand was leading the Magistrate's horse into the stables to give it food and water, preparing it for the long journey back to Sydney. When Hunter turned and faced the stallion Darcy was leading it panicked, rearing up and throwing the young man off balance.

Hunter threw up an arm, causing both Darcy and the horse to be frozen in time.

Patsy's jaw dropped. She turned and saw that Milly and the other horses seemed unaffected. "How did you...?"

Hunter was already moving toward the stallion. "I'll explain after. This beast is controlled by Nasqa." As Hunter got closer to the stallion, it showed signs of recognition but was held too tight in the time freeze to do anything of consequence. "We only have a few more seconds before it breaks free. Watch, and I'll show you how to deal with what you call a mind thief."

The horse was starting to show signs of struggled movement by the time Hunter was upon it. Without hesitation, she reached into its head, as though reaching into a bowl of liquid, and began to pull back. At first, whatever she was pulling at seemed to fight back, dragging her for a moment closer to the beast. It appeared the struggle would be sustained indefinitely, then Hunter pulled back hard, and a shadow that vaguely resembled a horse was dragged out and fell at her feet. The shadow rose up from the ground in an abstract form and appeared to beg for mercy. None was shown. The daisies that made up Hunter's garland broke away and leapt upon it, taking on animal-like characteristics. They tore the shadow apart and devoured it as though it were a favourite meal. One of the daisies burped before they all elegantly drifted back into place as part of Hunter's dancing garland.

Patsy was shocked. "You've killed it!"

"No, the parts of it still live, but not in this world."

"I don't understand. Mother and Nana-Neri say we can free people from being possessed by these creatures, but even the pixies don't know of ways to do what you've just done. Your flowers tore it apart. How can it not have been killed by your actions?"

Hunter looked toward the ground at Patsy's feet and smiled, as though Patsy's concerns were of no consequence. "Its parts are now strewn across the voids that separate the worlds. Sent to places where they can do no harm. Each part will remain aware for as long as it survives and have time to contemplate its actions."

Patsy returned the smile, but within herself she held back a feeling of discomfort. Something in her heart told her it was important to keep this feeling from rising to the surface.

For the first time since meeting Hunter, Patsy felt uneasy about her newfound friend. Looking at Darcy, she worried that the stablehand and stallion remained frozen in time, while all other life seemed to move on regardless. As if to reinforce the point, a kookaburra swooped from a tree outside the stables and grabbed a baby brown snake. Neridah had told her the Book of Wisdom explained how to do such things as time freezes, but that it was better avoided, as the consequences could be severe.

Hunter turned to Patsy. "Tell me more about this Book of Wisdom you just thought of again."

Patsy snapped back, "It's rude to read people's thoughts."

Hunter smiled then let out a little giggle, as though Patsy's retort was silly. "Is that what your grandmother tells you?"

"I don't need anyone to tell me that. It's pretty obvious, don't you think? Don't you prefer that your thoughts are private?"

"I'm happy to share my thoughts with you." She let out another laugh. "Or anyone else for that matter."

Patsy thought to herself, *I don't believe you.*

Hunter cast an angry glare in her direction. She hesitated for a moment, then, turning her attention back to Darcy and the horse, flicked her wrist. They came back to life. Darcy tipped his flat cap in a sign of respect before asking in a sing-song Irish accent, "Hey, Pats, who's your friend?"

Patsy smiled at the fourteen-year-old boy. She found herself wondering why she couldn't remember seeing him enter the stables. In fact, she struggled even to remember Hunter and herself arriving. Somehow, that seemed of little importance right now. She was always happy to see Darcy. There were few children or teenagers that she had the chance to meet, and she had enjoyed Darcy's company since he and his father had started working for the McIntyre family the week after her last crossworld encounter. "Hi, Darcy, her name's Hunter. She only arrived this morning."

Darcy couldn't help but stare at Hunter. He'd never seen such a beautiful young woman. "Hello, Miss Hunter." He extended his hand. "The name's Darcy, Darcy O'Sullivan."

Sensing his admiration, she adopted a coy expression and, knowing that he'd be unable to understand her without having the knowledge of how to listen, she replied in her native tongue, "Mouwn-kancher gainna-onger yonter." She smiled. "Mouwn-trember mouwn-limbray sauwn-dintar."

Darcy stood as if mesmerised. He removed his hat and ran a hand through his thick red curls. "I've not heard such a language before." He turned to Patsy. "I heard many languages when I travelled here from Ireland, but nothing remotely like your friend Hunter speaks. Do you know what she was saying?"

"She says she arrived a short while ago." Patsy giggled. "And, she says she might grow to like you.'

Hunter feigned embarrassment and waited a moment before turning to Patsy. "Nasqa! Sauwn-drendy ga abessee."

Patsy looked up at Darcy. "I'm sorry, we'll have to come back later. Hunter just heard Father calling."

"Oh, are you sure about that? When I left him just now he was having what seemed to be a serious talk with the Magistrate."

Hunter sent Patsy a thought. *We need to hurry.*

Patsy turned to Darcy as they started to make their way out of the stable. The memory of what Hunter had done to the Nasqa possessing the horse flooded back. If there were mind thieves, or Nasqa as Hunter called them, threatening the family home, then it was important to act. "We'll come back later, I promise."

Darcy called out, "I'll be looking forward to it."

*

Bandah followed Patsy and Hunter as they headed toward the stables.

Mrs Smith called after him, "What on Earth do you hope to achieve by following those two?"

"I want to learn whatever I can about this young woman."

"Fat load of good that'll do you. Mark my words, if that one senses you're watching her, she's liable to reach in here and grab you, then hurl you somewhere even worse."

The pixie looked over his shoulder and called out as he continued, "That's a risk I'm prepared to take."

The rotund fairy that was Mrs Smith got to her feet, cursing the pain that exploded in her knees. If only she'd been able to transform back to her fairy state before the arthritis had set in. She mumbled, "I don't believe I'm doing this." She leaned forward and beat her wings, lifting into the air as she called out, "If you're going to insist on this fool's errand, you'll be better off accompanied by someone with a bit of common sense."

Bandah paused in mid-air to allow her to catch up. "Could this mean that you've found a conscience lurking somewhere within yourself?"

"I'd just rather not spend eternity feeling responsible for your demise because of letting you run off on your own."

"Why, that almost sounds like you care."

"Hmmph."

They continued in silence until they reached the stables. Mrs Smith asked, "Can you hear them?"

He was struggling to focus on the hazy image of Patsy and Hunter at Milly's stall. "It's even harder to hear than it is to see. Their words are mixed with their thoughts, and I can't make out what Hunter's saying at all... her thoughts aren't making sense to me." He was startled when Mrs Smith placed a hand on his shoulder, turning him to face the stable entrance.

"Look at this. She's done a partial time freeze."

Bandah stared in disbelief at the sight of Darcy and the horse standing frozen in time. The nature of the time freeze made their images become clearer in the void. If the freeze was held for long enough, they'd start to become visible in adjacent crossworlds as well. "Can you see it? Can you see the shadow?"

"It's not, is it?" Mrs Smith asked.

"It's hard to say for sure from here, but I'm pretty sure it is. That's the Magistrate's horse. And if his horse is controlled by a mind thief, it's a sure bet that he is too."

"I can't see that it matters a great deal, and there's certainly nothing we can do about it from here."

Bandah shook his head. "Just when I begin to think there's hope for you—" He stopped mid-sentence when Hunter took him by surprise, looking down at him and smiling. "How can she know where we are?"

"I think there's a lot more we're going to discover that this young lady's capable of."

Bandah looked at her. "Young lady? Are you sure you're not letting your human experience affect your judgment?"

"I swear she's no more than a thousand or so years old."

"Yet she took us both by surprise when she threw us into this void."

"Aye, that she did." As she spoke, Hunter approached the Magistrate's horse and reached into it. "And I think we may have more surprises to come."

Bandah flew closer to see what was happening. His jaw dropped at the sight of the daisies tearing the mind thief apart. "No sentient being deserves this."

Mrs Smith scoffed. "Don't be so silly, it happens in the insect world all the time."

Before Bandah had the chance to reply, he was forced to leap aside as a fragment of the mind thief came through the barrier between worlds and into the void. "Whoa!"

Mrs Smith and the pixie watched in horror as more fragments entered the void. Some passed straight through and went elsewhere, while others landed at their feet or nearby. They backed away as the mind thief fragments started coming together. Bandah couldn't help but look up when Hunter's thoughts spoke to him. *Here's a little gift for you, pixie.* Her smile added to the insult.

Bandah stood as tall as his five-centimetre height would allow. "Again I ask, why are you here?"

Hunter looked away and ignored him as though he hadn't been heard. Mrs Smith sought to bring his attention back to their present predicament. "You might do well to watch what's happening here." Bandah took another step back as he watched the mind thief fragments coalesce, like mercury drifting together, barely audible screams of agony coming from each fragment.

Bandah turned to Mrs Smith. "I don't like the look of this."

Although the fairy was twice his height, she chose to take cover behind him. "You pixies have always been clever at dealing with these creatures. Do something."

CHAPTER 4

D arcy saw the Magistrate approaching and, knowing that Colin would want the horse to be given food and water, walked across from the stables. The Magistrate ignored him, coughing as he struggled to alight from his sulky.

Meredith whispered in her husband's ear, "Shouldn't you offer to help?"

Colin answered her with a cold stare, then stepped forward and turned his attention to the Magistrate, reaching out to offer a hand only when he saw the Magistrate no longer needed one. "Justice Johnson, welcome. I hope your journey from Parramatta was a smooth one."

"Spare me the platitudes, McIntyre. You know what that road's like, and I'm not here for pleasantries."

Colin said, "Perhaps the steam train would have been a better option?

I could have arranged for someone to meet you at the railway station."

"Hmph! I'm not inclined to trust those stinking metal contraptions. Spend half a day choking on coal dust and smoke while your bones are rattling along? I'll use a more natural mode of transportation, thank you very much." He looked across at Darcy. "You, boy, get my bags off this infernal buggy then tend to my horse's needs."

Darcy looked at Colin for approval, waiting for the gentle nod to come from his employer before following the Magistrate's bidding. Meredith gripped Colin's arm as she watched the drooling, obese form in front of her pull a dirty handkerchief from the pocket of his black coat to mop some of the sweat from his brow. His jowls trembled as he addressed Colin while his eyes drifted to leer at her. "What's she doing here? We have business to discuss."

Meredith took her husband by surprise. "My grandfather established this property and worked hard to make it what he passed on. I have every right to be present while its future is discussed."

Still leering, the Magistrate barked, "Nonsense! How about you make yourself useful, woman, and get me a brandy?"

Colin closed his eyes for a moment and sought to calm himself. Striking a magistrate, even one as foul as the Justice Johnson, would not help their situation. "Your Honour, while I appreciate that you are here to discuss business, both our interests will be better served if you refrain from speaking to my wife in such a manner. While I respect the fact that the decisions and agreements to be made will be between you and me, my wife has every right to be privy to such matters, and I'll not have you speak to her as though she were a common servant."

Having placed the Magistrate's bags by the man's side, Darcy set about freeing the horse from its constraints and taking it to the stables. The Magistrate turned away to cough before replying, "Hah!

What use is a wife if she doesn't behave as a servant who also bears your children?"

Meredith released her husband's arm. "Darling, I think it might serve our purposes better if I join Mother inside after all. I trust you'll do the best you can for the family."

Colin gave her hand a gentle squeeze before she offered an awkward smile and walked away. The Magistrate called after her, "Know this, woman. He'll do as I bid, or else I'll be taking it all."

Colin spoke through clenched teeth. "I'll have you know that I have friends on the Legislative Council."

"As do I, McIntyre. On top of that, I have an understanding with Governor Pritchard, one that allows me to do as I please with land throughout the Blue Mountains that has previously been claimed by squatters such as your good wife's grandfather." He turned his attention back to Meredith and mopped some spittle from the corners of his mouth as he watched her retreat to the house. "She's feisty, that one. You'd do well to teach her some manners."

Colin's fists tightened so much the knuckles were white. He struggled to maintain control. "You said you came here to discuss business. I'd prefer we restrict our conversation accordingly."

"Hmph, very well then. Help me with my bags and we'll adjourn to your library so you can sign over your pastoral lands. I trust you've organised appropriate lodging for me for this evening. I've no desire to make that dreadful journey twice in one day."

The prolonged silence that followed was broken by a magpie's song, its beautiful melody providing a stark contrast to the tension of their conversation. Colin took a deep breath. "There's a hotel in Blackheath that I'm sure you'll find more welcoming."

"You'll no doubt reconsider that when you appreciate the reality of your circumstance. Now, pick up my bags and we'll get into the warmth of your home where we'll see if your hospitality makes you worthy of remaining as a tenant on what will soon become my lands."

"My understanding was that we're discussing only the pastoral areas of the property."

"That was before you suggested I should find lodgings elsewhere. You'll find me a fair man to those who treat me with due respect. Now, pick up my bags, man!"

Colin could feel the blood pulsing through his temples. He wanted to say, *Pick up your own god-damned bags.* Instead, he swallowed his pride and picked up the Magistrate's bags. As they entered the house, Colin wondered how much longer he could withhold his rage.

*

Bandah and Mrs Smith watched on as the fragments of the mind thief came together.

Mrs Smith mumbled, "I really don't like this."

Bandah replied, "Let's just wait and see what happens. It's not like there's anywhere for us to go and seek cover."

The mind thief started to develop a form, one that included what could vaguely be perceived as a kind of orifice, or maybe even a mouth. Mrs Smith grabbed hold of Bandah's arm when it spoke, the words sounding more like different tones of whistling wind than spoken language. "Mosh-ko klon-ar?"

It made for a pitiful sight, seeing Mrs Smith hiding behind a pixie half her size. She dug her fingernails into his arm. "Can you make out what it's saying?"

Bandah was surprised. "You can't?"

"During those dreadful years in human form, it wasn't just my body that deteriorated. My memory of what I'd learned over the millennia paid a hefty price as well."

The mind thief fragment repeated its question, this time with greater urgency. "Mosh-ko klon-ar?"

Bandah looked at the grovelling shadow, then back to Mrs Smith's puzzled expression. He almost felt sympathy for the woman. If she was suffering from some form of dementia, she'd done a good job of hiding it till now. "It's pleading for help."

Mrs Smith released her grip on the pixie ever so slightly. "What do you mean?"

"I mean what I said... it's asking us for help. Mosh-ko klon-ar... it means, *can you help me?*"

"We can't trust it! It's a mind thief!"

He broke free of her grip. "Right now, we need all the friends we can get."

"But it's just a shadow of a being. It's nothing unless it's controlling another. It's like a virus."

"That's what we've always believed." He turned back to gaze upon the shadow. "But here's a fragment of such a creature that's reaching out, pleading for help." He paused as he watched it patiently wait for his response. "I think it deserves the benefit of the doubt."

"I still don't trust it."

The shadow reached out and touched Bandah's shoulder. "Mosh-ko klon-ar!"

Bandah replied, "Yes, we'll help you. And together, we'll help each other find a way out of here."

The shadow replied, "Ko zandiss"

Bandah turned to Mrs Smith. "He says we are kind."

Mrs Smith laughed. "You pixies are such foolish creatures. Don't you see? It may change its mind once it gets to know us better... when it finds a weakness to exploit. You're not seriously going to trust this abomination, are you?"

"Like with any creature, I'll trust it until it gives me cause to do otherwise. I'd advise that you do the same."

Mrs Smith took a defiant stance with hands on her hips. "Oh? And why would that be?"

"Because situations like this tend to bring out the best in all sorts of creatures."

Mrs Smith pointed at the shadow and sneered. "Even mind-sucking creatures like that thing?"

"Yes, absolutely. But you know what's even more amazing? This situation might just bring out the best in you as well."

A sound came from their shadowy companion that sounded reminiscent of a guttural laugh.

Mrs Smith looked at the shadow and smiled. "At least your new friend has a sense of humour."

Bandah snapped his fingers and said, "I have an idea!"

•

As Hunter and Patsy ran toward the house, some of the daisies on Hunter's garland broke free and moved a short distance ahead. Razor-sharp teeth emerged from around the flowers' centres in multiple rows that snapped wildly, as though eager for ripping into another mind thief, or Nasqa. Each flower that broke away would return to its place in the garland after a few seconds, unable to maintain their life force for long if they strayed too far from the host.

The girls raced up the steps to the veranda and through the front door. Cook approached the library with a tray of hot scones and was about to open the door when Hunter almost knocked the tray from her hands as she passed, throwing the door open with Patsy close behind.

Colin was in the process of pouring brandy for the Magistrate and himself. He frowned, put down the decanter and looked past Hunter to his daughter. "What's the meaning of this? Do you have any idea how important this meeting is? I'm disappointed, Patricia. You know better."

Patsy responded by pointing at the Magistrate. Colin turned and saw a look of abject fear on the man's face as he looked at Hunter.

The Magistrate tried to push himself back further into his chair as Hunter slowly approached. His voice trembled. "What are you doing here? What do you want?"

The daisies in the garland began swirling, their teeth gnashing so much it filled the room with a sound like dozens of mouse traps repeatedly snapping. Hunter's eyes grew wide. "Lis koo-sauwn vee, Nasqa?" *Why are you here, Nasqa?*

Surprised that he couldn't understand using the knowledge of listening Meredith had given him, Colin turned to his daughter. "Do you understand?"

Patsy nodded. She was about to offer a translation when she glanced at the Magistrate, noticing the dark, wet patch around his crutch where he'd wet himself.

The Magistrate's voice was punctuated by a shortness of breath. "The portal… we need to control it. I was sent to make sure we take control of the land around it." He cast his eyes toward Colin. "You need to make her leave, or she'll kill you all."

Colin took a sip on his brandy then turned to Hunter. "Tell me, what exactly are you intending to do?"

Hunter continued her slow walk toward the Magistrate. "I will free this man of the Nasqa that infects him and ensure it harms no one else, in this world, or any other."

Colin turned to his daughter.

"I've seen her do it, Father. She did it to his horse… she set it free."

Colin looked at the doorway and saw that Cook was standing frozen in time. He wasn't sure he liked what he was witnessing in his home. Turning back to Hunter he asked, "What have you done to Cook?"

"I am protecting her from her fears."

"Wouldn't it have been better to simply wait till she'd left the room?"

She was standing directly in front of the Magistrate, the Justice Albert Johnson. "You cannot waste time when it comes to dealing with Nasqa."

"And yet, here you are, revelling in the man's fear."

Hunter smiled. "It's not the man's fear, it is the fear within the Nasqa." She extended her arm and pushed it into the man's chest. The Magistrate screamed, slipping from his chair to the floor as she reached deep inside him and ripped out the shadow of the mind thief, throwing it to the ground. The daisies broke away from her garland and tore into it like a school of piranhas, ripping it into a thousand pieces. As the daisies swallowed the pieces they passed from our world into the void between worlds.

Colin clenched his fists. "I will not condone such violence taking place in my home!"

Hunter looked at him with a puzzled expression. "But it is Nasqa."

"I don't care what it is. What we've just witnessed can only be described as cruelty."

"You need not worry too much. In a few moments, you'll completely forget what you saw."

A voice from the doorway interrupted the conversation. "I won't."

Neridah stood, arms folded, in front of Cook in the doorway, Meredith by her side.

Hunter smiled. "Are you sure?"

Patsy placed a hand on Hunter's shoulder to get her attention. "We believe in showing respect for life, in all its forms."

Hunter pushed her hand away and took a step back. "Your actions suggest otherwise... all of you." She looked directly at Colin. "You wanted to greet my arrival carrying guns. Do they have a purpose other than to kill? If you respect life, why would you own such a thing?"

A groggy moan from the Magistrate drew everyone's attention, relieving some of the mounting tension in the room. Meredith rushed to him. "Are you okay?"

Leaning on his right elbow, he used his free hand to rub his eyes. "Yes, I believe I am. Perhaps better than I've felt in years." He looked at Hunter. "You, you freed me from hell." Aware that his weight was too great for Meredith to help him to his seat, he turned to Colin and reached out. "McIntyre, would you be kind enough?"

"Yes, of course." By the time he'd spoken the words, Colin was already lifting the man back into his chair.

The Magistrate took out his handkerchief and wiped his brow. "Thank you. If it's okay with you, I could certainly do with that brandy you were pouring."

Neridah approached the Magistrate. "How long were you possessed by that thing?"

He took his brandy and drained it in one go, then replied, "Since I first dined with Governor Pritchard almost two years ago." He extended the glass toward Neridah and asked, "Please?" Feeling sympathy for the man, she took the glass and refilled it as he continued. "The Governor, and all those around him, they're all under the control of these things."

He looked at Hunter and waved his finger as he searched for the words. "In all the time I was under that creature's control, I've not known it to feel fear… until today. As soon as you entered the room it felt terror."

Hunter shrugged. "My family have dealt with these Nasqa for countless generations. They have nothing worthwhile to offer."

"You're not of this world."

Neridah handed the Magistrate his refilled brandy. "Perhaps it's better for you to recover before pursuing this conversation further?"

The Magistrate nodded in agreement as he took the glass. "Probably the wisest words I've ever heard."

Meredith turned to Patsy. "Can you take Hunter to the stables and check that the Magistrate's horse has been attended to? I've no doubt the poor beast would have been spooked if it had to experience the same ordeal."

Patsy protested, "But, I saw Darcy tending to it—"

Colin snapped, "Patricia! I'll not have you argue with your mother. I still have matters of business to discuss with the Magistrate. Now go!"

Hunter was staring at the Book of Wisdom when Patsy grabbed her hand. "Come on." She looked back at her parents and made a show of saying, "It seems we're not wanted here." Hunter continued looking over her shoulder at the book as Patsy led her from the room.

They were already out the door when Meredith called out, "Hunter, could you please release Cook? I think the Magistrate could do with a hot scone now."

Hunter shrugged her shoulders in response. A moment later, Cook was entering the library with her tray of steaming hot scones. She looked at Meredith and Neridah with a surprised expression then turned back to Colin. "Oh, my goodness! Had I realised your good wife and mother-in-law were in here as well, I'd have brought in more… and a pot of tea."

Neridah watched Hunter as she left the room with Patsy. There was a lot that she didn't like about this girl's ways. She was not a good influence on her granddaughter. And there would be a hefty price to pay for the time freeze she'd imposed on Cook.

.

The Reverend Alfred Casey gave a nod to the gravedigger, signifying it was time to fill the grave. There were no mourners, no parents, no friends, no children. A lonely burial of someone who'd not yet reached their prime inevitably meant it had been preceded by a lonely existence. The Reverend always found these services difficult to perform, but he did his best to give the departed a final moment of dignity and recognition. At least on this occasion, there was someone to dig and fill the grave for him. But there'd be no marker other than the simple wooden cross that he'd plant at the head of the grave once the hole was filled. No one would ever know the name of the young man whose remains lay here.

Tonight would be better.

Tonight he'd be able to spend time with the one and only woman he'd ever loved. They'd dine together, talk, enjoy each other's company, and maybe even share a tender moment alone with just each other. A moment where they might share an embrace, or even a kiss, before he returned to Pulpit's Hill to retire for the evening.

There were at least four hours between now and when he'd need to make his way to the McIntyres', ample time to explore parts of the bushland he was still unfamiliar with. That was one of the things the Reverend most loved about living in the Blue Mountains. After all these years, there was still so much to explore. Today, he was thinking about a wallaby track he'd noticed about an hour's ride away.

He stood next to the bedraggled gravedigger filling the hole, then reached into his pocket and pulled out two shillings. They'd been all that was in the dead man's pocket, and the Reverend figured they were of little use to a corpse. "For your troubles." He placed them into the man's hand, causing his near toothless smile to light up his face.

He responded in a thick Irish accent. "To be sure, sir, you're more generous than most. I'll remember you in my prayers." He returned his attention to his work, smiling as he thought of how he'd enjoy spending his new-found wealth at the tavern in Springwood.

The Reverend headed toward the stables to saddle his horse. How long would he have to wait before Bandah returned with information about what was happening at the McIntyre household? How could he not be concerned knowing something had come through the portal? The last time the portal opened, he'd conspired with Colin and his family to rescue Neridah from Sellemae's lair, but it had nearly cost their lives.

With the bridle and saddle in place, he went to the barrel by the stable entrance and grabbed an apple for the horse, talking to the mare as she gratefully took it from his hand. "We'll have a good ride now, Elsa. But in the afternoon I'll be hitching you up to the sulky for the ride to the McIntyres'." The horse whinnied as though it understood, then the Reverend ruffled its mane affectionately before hoisting himself into the saddle. As he turned her to the stable entrance, Elsa seemed to read his mind. She let out a loud snort and took off in a canter.

The gravedigger, otherwise known as Sean O'Malley, tipped his hat as the horse passed through the small church graveyard. "God bless, Your Reverence, sir." He stood watching until the horse was out of sight, then put his shovel aside and stepped into the shallow grave. He hummed to himself as he brushed away the dirt from the dead man's clothing. Finding the pockets to be empty, he spat at the man's face, as though the lack of reward were an insult. Then, he spied the man's shoes. They were nothing special, but they were better than his own. Sean took pride in the fact that, as a result of his occupation, he hadn't paid for a single item of clothing in over ten years. A dead man buried beneath a few feet of dirt was unlikely to tell anyone of his theft.

As the gravedigger clambered back up from the hole, the mind thief that controlled him felt something. One of his own was calling out to any who would listen.

·

Mrs Smith shook her head in disbelief. "You're putting a lot of faith in this creature's supposed goodwill. Something, I might add, we've seen little evidence of."

The pixie asked, "Do you have a better idea?"

"I preferred your original plan, the one where we wait till your priest friend arrives and we see just how 'special' your relationship with him is."

"As much as I do believe that I'll be able to connect with Alfred when he arrives, there's no time for that now. That girl is a danger every minute she continues to run amok out there. And our new friend seems as keen to get out of here as we are."

"I still think it's crazy."

"What choice do we have? The mind thieves can communicate with each other even when they're in different crossworlds. Our friend can create a bridge, one that will allow us to communicate with the witches so they can create a sub-portal that frees all of us."

"You call it your 'friend.' Do you even know its name?"

Bandah sighed. It seemed pointless trying to reach the bitter old fairy.

The next moment, the shadow that was the mind thief remnants spoke in his defence. "Ak-bo-nasqa nub ney bask. Ak po-ee-dah, sass-op ardah." The shadow stretched out as though trying to embrace Bandah and Mrs Smith. "Ak kor poo-ee-dah. Ar-mosh treen-yer li-gak ye ar-dat."

Mrs Smith threw her hands up in the air. "Well, I don't know what the hell it's saying. You could at least let me in on the little secrets it's telling you."

Bandah bit his lower lip to keep himself from expressing his true thoughts. "He says the Nasqa don't need names. They are as one unless inside another."

"I can't see how that helps us."

"If you'll let me finish… he goes on to say that we three are as one. He says that he can reach out to others of his kind and ask that they tell the witches of our plight."

"It's little wonder you pixies generally travel together in your thousands. As individuals, you're so easily fooled."

"I trust him."

A scream of anguish from a short distance away drew their attention. It was the same sound that had pierced their ears when the mind thief fragments first came into the void. Without hesitation, they all raced to where Hunter's daisies were tearing apart the mind thief that had till now controlled the Magistrate.

The few fragments that fell into the part of the void they inhabited were even more tattered than those that had come through from the horse. Their shadowy colleague carefully moved to catch each fragment as it came through, absorbing them and growing in size and stature with each one that it captured.

Once the carnage was over, the creature had grown threefold in size. Stronger and more confident, its shadow rose high over Bandah and Mrs

Smith. "Ar-ee brunkt bow. Ar-mosh hoy nasqa jas. Ar-gosh ki lon-cun prac-bo-tunda."

Bandah's excitement was palpable. "It says it's stronger now, that it can feel another mind thief nearby that it will call to help us. It's a gravedigger! Alfred had a funeral to perform this morning. He'll be there… he should get the message."

Mrs Smith half raised an eyebrow. "I hope you're right."

CHAPTER 5

Hunter asked Patsy, "Why do you let them tell you what to do?"

"Because they know better than I do." Patsy stopped walking, wanting to ensure she had Hunter's attention. "What I want to know is, why have you let them tell *you* what to do? You've been alive longer than all of them put together, and you're much more powerful."

Hunter laughed. "Sometimes, it can be helpful to let people believe you respect them. They see in me a girl not much older than you. Even though they know otherwise, their thinking is influenced by what they see."

Patsy thought to herself, *You underestimate them.*

Hunter responded, *No, I don't think so at all. They underestimate me.*

Patsy put a hand on Hunter's shoulder. "You know what, Hunter? As much as I like you, I'd prefer that we keep our thoughts to ourselves."

Hunter's smile was so broad that it lacked sincerity. "But I thought we were friends."

While Hunter held her smile, Patsy couldn't help but notice the daisies in her garland turn toward her. Although they lacked faces, it was clear to Patsy they had a menacing intent. Aware that Hunter had noticed her attention drift to the flowers, Patsy looked her in the eye. "I'd like to be friends, but even friends have things that they keep from each other. I'm sure there are things about yourself you'd prefer I don't know."

Hunter stepped back, pushing Patsy's hand away from her shoulder. "What are you talking about? Do you feel there are things I've hidden from you?"

Patsy gave a reassuring smile. "There's so much about you that's a mystery to me, like the daisies in your garland. They tore apart a mind thief, not once, but twice! They seem bound to you, through some sort of loyalty."

In the back of her head, Patsy heard a voice call out, *Come and join us... be one of us. Join the garland of power.*

Patsy stared at Hunter's garland, searching for the origin of the invasive thought. Her suspicion of the source was confirmed when Hunter reached up and extracted one of the flowers, squeezing it between her fingers. She tried to hide the malice of her action behind a smile that changed to an expression of surprise when she realised Patsy could hear the tortured soul's brief plea for mercy. *Please, no! A thousand years of devoted service...* The thought never reached its conclusion as Hunter rubbed her fingers hard, breaking the daisy apart till its pieces fell from her fingers.

The tension was broken by Darcy's approaching voice. "Miss Hunter, I feel privileged to be crossing your path once more." He removed his battered flat cap, ran a hand through his hair, and straightened his worn waistcoat. "Some would call it fate."

Having been distracted from her train of thought, Patsy's memory of what had just transpired with the garland was gone in an instant. Hunter smiled at Darcy. "Py-sauwn trembar mouwn franze?"

The boy turned to Patsy and asked, "What did she say?"

Patsy giggled. "She asked if you think she's pretty."

Darcy blushed and found himself unable to look her in the eye. He fidgeted with the rim of his cap. "To be honest, you're truly the most beautiful woman I've laid eyes on."

Hunter reached out and gently lifted his chin, so he was facing her directly. She took him by surprise when she asked him in a deeply accented and broken English, "Do you, Mister Darcy O'Sullivan, like the flowers I wear in my hair?"

"Oh yes, my lady. They're like a gilded frame around a beautiful painting."

Hunter smiled as she thought to herself, *And sometime very soon, Darcy O'Sullivan, you'll be a part of that gilded frame.* While they stood staring at each other, Hunter asked, "Tonight... here, after dinner?"

Darcy fidgeted with his cap some more. "What, you and me?" He looked at the expectation in Hunter's eyes and shifted his feet, seeking the courage to come up with a more definitive reply. "The bottom of the garden can be lovely at night, and it should be a full moon. Would you care to go for a walk with me when we meet?"

Hunter and Patsy looked at each other, giggling behind their hands. Then Hunter turned back to Darcy and smiled as she replied, "Yes, I would like that. I would like it very much."

A voice called out from the rear of the stables, "Darcy O'Sullivan? Where in God's name would you be?"

Still blushing and fidgeting with his cap, Darcy looked over his shoulder then turned back to the girls. "That's my father calling, I guess I'd best be off." He looked at the ground for a moment, then looked into Hunter's eyes. "I'll see you this evening." He turned, placed the cap on his head, and walked at a brisk pace toward his father who'd stepped out from behind the stables. The middle-aged Jimmy O'Sullivan shook his head and smiled when he saw that his son had been in conversation with such an attractive young woman.

*

The Reverend Alfred Casey revelled in the thundering of Elsa's hooves as she pounded down the trail. There was little he needed to do to guide the beast. It was as though she knew where he wished to go. So much so, that when they reached the wallaby track he wished to explore, the mare came to an abrupt halt. He dismounted, then retrieved a wooden bowl from his saddlebag and poured half his water bottle into it. Holding the bowl up to the horse he said, "Don't worry, Elsa. I know this isn't much, but I won't be long."

Once Elsa had finished the contents of the bowl, he loosely secured her reins to a nearby tea tree then crouched low to commence his journey into the unknown.

The path was no doubt popular with wallabies and other wildlife as it was clearly defined at ground level. But a man of the Reverend's height had little choice but to bend his knees and back as he walked. He enjoyed the sound of every lizard or snake moving out of his path after they heard his approach. The magic of his journey was further enhanced by the continuous songs of the bellbirds inhabiting the area and the aroma of the rich rainforest soil.

After some twenty minutes, the forest grew darker. The Reverend felt glad to be wearing his coat as the temperature plummeted. He entered the deeper part of a gully, majestic tree ferns rising on either side of the creek that meandered through boulders twice the Reverend's size.

After clambering over a multitude of rocks, a well-defined pathway led up from the creek toward a cave-like opening in a massive wall of rock. Seeing signs of light at the other end, the urge to continue his exploration was impossible to ignore.

"I sometimes wonder about the foolishness of my pursuits." He crossed himself and entered the narrow tunnel, hands pushed against the walls on either side to counter the slippery nature of what was underfoot. After he'd moved forward just a few paces, the tunnel began to slope downward. He lost his footing and his grip on the walls, falling on his backside and sliding the rest of the way. Unable to control his passage, he bumped his head, and every other part of his body, as he accelerated toward the light.

His head bumped hard on a piece of rock jutting out from the wall and he felt like he was about to pass out when the rock fell away from under him and he hit the freezing cold water.

It took a few seconds for him to realise what was up, and what was down. When he recognised the rocks near his face as the bottom of the pool, he placed his feet against them and pushed up to the surface.

As his head broke through, and he captured a much-needed lungful of air, he looked around in wonder. Not one, but two waterfalls fed this pool. It was surrounded on all sides by steep walls. His only way out would be from where he came... unless he dared climb the sheer cliffs that surrounded him. He turned his head and saw that there was at least a shore on the far side where he could catch his breath before attempting to find his way back.

His wet clothing made the swim an unwelcome chore as he struggled toward the shore. He was almost halfway there when he heard a feminine voice next to his ear, "Do you have any idea what you've done?"

The Reverend flicked his head around to face the pixie, his long grey hair spraying water across the surface. "What in God's name would you be talking about?"

The pixie fluttered so close to his face that it forced the priest to go cross-eyed. "You sent him, didn't you? Isn't that what you always do?"

The Reverend took time to contemplate his response. "So, I'm assuming that you're referring to Bandah?"

"Of course I am. He's my cousin."

"Well, that would be of no surprise. It's my understanding that you would be one of thousands of cousins. What would your name be?"

She hovered in front of the Reverend just above the surface of the water. She was slim, although more shapely than the male pixies the Reverend was used to. "They call me Talia."

"You say that as though you prefer to go by a different title."

"My real name is Frydah, but they call me 'Talia' because in the tongue of the pixies it means 'rebel.' Why should that matter to you though, priest?"

"I've found trust works much better when two people understand exactly who they're talking to. I've not met a female pixie before."

"Although rare, we do exist, as do males among the fairies. Now tell me. Where did you send my cousin?"

"I didn't send him anywhere. However, he did make a choice to go the McIntyres' to investigate after someone, or something, accessed the portal between worlds."

Although the pixie's face was tiny, the Reverend recognised the anger in her expression. "And you let him go alone?"

The Reverend shrugged as he continued his journey across the pool, his feet having now found the bottom. The pixie continued to hover in front of his face as he dragged himself from the icy water. "What would you have had me do? In the time I've known your cousin, I've always found him to be single-minded. He wanted to know what was going on, and so did I."

"Why didn't you accompany him?"

"I had a funeral to perform." He found a rock to sit on and pulled off his boots. "I'm curious to know the reason for your anger. Bandah has always been a good friend of mine, and if he's in a perilous situation, I'd like to know of it also, so I can do what's in my power to help."

"For some reason, he's crossed over from this world."

"He does so often. I don't see why that in itself should have you so concerned."

Talia landed on his knee. "He hasn't shown up in any other crossworld."

"How can you be sure? My understanding is that there are countless crossworlds."

"But he's my cousin. I should be able to *feel* what world he's in. That's why we pixies are able to travel between the worlds with such confidence. The only thing that makes sense is that he's somehow trapped in the void between worlds."

"If that's the case, I understand your concern. The idea of being trapped between worlds is indeed frightening."

"I need your help to find him."

"How so? You're able to sense if he's in another crossworld. That's something I'm certainly not capable of."

"You have formed a bond with him we pixies call 'grundai.' You are closer than brothers. He has largely forsaken his own kind to be with you. Female pixies are rare, but what's even rarer is for pixies to form grundai bonds with those of another kind I can feel him if he's in another world, but I can't hear him from across them. My hope is, if he's in the void between the worlds, you may be able to hear him if he calls out to you." She flew up and sat on his shoulder, then took on a harsh and demanding tone of voice. "As his grundai partner, you have a duty to help."

"Bah! You fool yourself. It is my choice, not yours, whether or not I will help to find him. He is my friend, and he went on his own only because I was otherwise indisposed. Of course, I will help to find him, but because I wish to help my friend, not because of your demands." He looked up at the escarpment surrounding him. "But first, I'll need to find my way out of this deep hole."

"You won't be able to go back the way you came. It's far too slippery and treacherous. There is but one safe way for you to climb out of here. I'll guide you and help make sure you put your hands and feet only where they are safe."

"I guess I'd best put my boots back on then."

*

After Cook had left the library, Meredith closed the doors to ensure they had privacy to continue their discussion with the Magistrate.

Colin watched as the man threw down his brandy. "Can I offer you another, Your Honour?"

The Magistrate extended his arm with the empty glass in Colin's direction. "Please, yes. And you can refrain from the formalities while we're in the privacy of your home. Feel free to call me Albert." He turned to Meredith. "My lady, I must apologise for my appalling behaviour earlier. I treated you disrespectfully and in a manner that I deeply regret."

"That's quite alright. I understand that it was the creature who possessed you that spoke."

"But still, the words were delivered by my mouth."

Colin handed the Magistrate his refilled glass. "So, tell me, Albert, are you aware of what the creature was, and what it was thinking?"

He took a sip before replying, "Oh yes. Very much so. I've been a prisoner within my own body for years… until now. I was unable to control anything, but aware of it all. It's a wonder I have my sanity still intact." He leaned across and grabbed Colin's arm. "As I said before, in all that time, I'd never known the creature possessing me to feel fear… until today, when that young lady approached." The memory of the mind thief's fear made him throw down the rest of the brandy in one go. "It was terrified. It called her a 'boom-qua.' The closest words in English to describe what it means that I can think of would be 'under-god.' You need to ask yourselves this, is Hunter her name, or her title?" He turned to Meredith and Neridah. "It knew about you two and your daughter, Patricia… the trinity of witches. They see you as powerful, but also as vermin." He turned back to Colin. "I don't suppose I could trouble you for one more brandy? This is all horribly confronting."

Colin replied, "Yes, of course."

Neridah, not wanting to see Colin treated as though he were the Magistrate's servant, said, "I'll get it."

The Magistrate mopped his brow. "You need to be aware. Governor Pritchard is controlled by these 'Nasqa,' as they call themselves."

Meredith cut in. "That's what Hunter calls them too."

He nodded. "I sensed that their conflict goes back thousands of years and that the under-gods generally come out on top. But, I must tell you, as much as I don't think you should trust her, she may be worthwhile keeping around. Pritchard knows about the portal, and he wants to control it."

Neridah refilled his brandy glass. "We've dealt with mind thieves before. We can deal with them without Hunter's help."

Colin asked, "How did Pritchard learn about the portal?"

"You had a tutor who worked here... Mrs Bradshaw... was that her name?" When Colin nodded in agreement he continued, "She wasn't too happy about you freeing her, you know. But I digress. The Nasqa, or 'mind thieves' as you call them, communicate over vast distances using messengers... birds and the like that are also possessed. She'd let the Governor know about the portal as soon as she became aware of its existence, hoping it might create an opportunity for her. That's why your dinner guests were all taken over that night. After you'd freed her, she headed for Sydney, begging the Governor to have her taken over once more."

Colin asked, "Did he comply?"

"No. He took great joy in giving her false hope. He employed her to tutor his own children and saw to it that they made her life a living hell. I believe she's gone quite mad now and was recently admitted to a lunatic asylum. There's certainly no honour among the Nasqa."

Neridah asked, "But what about Pritchard and his plans... that is why you're here, isn't it?"

"Yes, indeed it is. And I must tell you, he won't give up on this."

Colin asked, "Will you personally be endangered on your return to Sydney?"

"No, there are only a few on the Legislative Council that are controlled by the Nasqa. On my return, I will make my change of allegiance as visible as possible. That will give me security. For all their powers, the

Nasqa can't override the reality of the political process. At least, not yet. But I warn you, Pritchard will not give up on trying to take control of that portal. The Nasqa will do whatever it takes."

Neridah said, "I think our more pressing problem might be what you refer to as an 'under-god.' I don't trust her intentions. My father travelled here from Ireland to continue the tradition of protecting the portal after it shifted its physical location from his homeland. I've no intention of letting that ancestral duty fail now."

The Magistrate replied, "Noble words, but I suspect they may be in vain. If this girl is feared by the Nasqa, you might just be out of your depth."

Neridah clenched her fists as she replied, "Do not underestimate what we are capable of when we come together."

There was an uneasy silence in the room for a few moments that was broken when the Magistrate burst out in laughter. "I swear, these creatures, as you say, have obviously underestimated you." He turned to Colin. "What would you wish me to do from here?"

Colin took a sip of his own brandy. He wasn't accustomed to drinking alcohol at this time of day, but the current situation made him feel comfortable about making an exception. "I think we should wait until this evening to make a decision, when the Reverend Casey joins us for dinner. I've always appreciated his counsel on such matters."

The Magistrate nodded. "I'm aware of him through the Nasqa's thoughts that I've overheard. Are you sure you trust him?"

"More than anyone else I know."

*

Sean O'Malley threw the shovel aside when he heard the plea for help. Maybe this would be his chance to shift to a more worthy host.

I need your help... the vermin let an under-god through, and I've been cast into the void.

Deep within Sean, his true persona held onto the grim hope that maybe this would be the opportunity for the thing that controlled him to move on and that he'd be freed from this curse of possession he'd lived with for so long.

The gravedigger walked up the hill and kicked in the door to the Reverend's house, hoping to find some money to take with him on his journey into town where he'd seek others to help him. Not being foolish enough to consider facing an under-god on his own, he knew he'd need money to buy drinks and food to help convince the occupiers of lowly bodies like his own to join him. He was aware of at least three such people in the barracks at Springwood alone, treated as madmen by some because their hosts resisted their possession. They remained in the corps only as a result of the protection offered them by the Nasqa-controlled captain who was the barracks' commanding officer. Maybe, if he worked it right, he'd even be able to enlist the captain's support.

He strode into the Reverend's house. It was a simple cottage, with one large room and a kitchen attached to the back. Although humble in size, its lathe and plaster walls were lined in wallpaper, and the doorways were framed in cedar. The furniture throughout the room was, for the most part, finely crafted silky oak. As O'Malley rummaged around, he cursed the priest. "Why would any man want so many books?" He pulled them from their shelves, whole rows at a time, sending most scattering across the floor.

Spying the piano, he thought there might be something hidden inside its stool and brought his foot down hard to smash it open. Nothing! He walked to the silky oak buffet, pulling its drawers out and emptying them of their contents.

He rubbed the coarse stubble on his chin before turning toward the kitchen door, kicking it so hard it nearly came off its hinges. He couldn't believe it. More books! This time, in huge stacks on the kitchen table. Why? Why would anyone want to waste time reading? He kicked the table over, then went through the cupboards. Nothing again.

Returning to the main room, he approached the writing desk, opened the cigar box and smiled a toothless grin. He'd finally found something worthwhile.

Looking around again he noticed two bottles of brandy sitting on the buffet. At least the cigars and brandy would warm him on his ride to the barracks.

He walked to the fireplace and lit a cigar from one of the burning embers, then grabbed a bottle, pulling its cork out with two of his remaining teeth. He spat the cork aside and took a deep swig from the bottle, followed by a drag on the cigar. He smiled as he picked up a few sheets of the Reverend's writing paper, then crouched by the fire as he set them alight. Shielding the small flames with his hand, he carried the burning paper across to where some of the books lay scattered on the floor, then let them fall. He stood and laughed when the first books ignited, flames rising as their pages distorted and curled as though tortured by the heat. Knowing the books would be reasonably slow to catch, he strode back to collect his bottles of brandy and the box of cigars, tucked them under his arm, then meandered to the door. He paused in the doorway to splash some brandy over the smouldering books, causing them to burst into flame.

By the time he'd collected his shovel and mounted his horse down by the graveyard, the Reverend's house was a blazing inferno.

CHAPTER 6

Neridah looked at the Book of Wisdom, wondering what it had to say about under-gods, then turned to Colin and asked, "Do you think it might be worthwhile moving the conversation to the drawing room? The sun should be shining through the windows now to make it warm, and it's such a beautiful outlook at this time of day."

The Magistrate waved dismissively. "Nonsense woman! The fireplace is burning and the brandy warms the soul. Drawing rooms are for women to practice their embroidery and talk of things that lack significance." The silence that ensued made the Magistrate realise how poorly his reply had been received. "I'm truly sorry, good lady. I must apologise. I've been possessed by that creature so long that I guess I've lost a degree of sensitivity."

Meredith responded on her mother's behalf. "Perhaps that sensitivity is something that had still to be learned beforehand?"

Not knowing where else to look, the Magistrate gazed at his shoes and let out a long sigh before raising his eyes to meet Meredith's. "Hmm, that could well be the case." Feeling humbled, he turned to Colin. "What say you, McIntyre, do we remain by the warmth of the fire, or adjourn to the drawing room?"

Colin looked at his wife, he knew her well enough to read in her expression that she agreed with her mother. Although he generally felt uncomfortable in the more feminine decor of the drawing room, he understood that resistance would cause him pain later that he could do without. "It's the best view we have over the property, and at this time of the afternoon, it's undoubtedly the warmest room in the house. If we settle in there for the next hour or two, we'll be well placed for a grand view of the sunset."

The Magistrate burped, then extended his hand. "Very well then. If you insist on treating me as a woman, I guess I've little choice but to acquiesce."

Colin helped the Magistrate from his chair while protesting, "That's not the—"

The Magistrate cut him off, grabbing at his chest and gasping for breath. His weight was such that Colin was unable to support him after the strength had gone from the old man's legs. The Magistrate collapsed to his knees. Meredith helped Colin ease him down so he was stretched out on the floor. Then, Meredith and her mother ran their hands over him to read his life force and ascertain what action they should take. The blank look on their faces told Colin everything he needed to know. The Magistrate was dead, and there was no bringing him back.

•

It was a two-hour ride at the best of times from Pulpit's Hill to Springwood, but Sean O'Malley was on a mission, and it didn't matter to him if his horse dropped dead of exhaustion when they arrived. He was sure the Nasqa at the barracks would be able to find some way to provide him with another one.

It would've been easier if he'd been able to enlist a lesser Nasqa to control his horse, a common path for the Nasqa to build their individual prestige. But that only worked if you held a high station, like a magistrate, military officer or governor. He pondered his ill fortune since arriving in this world. Always forced to take on the body of someone already close to the end of their life, helping find dirt on others that may help Nasqa inhabiting those of a more prestigious station. He felt deep resentment over having been sent to the Blue Mountains to keep an eye on the priest who'd caused trouble for the Nasqa when they'd helped Sellemae. As far as Sean was concerned the real reason he'd been sent was because the Nasqa controlling Governor Pritchard wanted to take over the land hosting the portal and didn't want the priest getting in his way.

Sean pulled one of the brandy bottles from his saddlebag, careful to time his movements to match the steady groove of the horse's gallop. He took a long swig then tossed the empty bottle aside.

He rode on. Salty sweat ran off his brow and stung his eyes. Rubbing them with his greasy fingers made it worse. At least the afternoon sun was at his back as he continued his eastward journey.

His horse was covered in frothy sweat and its breathing was laboured when Sean O'Malley reached a squatter's homestead. He rode to the stables, dismounted, and began transferring his saddle to a strong-looking chestnut mare that must have stood all of seventeen hands.

The owner of the homestead emerged, wearing boots and a coat. His square face bore strong features and deep-set eyes, framed by dark hair and thick sideburns. He carried a flintlock in one hand and a stock whip in the other. "Hey, what do you think you're doing?"

Sean continued saddling the horse.

"Did you hear me, man? To steal a man's horse is a hangable offence."

Sean turned to face him. "How far from here to Springwood Barracks?"

"You'll know that answer when you find yourself facing the Captain of the barracks… once I've bound you and led you in there on the back of my cart."

Sean O'Malley went back to ignoring him.

The squatter unfurled his stockwhip, making it crack. Both the mare and O'Malley's horse reared up. O'Malley continued ignoring the squatter and focused on calming the big horse. The squatter came closer, drawing his arm in readiness to crack his whip once more, this time with the intention of striking O'Malley. But the Nasqa was ready. O'Malley reached out and caught the whip, not even flinching as it wrapped around his arm and tore at his flesh. He pulled back hard, causing the squatter to fall to the ground and release his grip on the whip. He prepared himself to aim the flintlock and fire it at O'Malley, but he was too late. The gravedigger had jumped on the horse's back and rode it straight over him, crushing his right shoulder and pelvis.

He rode a short distance then, listening to the man's screams, decided to turn back.

He dismounted and approached the squatter.

"Please, for God's sake, man… help me."

O'Malley bent down and picked up the stockwhip and flintlock. "Now then, good sir, if I were to do that, you might go telling fibs about what happened here just now."

"I, I give you my word… no one will ever know. Just please… help me."

O'Malley watched the squatter's face contort as he tried to deal with the pain. He then sauntered back to his new stead as the man resumed his agonised screams. Once he was back on the horse, he fired the flintlock at the squatter's chest, bringing the screams to an abrupt end. He tossed the flintlock aside and said, "You certainly won't be telling anyone now." He stabbed his heels into the horse's side and rode off toward Springwood Barracks.

When he arrived at the gates twenty minutes later, the guards, who'd been sitting in the shade of a nearby tree sharing a bottle of rum, stumbled to their feet and rushed to block his path. One of them, a man with a mop of curly dark hair and a deep scar under his right eye, slurred his words together as he asked, "Who goes there?"

O'Malley replied, "What would you care?"

The guard burped. "We can't let you pass unless you've good reason to be here."

"I'm here to see the Captain."

The other guard, a lanky man who seemed less affected by the rum, looked O'Malley in the eye and said, "The Captain doesn't like your kind."

His colleague asked, "What would you be talking about?"

The lanky guard gestured toward O'Malley. "He knows what I mean." He stared at the gravedigger and communicated telepathically: *You lowly scum. You don't choose when to talk to us, we choose when to talk to you.*

O'Malley spoke his response. "When the Captain finds out the information I have for him, he'll be pleased you chose to let me through." He followed up the statement with a thought: *There's an under-god has come through.*

Looking to his colleague again, the lanky guard said, "We should let him through. He'll get what's coming to him when he meets the Captain." He turned back to Sean. "I'll escort you to his quarters."

·

Patsy said to Hunter, "Seeing we're clearly not wanted back at the library, let's go for a walk down by the creek. There's lots of lovely wildlife down there, and sometimes the fairies come out and sing."

"Okay, I'd like that."

As they made their way down the path Patsy said, "I can't believe that you're going to meet Darcy later." She giggled then asked, "Have you ever met with boys before?"

Hunter appeared puzzled by the question. "Oh yes, many hundreds of times over the years."

"Have you ever kissed one?"

For a moment, Patsy thought she detected a hint of anger in Hunter's eyes, but then the girl giggled as she had before. "Have you?"

"That's not fair. I asked you first. And besides, you're older than me. Why, my father would be horrified at the thought of me kissing a boy."

"But you are nearly twelve now. Have you never thought of kissing a boy?"

Patsy rolled her eyes upward and bit her lower lip while she thought of how she should respond. "I'm not saying… not until you've told me your answer."

"My father would be very angry if I were to kiss a boy that he hadn't approved of."

"See? We are alike." Patsy did a little pirouette as she continued down the path. "So, have there been any boys your father approved of you kissing?"

"What about you? Is there anyone you ever wanted to kiss?"

Patsy blushed. "I don't think I want to answer that."

"Is there a boy that you ever did kiss?"

Patsy's jaw dropped. "No! Of course not."

Hunter walked ahead, feeling free to let the violets grow in her footsteps now that it was just Patsy and herself.

Patsy looked at the violets. "How do you do that?"

Hunter stopped. "Do what?"

They were at the creek now, and Patsy took Hunter's hand, guiding her to the left, upstream and away from the pool with its portal. "The flowers... how do you make them appear in your footsteps?" She looked down at Hunter's feet, watching her stepping over rocks and in shallow pools at the creek's edge. Whether her foot hit soil, sand, rock or pebbles underwater, the violets always sprang up.

"I don't do anything. It just naturally happens when I take a step. The effort goes into stopping it."

"Does everyone do it where you come from?"

"Only those with the knowledge."

"It must be a very colourful world." As Patsy spoke, she noticed the foliage to either side of Hunter's trail of violets had died off. She turned to Hunter to ask about it then found herself distracted by the daisies in Hunter's garland. "What about your garland? Why do the daisies move around like that?"

"What do you mean?"

"They move like they're looking at me... like they're alive."

"I think you must be imagining things. Would you like a garland of daisies? I could show you how to make one."

They reached an area where the creek opened into a broad shallow area.

Patsy looked at the daisies in Hunter's garland. For now, the movement seemed restrained, but Patsy was sure she had seen movement among the flowers when she'd looked at them before. And there was something else… there were thoughts, individual ones, coming from each of the flowers. She thought to herself, *I wonder if there's anything in the Book of Wisdom about the garland… and about the flowers.*

"Patsy?"

"Oh, sorry. Yes, I suppose so."

"What's this Book of Wisdom you keep thinking about? Is that where you get your knowledge from?"

Patsy picked up a stone and skipped it across the surface of the water. "It's a book my family has learned from for generations. My grandmother says no one knows how old it is. No one even knows how many pages there are in it. No matter how many pages you turn, there are always more to follow."

"It sounds like a very special book. Can you show it to me?"

"I'd have to ask my grandmother first. She says it's sacred, and it should only ever be read by those with the duty of protection. Even my father's not allowed to read its contents. You have a duty to protect your world, don't you?"

Hunter picked up a stone, like the one Patsy had skipped across the water. "My father and I protect many worlds."

Patsy smiled. "Then it'll probably be okay. I'll still have to ask though."

Hunter crouched low and flicked her wrist, sending her stone skipping across the water. Each time it bounced off the surface, a spray of tiny flowers radiated out from the point of contact.

*

The Reverend Casey grabbed hold of the ledge. He knew that as soon as his left hand released its hold on a small crack in the rock, he would need to swing his body to bring his left arm over the top of the overhang, with nowhere for his feet to hold onto. It had taken hours to get this far, but the huge climb was almost over.

Talia stood at the cliff's edge. "Come on, Alfred. Hanging around isn't going to make it any easier."

The Reverend shook his head in dismay before responding. "Your comments may be better kept to yourself."

"And, if I were you, I'd be putting my efforts into the climb rather than providing a critique to the voice that's been your guide. Come on, your hand will just end up slipping if you keep waiting."

The Reverend knew she was right, but he didn't appreciate the reminder. He took a deep breath, closed his eyes, and focused. Energy from a dozen crossworlds surged through him. He released his left hand's grip on the rock and swung his arm around. He then reached up and brought it over the top of the ledge, leaving his feet swinging in the air. His grip was tenuous, so there was no time to catch his breath again. He pulled hard until he was able to bring his head above the edge, allowing him to reach out further with his right arm, enough to bring his shoulders and chest onto the safety of the clifftop. He gave himself a moment to draw breath before dragging his hips and legs up. Once clear of immediate danger, he rolled onto his back.

Talia clapped. "Well done. I didn't think you had it in you to do a climb like that."

"I'm grateful then that you showed the wisdom to keep such thoughts to yourself." The Reverend turned his head to the side and saw a column of smoke rising in the distance. "I'm not feeling good about the source of that smoke."

Knowing, as the Reverend did, that his home was the obvious source of the fire, Talia placed her tiny hand on his shoulder. "Sad as this loss may be, I believe you'll be facing bigger issues in the hours and days ahead. Right now, Alfred Casey, there are those who need you."

"Aye, that may be so, but how can you be so dismissive with regard to the fire? It's almost as though you expected it."

"Come on, Alfred, you did realise the gravedigger had been taken by a mind thief, surely?"

The Reverend tightened his fists. He didn't appreciate the obvious being pointed out to him, particularly when he had only just worked it out for himself. There was no point taking it out on the pixie though, she was trying to be helpful. Were it not for her, he'd be languishing at the bottom of the hole. He felt quite sure he would've struggled far more to find his way out without her help. "In hindsight, I should have suspected. I just cannot help but trust in people until given reason to do otherwise."

Talia paused and looked up to the sky for a moment before shaking her head and turning back to the Reverend. "Ah, such a rare trait, particularly in humans. Bandah's always been the same way. I can see now why he likes you… and why he feels protective of you."

CHAPTER 7

Colin, Meredith and Neridah stared at the Magistrate's body in stunned silence.

Neridah stood up and said to no one in particular, "Well, that makes things a little more complicated."

Colin glared at his mother-in-law. "A man has just died. Must you always be so lacking in sensitivity?"

Neridah rolled her eyes and let out a sigh. She looked into space for a moment with her hands on her hips as she collected her thoughts.

Meredith bowed her head, closed her eyes, and rubbed a hand against her brow. She didn't want to listen to Colin and her mother arguing, not now. It was painful at the best of times. At least her mother was pausing to choose her words now, as opposed to her usual reactive manner.

Neridah glanced at the Magistrate's corpse then looked back to Colin.

"I'm not wanting to argue, and I don't wish to be disrespectful. This man would have died years ago were it not for the mind thief."

Meredith concurred. "Mother's right, darling." She stood up to be on the same level as her husband and mother. "I can feel it too. His heart failed after the creature had left him. It turns out his body was incapable of surviving on its own."

Colin nodded as he remembered times when his wife had told him of someone's cancer long before the sufferer or their physician had known of it.

Neridah looked back to the corpse. "Lungs, kidneys, liver, bones. The man was riddled with it."

Colin asked, "Why was he able to live while under the mind thief's control then?"

"The mind thieves control the whole body and everything in it. They can make a disease slow dramatically in its progress. Or even hold it in a kind of stasis. This man was likely at death's door when first taken over."

"The pain must have been unspeakable."

"The mind thief wouldn't have felt that... he'd have left that for the Magistrate to deal with."

"Do you think he knew?"

"A cancer that advanced? Yes, but he must have kept it to himself. I doubt the mind thief would have chosen him as a host had it known beforehand."

Colin replied, "Unless it was concerned more about what the Magistrate's title would allow it to achieve. I wonder how long the mind thief would have remained in his body after the papers transferring my title on the land were signed."

Neridah nodded in acknowledgment. "You may be onto something with that."

Colin put his hand on Meredith's shoulder. "I'll go to the stables to fetch Jimmy and his son. They can help carry him through to the kitchen. Then we can wrap him in wet blankets and place him in the larder overnight. In the morning, I'll take him to the barracks at Springwood. They should be able to deal with transporting him to Sydney from there."

.

Patsy looked at Hunter and asked, "Can you teach me how to do that?"

"What? Skipping stones? I just followed what you did. It's you that's taught me something."

Patsy smiled at the idea that she could have taught Hunter even the smallest thing. "It's not that. It's the flowers that came out as the stones skipped. Can you teach me how to do that?"

Hunter feigned a look of bewilderment. "But that is something that just happens, like when I walk. I don't know that I could teach it when it's not something that's willful."

Feeling patronised, Patsy folded her arms in a gesture of defiance. "I don't believe you. You're able to stop the violets in your footsteps if you try. So, that shows you know how and why they happen. I think it's the same with the flowers when you skip stones."

Hunter narrowed her eyes but said nothing.

Patsy asked, "Is it to do with your garland?"

Some of the flowers in the garland turned in Patsy's direction. Hunter frowned for a moment then softened her expression, letting out a small laugh before replying, "Why would you think that? It's just some flowers woven together."

"But they move... and they think. I know they do."

Hunter remained silent, but thoughts ran through Patsy's head. *You must not think such things. Forget you ever thought of them.*

Patsy replied, "I don't like it when others use thoughts to try and tell me what to do."

Hunter screwed up her face as though confused. "Why would you say that? Are you accusing me?"

"No, it's not you." Patsy pointed at the garland. "It's them."

"Why would you say that?"

"I can hear them. They're telling me not to think about them and trying to make me forget."

This time, Hunter didn't respond. She stood and looked at Patsy. *How could she know?*

Patsy's breathing was getting heavier. "They've done it to me before. There's something you did at the stables, and now I can't remember. I remember things then forget them again. And you wanted everyone to forget what you did to the mind thief you took out of the Magistrate."

Hunter looked at Patsy with a cold stare. "And they will forget. By the time the man is wrapped in blankets, they'll remember only that he had a heart attack. But you won't forget. I can see now, you're different. You're like—"

Patsy stamped her foot, putting a crack in the rock she was standing on and sending out a shockwave that knocked Hunter to the ground, making a splash as she landed on her backside in a shallow puddle. Patsy's teeth were clenched as she said, "I told you before, don't patronise me."

•

After Colin left the library, Meredith said to her mother, "I'll go and ask Mrs Banks to organise some blankets. Are you happy to stay with the

Magistrate until Colin returns?"

Neridah replied, "Yes, that's fine. I wanted to look something up anyway."

"What, in the Book of Wisdom? Do you think that's wise when Colin will be back soon with Jimmy and his boy?"

"I'll be very quick."

Meredith stared at her mother as she backed out of the room. Sometimes she saw her mother's teenage appearance and wondered if she had the immaturity to match. It was little wonder her husband and mother clashed so much. "I'll close the door, so you have a moment of warning when someone enters. At least that might give you time to close the book."

Neridah smiled. "Thank you, that's very thoughtful."

As soon as Meredith had closed the door, Neridah went to the writing desk and opened the secret compartment that held the key to open the Book of Wisdom. There was very little time, but she had a plan to change that. Hunter had imposed a time freeze on an individual, but what she wanted to do was different. She wanted to isolate time within the library. Yes, there were still consequences, but not so great as when imposing a time freeze on others. All magic had consequences anyway. She'd seen the page she was after before. Her own mother had warned her against its contents. The words were still clear in her head. *Spells that invoke the changing of time extract a heavier price than most other spells. You could take time away at a critical moment for another or cause a delay where none should exist. The consequences can be catastrophic, and there is no way of ever knowing what you may have been responsible for.*

Neridah went to the book and unlocked its clasp, throwing the book open to roughly where she remembered the page was when she'd asked her mother about it as a child.

The cost is potentially so great you'd have to wonder why anyone would want to learn about such things. There would have to be no other choice.

It was clear to Neridah. There was no choice.

She didn't trust this powerful and timeless entity that presented itself in such a youthful body. And that garland. There was something very disturbing about the garland.

What annoyed her most of all was that she could feel the foggy mask that hid many of her memories relating to Hunter. If she didn't use the spell to alter the passage of time within the library, she may lose the memory of what she needed to learn.

Neridah was seeking time to look up and read about the garland, without interruption. And she wanted to look up other concerns she had about Hunter, things she couldn't quite put a finger on.

She looked down at the page. It was exactly the one she'd hoped for. That's how the Book of Wisdom worked for those who knew its secrets. It sensed what you needed to know and guided your hand to the page.

Neridah took a deep breath before reciting the incantation. "Ka Dae marsie karn, com-ba swa-ba keb vog." *The time right here must stop, until I swing my arm aloft.*

Being in the library, Neridah was isolated from the sounds of nature that might let her know whether the spell had worked. There was no choice but to trust that it had. She'd gone beyond boundaries that she'd held sacred before today, but there were no regrets.

She placed one hand to the left extreme of the book, and the other to the right, closed her eyes and thought of what she needed to know. *Garlands that live, garlands that dance.* She kept the thought running through her head as she moved her hands along the edges of the book's pages, waiting for the sensation that would tell her where to open the book. The pages felt as though they were moving under her touch, as thousands of them flipped in and out of existence. Of the millions of pages that co-existed across so many crossworlds, it was likely only one would have the information she sought. The movement stopped. The page Neridah needed had made itself known to her right hand. She opened her eyes and carefully opened the book to that page. It revealed an illustration of a garland of daisies, almost identical to the one worn by Hunter.

The text was In a language unfamiliar to her, an indication of how far into the history of the book she'd had to search. If she was patient and waited a few minutes, her eyes would adjust and learn to see the words as ones that she understood.

She ran a finger over the ancient illustration of the garland, then turned her head in response to a knock at the door. The spell hadn't worked! She tried to sound relaxed as she called out, "Who is it?"

She closed the book as gently as she could while the reply came. "It's Mrs Banks, ma'am. Mrs McIntyre requested I bring blankets."

"If you give me a moment, I'll get the door for you." She turned the key in the book's lock then returned it to the secret compartment of the writing desk on her way to the door.

She adjusted her dress and took a moment to settle her breathing before opening the door.

There was nobody there.

*

Captain Taylor poured Sean O'Malley a glass of rum. "You were right to come to me with this information."

"So, we'll be riding there this evening?"

"No."

"Begging your pardon, sir, but there's an under-god there, and it's tortured not one, but two of our own."

"You speak recklessly, almost as though you let the alcohol affect your thinking as it would your host. The Governor has plans for that property. He sent our kin there for a reason. We'll not be doing anything rash without his consent."

"Hah, you say that from the comfort of your position in these barracks." He leaned across the desk and pointed an accusing and trembling finger at the Captain. "What if it were you that were torn apart and thrown into the void?"

Captain Taylor watched the finger as though he was keeping his eye on a mosquito. "And what would you have me do to this under-god?"

O'Malley threw his arms into the air. "Kill the body it inhabits and let it know how it feels to suffer."

Captain Taylor walked to the window then glanced over his shoulder at the decrepit gravedigger. "This attitude you're displaying, it's why you've been designated the host you have rather than one of higher station. I will acknowledge you've done the right thing to report this matter to me rather than recklessly pursuing your own vengeance. But mark my words, try to tell me what I should do again and you will find yourself given a far lesser creature to control."

As if to emphasise the point, he opened the window and let out a quiet whistle. A few seconds later, a screeching flying fox appeared at the windowsill. He spoke to the host in the language of the Nasqa: "Pra-li-ar mondee. Har-gen bo-dah ok-gen li-scew bo-gardae pee-lone buckah gu-dah boom-qua. Gi-gen boobi-gen yandee re-ak li-kae." *Go to our leader. Tell him the one he sent to secure the portal has been disabled by an under-god. Ask him what he wishes for us to do.*

As the mind-thief-controlled primate flew away, he sent it another thought. *Bring me a response before dawn, and the gravedigger's body will be yours to control.*

The flying fox screeched its approval then flew into the night.

Unaware of the Captain's offer, Sean O'Malley finished his rum then burped loudly.

*

The sun was getting lower by the time the Reverend and Talia made it back to his horse. "It'll be getting dark by the time I reach the McIntyres' now."

Talia said to him, "Not if we go straight there."

He mounted the horse as he replied, "I'll not go there till I've had the chance to check and see if anything remains of my home and church."

"Honestly, you humans! I'll never understand why you worry so much about that stuff."

"Your manner of speech is much like your cousin. And just as dismissive. Regardless of what you may think, I'll not ride to the McIntyres' until I know what remains for me. If you wish for my help in finding your cousin, then I suggest you try to be more patient." He kicked his boots into Elsa's side and the horse took off.

Talia flew just ahead of the horse. "Some friend you are."

The rest of the ride to the Reverend's home was punctuated by a tense silence.

When they reached the graveyard, the Reverend pulled up Elsa at the spot where he'd stood performing his lonely burial service earlier in the day. He shook his head as he looked at the partially covered body with the missing shoes.

Talia landed on his shoulder. "Please, tell me you're not. That can wait till the morning, surely?"

The Reverend turned to her with a cold glare. "I'll not leave the body here uncovered overnight. It's a wonder the scavengers haven't already taken their share."

"Does it really matter?"

The Reverend ignored the question. He dismounted and led Elsa up to the smouldering remains of his home. At least the church and stables were still intact. Leaving Elsa to graze on the grass a few metres from the charred remains, he walked into the ruins, making his way toward where his bed had been. The woollen blankets and stuffing of his mattress had retarded the flames just enough that the floorboards beneath them were blackened but not fully destroyed as most of the timber structure had been. He used his boot to brush away what remained of the mattress from a spot near where the wall had been. There were two short boards of identical length. He crouched down and lifted them, revealing a silky oak box. No bigger than a loaf of bread, it showed no obvious signs of hinges or a lid.

Talia flew over and fluttered in the air near his face. She looked toward the box with its intricate marquetry. "So, that's why it was so important for you to come by here?"

"Aye."

"What's in it?"

The Reverend turned his cold gaze to the pixie. "That's of no concern to you." He walked back to Elsa and led her to his sulky by the stables. He then secured the box to the seat with a length of rope before grabbing a shovel and making his way down to the graveyard, insistent on finishing the job he'd paid Sean O'Malley so generously for.

Talia watched the sun sink lower. As the Reverend laboured she shook her head and mumbled, "Humans."

CHAPTER 8

Hunter sat in the shallow pool shivering. "It's so cold… and my dress!" She threw her hands up in the air. "It's wet!"

The daisies in her garland were tearing themselves outward, snapping back in like they were bound to Hunter's head by rubber bands. As they reached out, tiny squeals escaped their central cores.

Ignoring the writhing daisies, Patsy extended a hand, offering to help Hunter to her feet. "Come on, you'll dry off quicker if we go into the paddock and take in the afternoon sun."

Accepting her hand, Hunter looked up at Patsy and rose to her feet. "I don't understand why, or how, you did that."

"You were acting like I don't matter. As though you can make me think and do what you want me to. I want to be friends, but friends don't do things like that to each other."

"You want to be friends? You made me fall. You took me by surprise." Back on her feet, she pointed to the puddle. "I was unable to protect myself from the wetness and the cold of the water."

Patsy shrugged her shoulders. "You made me angry." She looked up at the sky. "My grandmother says that when I get angry the impact is probably felt across all the crossworlds."

"I think your grandmother is good at exaggerating."

Patsy thought about it for a moment then replied, "Maybe, but I think most of the time she's right." Again, she took Hunter's hand. "Come on, you really need to dry off. Let's go up to the paddock by the house. We can sit in the sun." Patsy smiled. "The way you're shivering, you'll likely catch a cold otherwise."

Hunter's teeth were chattering. "If a sickness tries to take hold of me, I will purge it as though it were a Nasqa." She dragged her legs forward and out of the puddle, using her free hand to try and pull the wet dress away from her legs. "It feels so horrible; the way it sticks to the flesh." She had to stop walking for a moment. Her head went back in an involuntary action. Her eyes closed, then she lurched forward and let out a sneeze.

Patsy replied, "I don't mind so much getting wet, and it's been ages since I caught a cold." She laughed to herself at the thought of Hunter trying to get rid of a cold the way she'd dealt with the mind thief. "Colds aren't like Nasqa. Mother says that, one day, people will learn that sickness is caused by lots of tiny creatures that invade the body."

"Then I will rip them out one at a time."

Patsy led Hunter through a shortcut to the paddock. It meant risking tears in their dresses as they followed narrow wallaby tracks, weaving through tea trees and tree ferns. Patsy preferred it to the pathway, and she was concerned about the need to get Hunter into the full sun as soon as possible. She thought about what Hunter had said. "That'll keep you busy. Mother says there are thousands and thousands of them."

"How does your mother know what people will learn in the future?"

"It's in the Book of Wisdom."

This book, it even has knowledge from the future? Father was wise to send me here, for more reasons than just seeking out Alfred.

As they scrambled to the top of the bank and entered the sunlit paddock, Patsy asked, "Why are you so interested in the Reverend Casey?"

Hunter's daisies turned to face Patsy, staring at her in surprise as Hunter replied, "I thought you didn't like us reading each other's thoughts."

"But they were so loud, I couldn't help but hear them. It was like you were screaming them out for the world to hear."

"It must be the wetness. I'll try to keep them more quiet in the future." She reeled back then let out another sneeze.

Patsy sat down in the sun. "You haven't answered my question."

Hunter joined her, choosing to lie on her belly so the sun would be on the wettest parts of her dress. Violets sprang up all around where she lay. "As I said before, in my world, it's rare for men to have the knowledge. When Alfred and your grandmother closed the portal, they used power from so many worlds that it left memories of what they'd done drifting into portals within many of the worlds they drew power from." Hunter paused, then rolled over onto her back. Her dress was already dry, as though the flowers had absorbed the moisture as they grew. "At first, my father was angry that someone would dare to draw power from our world. But then, when he felt the male presence in the memories, he saw hope for the future in them."

"In what way?"

"I won't say more till my father has met with Alfred."

"I don't know that the Reverend is keen to cross worlds again. He's only ever crossed once, and that was solely for the purpose of rescuing my grandmother."

A smug smile spread across Hunter's face. "He will."

*

Standing in the doorway to the library, Neridah heard Colin's voice approaching the front door of the house, closely followed by that of the Magistrate.

How could this be? She looked to where the man's body should be… it was gone!

Had she gone back somehow in time?

Desperate not to have to face Colin in this situation, she slipped out of the library and raced toward the dining room door, managing to get through just before she would have been seen by the two men.

"How about you get your mother-in-law to join us in the library, McIntyre? Rumour has it she's even better on the eye than your missus."

Colin walked on beside the Magistrate in grim silence as they entered the library.

Neridah struggled to maintain control. She could feel the blood pulsing through her temples. Although aware he would soon pass away, she couldn't help but think of what she would like to do to that man.

She was lost in imagined justices being carried out when she was confronted by something she'd never imagined herself having to deal with… the sound of her own voice approaching.

"Seriously, Meredith, we have to intervene. From what you tell me, there's something about the Magistrate that just isn't right. I wouldn't mind betting he's controlled by a mind thief."

The strangest part of it was that she remembered speaking those words. She knew what would happen next and, more importantly, where she should hide to avoid being seen. She knew that Patsy and Hunter would race past the doorway any second now… rushing to the library… that Cook would enter the corridor from the kitchen door next to the stairs carrying a tray of scones… and that Cook's appearance would cause Meredith and the other version of herself to hesitate before entering the library themselves.

Concealing herself behind the door, she watched Meredith and the other version of herself march through the dining room.

Her breathing became heavier and she felt faint. This couldn't be real. She had to call it out for what it was.

She must have passed out and was having a dream.

The best remedy, the only remedy, was to bring this dream to an end. She had to reach out to the image of herself.

Neridah stepped out from behind the half-closed door she'd been hiding behind and prepared to make her presence known, only to go mute when Meredith looked over her shoulder, made deliberate eye contact, and placed a finger over her lips.

*

Colin shook his head in despair. "I shudder to think what they'll think in Sydney when they learn of what's happened."

Darcy and his father remained silent while they shared the burden of the Magistrate's weight as they carried him through to the kitchen.

Cook was ready for them. "I cleared the table as soon as I heard of what happened. Mrs Banks has brought ample blankets to wrap the poor fellow. She told me no one answered when she knocked at the library door, so she brought them straight here. I've already moistened them for you."

Colin said. "Thank you, Cook. I wouldn't have expected anything less."

Ferdinand had followed the men in. What sounded like a meow and a purr to the others was clear to Colin. "You can tell, can't you? This isn't what it seems."

Colin looked at Cook. "Can you do one more thing for me? Can you please get that cat out of here?"

A few seconds later, Darcy and his father heard a sigh escape the dead man's lips. Jimmy O'Sullivan put a hand on his son's shoulder and said, "This happens sometimes. It's not something to worry yourself about."

Having learned the art of listening, Colin had heard a word within the dead man's sigh: *Flee.*

He rubbed a hand against his brow as he processed what was happening. For some reason, his memory of the day's events was hazy. As far as he could recall, the Magistrate had arrived earlier than expected, then there was a hole in his memory regarding what had happened before the man had a heart attack and passed away during a heated discussion in the library. He remembered sending Hunter and his daughter to the stables. It must have been to spare them having to deal with seeing the corpse. Come to think of it, even the memory of Hunter's arrival that morning was vague. Bringing himself back to the moment, he turned to Jimmy and asked, "Will you and Darcy be good enough to help Cook wrap him in the blankets and carry his body to the larder?"

Jimmy replied, "Aye, Mr McIntyre, consider it done."

Cook asked, "What about dinner, Mr McIntyre, sir? Are you still expecting the Reverend Casey?"

Colin replied, "Yes, we've no way of contacting him now to change the arrangements. So, we'll continue as planned. I expect he'll be here soon."

Cook looked at Jimmy and Darcy. "Well then lads, we'd best get done here so I can continue preparations." She turned to Colin as he was leaving the room. "Dinner should be ready in a bit over an hour."

*

As the sun fell below the horizon, Patsy and Hunter made their way back to the house. They'd shared an uncomfortable silence after the discussion about the Reverend. Despite that, Patsy still enjoyed the company of this amazing girl who came from such a different world.

They entered the back door leading into the kitchen just after Jimmy and Darcy had carried the Magistrate to the larder. Cook looked up from the soup she was preparing and said to Patsy, "It's about time. I boiled the water for your bath ages ago, young miss."

Patsy rolled her eyes. "Urgh! Do I really have to? What's Hunter meant to do?"

Cook folded her arms. "It's one thing your mother has always been strong about, that you should bath daily, before dinner. What Hunter does in the meantime is not my concern." She looked at their guest and asked, "Perhaps you'd like to have a bath too, Miss Hunter?"

Hunter looked at the bathtub and giggled, then said to Cook, "I bathed in the creek earlier."

Cook put her hands on her hips. "Oh, did you now? It's a wonder you haven't come down with a chill then. What, with how cold that water is and all."

The two girls looked at each other and snickered behind their hands. Patsy said, "I'm sorry. It won't take too long."

Hunter smiled and replied, "It's okay. I can go back to the stables. I liked it there."

Patsy giggled again, then tilted her head to one side as she swung her shoulders back and forth. "You just want to see Darcy again."

Hunter smiled, then looked at Cook. "I'll come back soon. I promise I won't be late for dinner."

Cook shook her head then turned her attention back to the soup as Hunter left the room. "I'll not say that I approve of a young lass like her going off to the stables to meet a young man like that."

.

It was already dark when the Reverend arrived at the McIntyres' for dinner. Darcy came out and greeted him as he dismounted from his sulky. "I'll look after Elsa for you, Your Reverence." He extended his hand, which the Reverend warmly received, grasping it in both of his own. Darcy smiled. "It's good to be seeing you again."

The Reverend put a hand on the boy's shoulder and said, "Aye, and it's good to see you as well. How's your father?"

"Getting older, but up to no good regardless." The voice came from Jimmy O'Sullivan as he emerged from the shadows near the stables. He addressed Darcy, "Come on, son, let's take Elsa so the Reverend can go inside and relax. I believe he had a funeral to deal with today."

The Reverend untied the cord holding his silky oak box in place so that the stablehands could feel free to take the horse and sulky. "There's no great rush, Jimmy. It's good to see you. I'm more than happy to share a moment of my time with the likes of you two scoundrels."

They all turned their attention to the McIntyre residence as the front door opened to frame Neridah's silhouette. Jimmy looked at the

Reverend and said, "We can catch up another time." He gestured to his son. "Come on, let's give Elsa the food and water she deserves."

The Reverend stood speechless as Neridah slowly approached.

She wanted to run to him, but not while the stablehands were still nearby. Once they were out of sight, she picked up her pace for the last few steps then threw her arms around the Reverend. "Oh, Alfred, I've missed you so much."

The Reverend couldn't help but reciprocate, enjoying the warmth of her as they embraced. "Aye, and I've missed you as well."

Neridah took in a breath then stepped back, looking the Reverend in the eyes. "I can smell smoke on you." She pulled back further and looked him up and down. "And your clothes are torn! What happened?"

He lifted a hand and ran it through her hair, just behind her left ear. "I've had a difficult day, and I'm afraid I don't have a home to go to tonight."

She embraced him once again. "Oh, my poor darling." She took a step back, still holding him. Her eyes made her look akin to a lost puppy.

He held up the silky oak box. "This is all I have left."

Again, she pulled herself close to him. "You know there's always room for you here."

The Reverend's response was deliberate and cold. "I think that's a decision for Colin to be making, don't you?" He stared deep into Neridah's pleading eyes, careful not to offer encouragement. "It's certainly not my place to accept such an offer without his approval."

Neridah pulled away, letting her hands fall by her side. "Why do you do this? Every time there's an opportunity for us to be together, you find a reason why we shouldn't."

"I took vows."

"Yes, I know the story." She wiped a tear away from her cheek then pointed a finger into his chest. "You took vows so you'd have the strength to one day save me; something you dedicated your life to." Her teeth clenched. "And you did it!" She grabbed hold of his arms at the elbow and shook them. "You saved me." She was taking several short and rapid breaths between each phrase. Venom dripped off every word. "Isn't that what your precious vows were all about?"

The Reverend's expression remained the same, as though carved from stone. He asked, "Don't you want to know what happened?"

She threw her arms in the air, like an adolescent throwing a tantrum. "Arrgh! You just don't get it! Do you seriously think you're the only one who's had a hard day?"

The Reverend could feel his blood pressure rising. "For the love of God! My house burnt down, woman." He gestured toward the two-story homestead with a slight movement of his head. "I believe yours is still standing."

She clenched her fists and stamped her foot before speaking through tears. "It's not my house. I just grew up here. Then, when you finally get around to rescuing me after forty long years of waiting, I discover it's now owned by my daughter's husband. And in case you hadn't noticed, he doesn't like me very much."

The Reverend looked away from her and stared at the house. He had no desire to continue having what was bound to be a circular argument. It was painful enough that he loved the woman. Did she have to make it so much harder? As he looked at the house, Talia appeared at his shoulder.

Neridah pointed at the pixie. "Oh, it gets better. You've got a new pixie travelling companion… a female one at that."

The Reverend ignored her as Talia looked at the house and asked, "What do you think?"

He responded in a soft, deadpan voice. "I'm thinking that something out of the ordinary might have taken place here today."

Neridah replied, "What? Like a timeless young beauty, with powers beyond anything I've ever seen, coming through the portal? Or a magistrate arriving from Sydney to strip Colin of half the property, then suddenly dying? But then the best part was when I tried to do a time freeze spell and found myself thrown back in time and had to watch myself do what I'd already done... topping it off with having my daughter bid me be silent!"

Talia asked her, "You did a time freeze spell?"

The Reverend shook his head in disbelief. He tugged at his beard while searching for the best response, only to be saved when Colin called out from the veranda, Meredith standing by his side. "Alfred, it's good to see you. No doubt Neridah has told you of our eventful day."

"Aye, that she has."

Neridah put her arm through the Reverend's. She looked up at him and smiled as she began leading him to the house as though no cross words had been spoken. "Poor Alfred's had a difficult day as well. Far more difficult than ours. It seems his house burnt down. I told him he's more than welcome to stay here."

Colin and Meredith stepped down from the veranda to approach the Reverend. Colin said, "Oh my God, Alfred, that's terrible news. Come inside and tell us about it over a brandy. And I insist you take up residence here until your own home is ready for your return."

The Reverend tipped his hat and replied, "Thank you. I'll gladly accept your offer." Neridah's grip on his shoulder tightened. She couldn't contain the smile that broke out in a broad grin as she began to blush. The Reverend continued as though he was unaware of her excitement. "I must ask you though, Bandah left my company this morning to investigate the girl Neridah says came through the portal this morning." He gestured toward Talia. "His cousin, Talia, came to me later in the day. She was most concerned, having concluded he'd vanished from this world and all others she can feel."

Talia flew out to be closer to Colin. "Actually, I lied when I told Alfred I'm Bandah's cousin. I'm actually his wife."

Meredith raised an eyebrow. "It seems we've got lots to talk about."

·

Hunter made her way down the path to the pool and its portal. She had no intention of going to the stables just now. Looking over her shoulder, she noticed the Reverend's sulky arriving. In the darkness, she was confident that no one would notice her. Although the sunlight was gone, she could still see the path, her eyes adjusting to the dark like those of a cat. The crickets began singing praise to her as she walked by, causing her to raise a finger to her lips. They went quiet in response to her unspoken command.

She stood at the water's edge. "Albiorix come, Albiorix come..." She continued the mantra as she raised her arms. Water in the middle of the pool began spinning in a vortex, droplets breaking away from the surface and rising several metres in the air. "Albiorix come, Albiorix come..."

More and more droplets rose above the vortex and came together until they formed the shape of a man. He had a heroic figure and wore a robe not much different from Hunter's dress. His chiselled features were framed by a mane of hair and a long beard, much like the Reverend. As Hunter lowered her arms, the watery figure spoke: "How goes the hunt, daughter?"

"The priest has just arrived."

"Splendid! When shall you return?"

"I shall bring him in the morning."

"That is good."

Hunter asked, "What of the trilogy of witches?"

"They are not your concern."

"The daughter is powerful. She made me fall."

The watery figure paused to reflect for a moment, then his brow furrowed before he continued: "Surprising as that may be, it is of little consequence."

"Also, Father, their book of spells seems to have great power within its pages. Perhaps I should bring that as well?"

The watery figure thrust an arm toward Hunter. The ground beneath her feet shook and she fell to the ground. "I am Albiorix! It is not for you to make suggestions. I sent you to bring the priest. We are under-gods! We have no need of books, they are for lesser creatures."

Humbled, Hunter rose to her feet. "I shall return in the morning with the priest."

"Good. Now go." The figure of Albiorix fell back to the pool as the vortex came to a stop. Within seconds, the surface appeared still. Hunter turned and walked up the pathway.

CHAPTER 9

C olin and the Reverend sank into the library's high-backed leather chairs. The Reverend's silky oak box was on the floor next to his chair. Neridah had chosen to sit on the settee with her feet up. After closing the ornate cedar door so they had privacy, Meredith poured Colin and the Reverend a brandy before taking a seat near the writing desk. Talia was hovering above the Book of Wisdom with her hands on her hips. "So, this is the famous book, huh?"

Neridah looked across and frowned. "What do you mean by famous? The only people who have ever read its pages have been those of our bloodline."

Talia flew up to her. "Ah, but here's the riddle for you. Your bloodline has been around for a long time. The book is older than humanity, at least in this world. The book co-exists in thousands of worlds but in each world it is also unique, reflecting the differences between those worlds. There have been legends told about it for tens of thousands of years. Much of our knowledge has come from those with access to its wisdom in other worlds… wisdom that custodians of the book have chosen to share with us. We—"

She was interrupted by the Reverend. "Hush… did you hear that?" He stared at the ground near his feet. "I could swear that I heard something just now. For the briefest of moments, there was something there." Talia immediately flew over to inspect the area of his eye line. "Can you feel anything of your husband?" asked the Reverend.

She looked up and shook her head. "I wish I could say otherwise, but no."

Colin said, "After a day like we've all had, it's easy to let our minds play tricks with us, to imagine the things we wish for to the point where it feels as though they're real."

Talia stared at Colin in disbelief, then turned to Meredith. "You actually chose to marry this man?"

Colin snapped, "I don't care if you're a pixie, a human, or some kind of god. When you are a guest in this household, you will treat me, and all the other occupants and guests, with respect."

Talia was about to speak when the Reverend asked Colin, "You wanted to know more about today's happenings?"

Colin nodded to the Reverend. "Please, I'm eager to hear your story."

"My day started with Bandah interrupting me while I bathed. He told of someone coming through the portal and his wish to learn about who or what it was. When I told him of my busy day, he insisted on coming here to see for himself."

Colin said, "I never saw him." He gestured to Meredith and Neridah. "Did either of you?"

Neridah said, "I've sensed gaps in my memory today. I wonder if one of us might have encountered him, but the memory is gone."

Colin said, "I haven't felt that." He turned to Meredith. "What about you?"

Meredith shrugged her shoulders. "I can't really say." Neridah stared at her, sure that she was keeping something to herself.

Colin put his hands together below his chin, the index fingers forming a steeple. "What of your house though, Alfred? I want to know how it came to be that it's burnt down."

The Reverend was about to speak when he looked to his shoulder. "There it is again."

Talia flew up to his shoulder and bent over, sniffing as though she were a bloodhound. Realising the whole room was watching her, she looked up and said, "There's nothing I can grasp onto to say where he is, but I can feel him. I'm sure that Bandah is with us." She flew toward Colin. "It has to be that girl, the one who came through the portal today." She turned and looked toward the base of the Book of Wisdom's stand. "There's something else too… I can sense a mind thief."

They all looked up when there was a knock at the door. Meredith called out, "Who is it?"

Mrs Banks replied, "It's just me, ma'am. Cook asked if I could let you know that she's about to serve dinner."

Colin stood up. "Oh well, it seems we'll have to hear the rest of Alfred's tale over dinner."

Talia protested, "But, what about Bandah? He's in here… I'm sure of it."

Colin replied, "Well then, you can stay in here and seek him out while the rest of us eat."

•

Patsy was waiting at the kitchen door when Hunter arrived back at the house. "Come on, Cook's already serving up dinner." She looked at the direction Hunter had come from. "I thought you were going to the stables?"

Hunter looked up with a half-smile. "I'll be seeing Darcy later... and I found myself missing home when the light had faded, so I went down to sit by the creek for a moment."

"In the dark?"

"Darkness doesn't bother me." She paused and sniffed the air.

"Doesn't it smell wonderful?" Patsy led her through the kitchen then looked over her shoulder. "I enjoy the smell of dinner almost as much as I enjoy eating it."

When they entered the dining room, the others were already seated, and Cook had placed Hunter and Patsy's bowls of soup on the table ready for them. Patsy pulled a chair out for Hunter. "Here, you can sit where I normally do."

Hunter almost looked nervous as she took her seat. When Patsy was seated as well, she looked down at the bowl of soup. She turned to Patsy and asked, "What's in it?"

"All sorts of things. Cook's friend, Mr Donaldson, gave her the recipe when he came back from a trip to the goldfields near Bathurst."

"What sort of 'things' are among the 'all sorts of things' you speak of?"

Patsy used her spoon to scoop out a piece of mutton. "Well, to begin with, there's mutton, and carrots, and corn. Cook says it's the ginger and mutton that give it most of its flavour." Patsy tore off a piece of the damper sitting on the plate next to her bowl of soup. "I like to dunk bread in it, especially while it's hot."

The rest of the table was silent. Colin let out a little cough to draw his daughter's attention.

Patsy put the bread back down on its plate. "Oh!" She was struggling to hold back a snicker. "Sorry, Father."

Colin gestured toward Hunter then moved his arm toward the Reverend. "Hunter, I'd like you to meet the Reverend Alfred Casey."

Hunter smiled. "Hello, I've been looking forward to meeting you."

The Reverend raised an eyebrow. "Oh, and why would that be?"

"My father thinks you're very important."

"Does he now?"

Meredith interrupted, "We can discuss such things with more clarity on a full stomach. Can I suggest we start on the soup before it goes cold?"

Hunter stared at the Reverend. "Why did you bring a pixie with you?"

The Reverend took a sip of his soup before responding. "I don't know that it's any of your business whether or not I share the company of a pixie on my journeys, young lady."

"I'm not young. I'm older than you could imagine."

"Then perhaps you should display more wisdom when choosing your words." The Reverend tore off a piece of damper and dunked it in his soup. He was about to take his first bite when he paused, then turned to Colin and asked, "What time do you intend to leave in the morning for the barracks?"

Colin finished chewing a piece of mutton and swallowed before replying, "Before sunrise. I don't want to be arriving with a body that has started to create a stench around it."

The Reverend asked, "Would you like some company on the journey? I've no commitments for the morning, and I believe the distraction would serve me well."

Hunter snapped, "No! You can't! You have to meet my father!"

Neridah couldn't resist a quiet comment. "This'll be interesting." She continued eating her meal as she watched. The others appeared as though frozen in time, fearful of how the Reverend might react. "It's normally Patricia who gets scary when she's angry."

Patsy pricked her ears up. She was surprised her grandmother would make such a comment. "Hey! I'm right here you know... at the table. It's not like I can't hear you."

The Reverend cast a cold stare toward Hunter. "Understand this, Miss Hunter, there is nothing and no one, on this world or any other, that will make me do something unless it is my own choice to do so."

Hunter returned the stare, made all the more threatening by the way the daisies in her garland turned toward the Reverend. "You will come with me in the morning to visit my father, and it will be your choice."

The room waited for the Reverend's reply in silent anticipation. "What is your father's name?" he asked.

"Albiorix."

"I thought as much." He pointed to her garland. "You'd do well to train your flowers to remain calm. They don't help you pull off your deceptions."

"You know my father?"

"I know of him."

"Then you'll agree to visit with him?"

"I'll decide what I wish to do when I'm ready." The Reverend broke off eye contact and returned to eating his soup.

Hunter looked around and asked, "Where's the pixie you brought with you?"

"Trying to figure out what you've done to her husband."

Neridah interrupted, "I thought Albiorix was just a legend."

The Reverend turned to her. "Aye, and legends are generally born from some form of reality. Before she died, your mother summoned me to her deathbed. There was just one thing that she asked of me: *Should my daughter return, protect her from the one called Albiorix who wears the crown of dancing daisies.*"

Hunter said, "I think it's best if you all just forget this conversation and enjoy the soup your cook has prepared."

Colin said, "To be honest, I haven't followed much of the conversation at all. I've been trying to listen, but I guess the long day has rendered me too tired to keep up."

Meredith added, "I must admit, I'm struggling a bit too." She smiled and grasped her husband's hand to reassure him.

The Reverend didn't bother to look at Hunter as he said, "I'll make two things clear to you, Miss Hunter. The first one would be that your parlour tricks don't work on me. The other is that you should avoid making the mistake of underestimating what these women can do. If you make them angry, I guarantee you'll regret it."

Patsy smiled and touched Hunter's arm. "He's right you know… on both counts. I could feel you trying to fog my understanding of the discussion, but it didn't work." She let out a little laugh. "I actually think it's kind of funny now."

Neridah gave Patsy a puzzled look. "I'm not quite sure what you're talking about."

Meredith chimed in, "I'm not following the discussion either."

Colin gestured toward Patsy and said, "At least there's a little laughter at the dinner table for a change." He raised a glass. "I propose we change the subject and enjoy the evening. After all, poor Alfred has had to endure the tragedy of his house burning down, and in the morning, he'll be transporting through the portal to meet with Hunter's father. As for myself, I'll be up before the dawn tomorrow to deal with the Magistrate, so I'll be looking to retire shortly after dinner. So, let's enjoy each other's company while we can."

The Reverend cast his eyes toward Colin. "A man has died today in your home. It's unlike you to be so frivolous of such matters."

Although Hunter was still looking into her bowl of soup, the flowers of her garland all seemed focused on Colin. He looked at the Reverend and said, "I'm really not sure what you're talking about."

Meredith glanced at her husband as she mopped her lips with a napkin, choosing to remain silent rather than draw the attention of Hunter and her garland. She was unwilling to even think about her concerns.

Neridah squeezed the Reverend's hand. "I'm so glad you've agreed to go with Hunter to meet her father." While Hunter smiled and cast her eyes down to her soup, Neridah glanced at Patsy and gave her a knowing wink. Patsy gave the gentlest of nods in return.

Hunter looked up from her soup and toward Colin. "I tire of this meal. It's not the sustenance on which I thrive." She made an attempt at politeness. "If it's okay with you, I'd like to leave the table now, so that I can go outside and dance. I've spent all day withholding the violets when I walk, and long to let them out while dancing."

Patsy leaned across and cupped her hand over Hunter's ear as she whispered, "Father never accepts the idea of someone leaving the table while others are still eating. He says it's very rude."

Hunter smiled as Colin replied, "Of course. Do as you must." As she got up and left the table, she looked at Patsy with a wry smile.

Patsy asked her father, "Can I join her? I think I've had my fill."

Hunter was halfway to the door, her daisies still facing those at the table. Colin leaned back in his chair, a puzzled expression on his face.

"Patricia, you surprise me that you'd even ask such a thing while we're all still eating."

"But Hunter just—"

Seeing her husband's anger rising, Meredith placed a gentle hand on his wrist and looked across at her daughter. "Patricia, you know better than to talk back to your father." She was looking forward to Hunter leaving the room, hoping that once that had transpired, Colin might regain control of his thoughts.

Her heart sank when, even after Hunter was gone, she observed the tiredness and confusion in his eyes.

*

With Elsa brushed down and happy in a stall, feedbag around her neck, Jimmy placed a hand on his son's shoulder. "I'll be off to our quarters. Mrs Banks intimated she might enjoy sharing a rum together before dinner, and that's an offer too good to refuse. She's been widowed a long time and deserves to spend time in the company of a gentleman like myself."

Darcy smiled and said, "Have a good time then. I'll do my best to make sure I embarrass you when I come up to join you for dinner."

"Oh? Will you now? I'd be minding my own business if I was you… else I might come snooping when you meet your new lady friend."

Darcy looked at the main house, then turned back to his father. "The McIntyres and their guests will be done with their dinner soon. I expect Hunter might come out anytime now. She told me she'd meet me here after dinner."

"Well then, I guess I'd best be getting out of your way." Jimmy laughed to himself as he walked into the darkness. It was a long time since he'd enjoyed life so much. Working with the McIntyre family had given him a great deal of joy and satisfaction.

No sooner had Darcy's father left the stables than Hunter appeared, seemingly out of nowhere.

Darcy removed his flat cap, fidgeting with it as he said, "Miss Hunter? What a surprise. I wasn't expecting you quite so soon."

She turned a shoulder toward him, bringing her chin down in a slow and deliberate movement. "I was getting anxious. I needed to come outside into the fresh air." She moved closer to him. "Do you like to dance?"

The very suggestion reminded Darcy of how he had danced with his family in Ireland. Special memories of his mother flooded through him; of how much she'd loved to dance before she fell ill. He stuttered a little as he replied, "W-w-well, yes. I love to dance!" He looked around and spread his arms. "But sadly, Miss Hunter, there's no music."

Hunter touched his cheek. "Listen, Darcy O'Sullivan, can you hear them? The cicadas, the crickets, and the frogs?"

"Well, yes, but—"

Hunter pulled away from him, spinning in pirouettes as she moved out of the stables. Violets sprang up wherever her feet touched the earth, causing Darcy to wonder if perhaps he were caught in a dream. She kept her head looking back at him, gesturing with her hands for him to follow.

Watching the gracefulness of her movements, Darcy shifted his weight from one foot to the other in an effort to build courage. Dream or not, he felt compelled by this young woman who was so full of the magic of life. It seemed only natural to him that one so beautiful should leave flowers in her wake.

As Hunter danced her way into the open, her movements brought the divergent sounds of nature into time with each other, as though she was conducting an orchestra. Crickets, frogs, flying foxes, all came together in harmony. The sounds made him want to move his own legs in time.

Unable to contain himself any longer, he threw the flat cap aside and took long strides out of the stables and into the night. Hunter was rim lit by the rising moon's soft light, appearing more beautiful than ever as she glanced over her shoulder and smiled at him. He didn't even notice that it was her thoughts he was hearing now rather than words: *Come, Darcy O'Sullivan. Come dance with me.*

He joined her in the moonlight, his legs rising and falling in time with the sounds of the night, sounds that filled his head and left no room for thoughts other than the need to dance and be close to this mysterious young woman.

Hunter spun around and laughed, her daisies freeing themselves from the constraints of the garland and dancing through the air in a circle around her.

As the tempo increased, Darcy became breathless.

Yet still, he danced.

The daisies grew larger, creating a wide circle around their host; a circle Darcy was now part of.

Faster and faster he moved, unable to breathe, yet unable to stop.

The violets from Hunter's footfalls had spread beyond the area of their dance, turning the paddock into a sea of colour.

Darcy looked around the circle as he continued his dance and saw that what had once been daisies were now fantastical creatures, the like of which he'd never seen.

One beast appeared as a tree with the facial features of a man that was somehow free of the ground, yet able to move its roots at will, like so many legs.

Another appeared similar to a human, but with a more slender appearance that lacked clothing or hair.

As best as he could tell there were eleven such creatures, each one different in appearance, and all consumed by the music of the night as the tempo increased still more.

He looked around the circle and noticed the disparate creatures had all joined hands, including himself.

Hunter laughed as she danced in the centre of it all, her whole body glowing in the light of the moon. Or was it something other than the moon that lit the dancers?

It was Hunter.

She had become the light.

She was chanting now: "Fusta abra-mouwn mouwn-be dis lessdee." To his surprise, Darcy could understand her unusual language as though it were English. *Dance for me, my little pets.*

The pace grew faster, and from out of nowhere, a single thought sprang into Darcy's mind. At first, he couldn't make out what it was until it grew enough to take over his consciousness.

Break free.

It was too late. The fantastical creatures had already begun to change. They were no longer dancing on the ground but moving through the air.

Hunter brought her hands down in a swift and sudden movement that caused the music to stop. In that instant, Darcy, and the other dancers from the circle were drawn in towards her as though she were a magnet. As they drew closer, Darcy watched the other creatures transform back to the daisies they'd been before. He was compelled to look outward, as were the others, then he felt the warmth of Hunter's hair against his back, a sensation that spread from head to toe.

Realising all too late what had become of him, Darcy tried to scream, his tiny daisy voice barely audible to even the others in the garland.

Hunter smiled as she walked to the house.

The mass of violets where she'd danced wilted and withered away to dust after she'd taken just a few steps.

.

Having no interest in joining the others for dinner, Talia remained in the library. She'd come to the McIntyre property with a specific purpose and could feel the echoes of what happened earlier in the day. There'd been an altercation with a mind thief, of that she was certain. She could almost taste it. But there was more. In all her lifetime, she'd only ever once felt the after-effects of a time freeze spell. And here, in this room, she could feel the evidence of three of them having occurred almost back-to-back, the last one having gone wrong. She could tell it all by the stench of the time leakage. Humans weren't inclined to pick up on such things.

Talia sat down on the chair where the Magistrate had suffered his heart attack. There was another echo she could feel, almost like it were a memory. She could feel its distress lingering all around her. Fear, abject horror of what some creature had faced. Her heartbeat quickened and she struggled to breathe. She stared at the space Hunter had filled just before reaching into the Magistrate. Pain tore through her chest until she pulled herself away and flew to the other side of the room.

She landed on top of a bookcase and lay on her back as she let her breathing return to normal. Having felt the echo of its pain, she could feel the presence of the mind thief still lingering, as though it were occupying the space within the room, but in a different crossworld. The more she dwelt on it, the stronger the feeling became. In the back of her mind, she heard the words, *Ellise-ar.* It was the language of the mind thieves… a language she rarely came across.

She knew that *ar* meant *I* or *me*.

But *ellise*… what did that mean?

She was sure she'd heard it before, but it must have been thousands of years ago.

Talia took her mind back to a world she'd dwelt in for a few centuries, just after she and Bandah had married. Then it came to her: *Ellise*, to *come*, or *follow*. There was a mind thief co-existing in this spot, but not within this crossworld, and it was asking her to follow.

There could be only one reason a mind thief would want anything to do with a pixie like her. It must have befriended Bandah. And if that were the case, they must both be trapped in the void between worlds. "Is Bandah with you?"

There were a few seconds of silence and then, *Ellise-ar.*

Talia bit her lower lip and looked down. "I can't believe I'm saying this… okay, I'll follow you."

Boe-esta.

Talia thought about the words then nodded. "You want me to stay low? That makes sense."

The mind thief led her out the front door, then down the side of the house and across the paddock to the stables. It was leading her toward where the other incident had taken place but paused before reaching the stables because of the conversation Darcy and his father were having nearby. When Jimmy O'Sullivan made his way to the servants' quarters, she expected Darcy would do the same.

Then Hunter appeared.

Talia hid behind a tuft of grass and watched the dance of the garland play out. She had to stay as quiet and still as possible to ensure she wasn't seen. For the first time she could remember, Talia felt scared—so scared she was worried the sound of her heartbeat might give her away.

She started to think it might be safe to draw a breath when Hunter started walking back up toward the house. Then, Hunter turned and looked straight at where she was hiding in the darkness. "Another pixie?"

Hunter reached out toward Talia, then pulled back, causing the pixie to be drawn straight to her. Unsure of what else she could do, Talia defiantly asked, "What have you done with my husband?"

Hunter feigned a coy expression. "Oh, how sweet! The two of you are married? And now you've come looking for him?" She smiled. "I so like it when I can help others find what they're looking for." She flicked a finger toward Talia and the pixie vanished.

*

Captain Taylor kicked Sean O'Malley's chest. "Wake up! We've word back from the Governor."

The gravedigger groaned. "I think you just broke a few of my ribs." His hand released its grip on the empty rum bottle it had clung to while unconscious.

"You make me sick. The way you let yourself sink into the embracing effects of drink and pain that your host experiences. You wonder why you haven't been entrusted with a host of higher station?"

O'Malley snarled at the Captain. "There's little else to get joy from when you're sent into the body of a gravedigger."

"Pitiful... truly pitiful."

"You criticise me, while you bathe in the glory of your status. I see so much hypocrisy in your words."

The Captain replied with another kick. This time his boot connected with O'Malley's face, knocking one of the gravedigger's few remaining teeth out as his head was flung back against the wall.

O'Malley wiped the blood and spittle away with a dirty sleeve. He glared at the Captain in the dull moonlight that shone through the room's one small window. "We could have this fun all night, but I'm curious as to what Governor Pritchard had to say."

Captain Taylor took a seat and put his feet up on his desk. He looked down at O'Malley and wondered why he'd allowed the man to sleep on the floor of his office in the first place. "He said we should act. He wants us there before dawn... before they have a chance to move the body. That way, we can make it look as though we were going in to protect the Magistrate. We can go in with force, eliminating McIntyre and making the seizure of his properties seem more reasonable to the good citizens of the Blue Mountains."

"What of our brethren?"

"That's none of our concern."

"Oh? Is it not true that without his call for help, we'd be none the wiser of what has already transpired at that property? And what of the under-god?"

"We will be going in there with twenty armed troops. Our target is McIntyre, not the under-god. The Governor believes she will ignore us if she knows we are only interested in the seizure of his land."

O'Malley shook his head as he thought to himself, *And you thought I was a fool.*

The Captain stood up and began walking to the door. "Sleep while you can. In a few hours, we'll be on the road to Blackheath and the McIntyre property."

*

Talia was winded when she hit the ground. She felt familiar hands lift her head and cradle it in a loving caress, then a voice she hadn't heard in decades said, "Oh, my poor—"

Bandah was cut off by Mrs Smith. "Well, that was some rescue. Did it ever occur to that wife of yours that she might want to take more care while watching that under-god thing?"

Talia, shocked by the interruption as much as by being forced into the void, looked at the aging fairy. "Who, or should I say *what*, are you? And who gives you the right to talk to me like that?"

Bandah's voice had a patronising tone. "Now, my—"

"Don't you start with that. I've barely seen you since that priest became your grundai." Talia sat up and looked at Mrs Smith, then turned back to Bandah.

Bandah looked at his wife and gestured toward the fairy. "Talia, meet Mrs Smith."

Talia got to her feet, staring at Mrs Smith. "Mrs Smith? Rather an odd name for a fairy, isn't it?"

Bandah shrugged his shoulders. "She's an odd fairy."

"I can see that." Talia made a small reflex jump as she caught a glimpse of the moving shadow to her right.

A sound almost like a voice came from the shadowy creature: *Ar-elliah*

Bandah nodded toward the mind thief as Talia pushed herself against him for safety. He put his hands on her shoulders, his cheek next to hers. "He says he's your friend."

"How do you know it's a he?"

"I don't, but the last body he inhabited was male, and I prefer 'he' to 'it.' Since he's been helping us, I've come to the conclusion that even a mind thief deserves a little dignity."

Mrs Smith folded her arms and rolled her eyes. "Here we go again. Are all you pixies such bleeding hearts?"

Talia glared at her. "Definitely not." She flicked a glance at Bandah. "Just him." She shifted her weight onto one foot, put a hand on her hip, and pointed at Mrs Smith. "I'm still puzzled as to how a fairy ends up looking so old and wrinkled. From my experience, fairies still look young after tens of thousands of years." She turned back to Bandah and took a step back. "And as for you… I want an explanation. What exactly is going on here? How can this girl, Hunter, be able to do this to us? Who is she?" She pointed toward the paddock. "You did see what she did to the stablehand?"

"Our friend calls her an under-god. The mind thieves, or Nasqa as they like to call themselves, they fear these under-gods more than any other creature."

The mind thief, being the combination of remnants from two such creatures, now rose high above its companions. It stretched out as though trying to listen to a distant voice, then let out a moan that sounded like wind whistling through trees. A sequence of sounds from what could have been considered a type of mouth followed. *Gak ye-ar-dat elka di-cun, fell-gosh os sess jai-bo-stae*

Talia asked Bandah, "Did you understand that?"

"He says that others of his kind are coming to help. That they'll be here before dawn."

Talia looked toward the shadow as she addressed Bandah. "You're not seriously going to trust them. Please, tell me you're not."

Mrs Smith approached her and placed a hand on her shoulder. "I never thought I'd live to hear it. A pixie making sense!"

Talia pushed Mrs Smith's hand away as Bandah replied, "I can't see we've any other choice. I've tried to reach Alfred with little success. When you arrived, I had new hope, until you found yourself in the same predicament." He turned toward the shadow. "The Nasqa's plan is our only choice. And I, for one, trust him."

CHAPTER 10

Colin and the Reverend had already adjourned to the library, leaving Neridah, Meredith and Patsy at the dining table.

Meredith folded her napkin and placed it on the table then turned to Patsy. "I think it's time you retire for the night."

Patsy protested, "But what about Hunter? Can't I wait until she's back, so I can show her to her room?"

"Patricia, I'm more than capable of showing Hunter to her room. Mrs Banks has already prepared it for her. We all need a good sleep tonight, and your father will be leaving before the dawn. I've no idea how long Hunter will be gone while spreading her flowers, and to be quite honest, I don't really care." She stood up as she continued. "What I do care about is that you've had a long day and need your sleep."

Patsy crossed her arms in an act of defiance. "I think you're going to join Father and the Reverend in the library to talk about things you don't want me to hear. You want to talk about what worries you about Hunter, and you're glad to have the opportunity to send me to bed before she returns."

Neridah swallowed her last morsel of the apple pie Cook had served for dessert before suggesting to Meredith, "She's right on all counts, you know."

Meredith couldn't believe it. Why couldn't her mother offer a bit of support from time to time, rather than always taking Patricia's side? The girl wasn't even in her teen years.

It was as if Neridah had read her daughter's mind. "She's almost twelve... you do realise that?" Neridah pushed her plate away and stood up. "I think there could be much to be gained if the three of us consulted the Book of Wisdom together."

Patsy's jaw dropped. *Yes! Oh please,* she thought. She'd spent many hours going through the Book of Wisdom with her mother and grandmother, but never before when there was something particular to research. She liked Hunter, but for reasons she was struggling to remember, the garland bothered her.

"We can't. At least, not until Colin and the Reverend have retired."

Neridah waved a dismissive hand at Meredith. "Alfred's house burnt down today, and Colin's day has been filled with stress. If they're not both ready to retire within the hour, I'll be most—" She stopped mid-sentence when she noticed Hunter's silhouette in the doorway. She put a hand to her chest and asked, "Hunter, how long have you been standing there?"

"Long enough." She walked into the room and looked at Patsy. "I thought we were friends."

Patsy looked puzzled. "I want to be friends, but you do make it difficult."

"Well, you don't need to worry, I'll be gone before sunrise. Can someone show me to my room? I'd like to get some rest now."

Patsy thought she could hear a tiny voice calling to her... so tiny it was more a distant whimper than a voice.

Pats, help me.

Noticing Patsy's distraction, Hunter stared at her. "Is something wrong?"

"No, I just thought I heard something."

Meredith made her way toward the doorway. "Come on, Hunter, I'll show you to your room."

As Hunter and Meredith left the room, Patsy tried to remember what it was she'd heard a moment ago. It was lost.

Patsy and Neridah watched the backlit forms of Meredith and Hunter make their way to the stairs. Once they were out of earshot, Neridah asked, "Have you struggled to remember things today?"

"Yes... in fact, just now, I thought I heard something, but can't remember what it was."

"I fear it's happened to all of us. It's like parts of the day are shrouded in fog. Colin seems to have been particularly susceptible, to the point where he's just not himself."

"I want to like her, but she keeps making me angry. I made her fall in the creek earlier."

Neridah smiled at the thought.

*

As they made their way up the stairs, Meredith said to Hunter, "Your plan will never work."

"What plan?"

"It's not really your plan, it's your father's."

How can you dare presume to know what my plans are?

Meredith turned to her and smiled. "It's written into the future's history. You and Albiorix will fail."

You will forget!

"No, I won't forget. I'm prepared for you, Hunter. Or would you prefer I use your real name rather than your title?" Meredith opened the door to Hunter's room. "You'll find a chamber pot under the bed if you need it. I hope you sleep well. You'll need it."

Hunter stared at Meredith's sardonic smile as she entered the room. "Not as much as you will." She walked toward the bed, then turned and added, "By this time tomorrow, you will go to my father begging to join in his service."

Meredith smiled and said, "You underestimate us." She pulled the door shut and made her way back downstairs.

*

The Reverend rejected Colin's offer of a brandy. He looked down at some of the cuts and bruises on his exposed forearms. "It won't do much to repair the damage of today, and certainly won't help me in my search for what's become of Bandah."

"I understand. However, I think I might indulge in one more, if for no other reason than to help me sleep while there's a corpse in the house." Colin took a seat and said, "Come with me in the morning, Alfred. On the way back from Springwood, we can order you some new clothing. I'll happily pay for it on my account. There's not much here I can offer you. Your shoulders are so much broader than mine."

The Reverend raised an eyebrow, curious that Colin seemed to have forgotten his earlier assertion that the Reverend would be accompanying Hunter in the morning. He nodded in appreciation. "You're a good man, Colin McIntyre. While I appreciate your welcome, I have much to attend to, and I've no intention of imposing on your hospitality longer than absolutely necessary." He looked at the ceiling. "The longer I'm here, the harder it will be to convince Neridah that my place is elsewhere. I'll be needing to organise a tent to see me through until my home is rebuilt."

"Hmmm. I wonder. Is that concern about how Neridah will feel, or about how you might struggle to leave her?"

The Reverend made a sweeping and dismissive gesture with his arm. He was unconvincing as he retorted, "Nonsense man!" He was about to continue when he heard something like a muffled voice next to his chair. "Did you hear that?"

Colin looked puzzled. "Hear what?"

"It was like a voice, but I couldn't make out a word."

"Bandah?"

"Perhaps." The Reverend looked around. "I would've expected the pixie woman to return by now."

Colin rubbed his brow, as though he had a headache. "I have to say, I'm struggling to stay awake. Everything feels a little hazy."

"Perhaps you'd do well to retire for the evening."

Colin held a hand against his forehead. "I'll be fine, really." He sat up straight in his chair, as though he'd had a sudden surge of energy and inspiration. "It just occurred to me. If you want to find out what's happened with Bandah, perhaps you should go with Hunter when she leaves tomorrow. Maybe her father can give you the answers you need."

The Reverend stared at him. "Those aren't words I'd expect to hear come from you, Colin McIntyre."

Again, Colin found himself rubbing his forehead. "What? That I'm struggling to stay awake?"

"No, it's what you said after."

"I've… no recollection of saying other than that I'm tired. Things are a little hazy." He looked up and saw Neridah standing behind Patsy in the doorway, her hands resting on the younger girl's shoulders.

Neridah said, "We thought we might join you for a few moments before Patricia goes to bed and you retire."

Colin looked at his daughter's smiling face. "Yes, of course, come in… both of you." He rose from his chair, far slower than Patsy was used to seeing him move. "I'm afraid, however, that I may have to leave you in Alfred's care. The day seems to have caught up with me and I need to rise well before the dawn."

Patsy and her grandmother stepped forward into the library, creating space for Colin to stagger past them. "Goodnight, Father. I hope you feel better in the morning."

Colin gestured with his hand as he passed them. "Yes, of course. Goodnight, pumpkin." It had been years since Colin had called her pumpkin. He paused at the bottom of the staircase and looked back at his daughter. Despite his extreme tiredness, her smile was infectious. The subtle grin that spread across his face helped him straighten as he made his way up the stairs.

The three remaining in the library waited until they heard the door to Colin's bedroom close before they dared to speak. Then Neridah walked up to the Reverend and said, "Tell me, Alfred. Tell me you're not going to do it."

"How can I tell you such when I've still no idea myself of what I'll be doing?"

Patsy asked, "Shouldn't Talia be back by now?"

The Reverend said, "Aye, it troubles me greatly." He turned back to Neridah. "That's why I'm feeling such uncertainty. It may be that the only way to find answers is to follow Hunter back to her own world."

Neridah grabbed his shoulder. "Then I'll go with you. Together we're so much stronger. Remember when we shut the portal?"

The Reverend shook his head. "No. That cannot happen. You cannot go breaking up the Trilogy at such a time. The power of you three women working together is far greater than the power you and I share."

They all turned to the door when Meredith entered. "Do you really think it's wise to have these discussions so openly when Hunter is upstairs? You do know she hears our thoughts?"

Patsy said, "I can read her thoughts too. And I made her fall into the creek when she made me angry."

The Reverend raised an eyebrow.

Neridah was about to speak when she heard frantic knocking at the front door. Meredith said, "I'll see who it is." She walked through the library doorway and into the corridor calling out, "Who's there?"

A panicked voice with a thick Irish accent replied from beyond the door. "It's Jimmy O'Sullivan, Mrs McIntyre. I'm sorry to be troubling you at this hour."

Meredith opened the door. The others were huddled in the library doorway, curious as to what the problem might be. "That's okay, Jimmy. What's wrong?"

As a sign of his respect, he took off his flat cap. His eyes were wide with desperation, and a tear ran down his cheek. He rubbed his chin as if it would help him find his words. "It's my boy, Darcy, Mrs McIntyre. He went walking earlier this evening with your young guest and hasn't returned. I saw through my window when your guest returned to the house, but when I went back to our shared quarters, Darcy was nowhere to be seen."

Neridah made her way to the front door. "And where were you while your young son went walking with our house guest? Do you think that's responsible, especially with a girl who appears so young?"

Jimmy stared at the ground. "I'm sorry to say that I was with Mrs Banks, sharing a wee rum before dinner." He looked up with eyes full of sorrow. "There was nothing more than a shared drink and some laughter, honest to God, ma'am." He looked directly at Neridah. "Honestly, Mrs Corrigan, I trust my son's good intentions. He rarely gets to see girls other than your granddaughter, so I was happy for him."

Neridah glared at Jimmy. Every time she heard the name Corrigan, it reminded her of the short-lived and loveless marriage she'd never wanted.

In contrast, Meredith smiled as she placed a reassuring hand on Jimmy's shoulder. "You're a good father, Jimmy. And I'm glad that you and Mrs Banks are spending time together." She looked over her shoulder and called to Patsy, "Did you know of this liaison between Hunter and Darcy, Patricia?"

Patsy looked down to hide a guilty smirk. It took great effort to feign a look of innocence as she looked up. "Well... sort of..."

The Reverend said, "Mr O'Sullivan deserves to know what you know." He gestured toward the front door. "Go on, lass."

She looked at Jimmy and said, "I don't know that there's more I can tell you other than what you already know. She asked if he thought she was pretty, and then Darcy asked if she'd like to go for a walk after dinner."

Jimmy choked back tears. "Darcy's dinner is still waiting on the table..."

Patsy tried to say something, but the sudden realisation of how serious the situation was left her speechless.

Neridah turned to Meredith. "I think we should go upstairs and ask Hunter what she knows."

Meredith nodded in ascent.

Patsy said, "I'll join you."

Neridah and Meredith replied in unison, "No!" Then Meredith put her hand on Patsy's shoulder. "It's better that you stay here with Jimmy and the Reverend."

"But I know her bet—"

Neridah interrupted her, "Patricia, you know better than to argue with your mother." She turned to the Reverend. "Perhaps Mr O'Sullivan would be more comfortable if you and Patricia sit with him in the parlour while we learn what Miss Hunter knows of Darcy's whereabouts?"

The Reverend nodded. "Aye, come on Jimmy, or you'll be catching a cold standing out there."

As the Reverend ushered Jimmy into the parlour, he glanced over his shoulder, sure that he'd heard something, yet unable to say what it was. He turned to Patsy and said, "Perhaps you can see if Cook is still in the kitchen, and if she is, you might ask her to prepare a pot of tea?"

Patsy turned and dragged her feet as she left the room. "Okay, if I must."

The Reverend glared at her. It never ceased to amaze him how much he could see Neridah's attitude as a young girl reflected in Patsy.

*

Neridah and her daughter lifted their dresses as they ascended the stairs, conscious of avoiding the risk of tripping on the hems. Their silence and grim expressions betrayed their shared understanding of the seriousness of the situation.

On reaching the top of the staircase they turned toward the guest room and walked toward it, yet with each step, the room seemed just as distant as before. Mother and daughter looked at each other and quickened their pace.

Again, they found themselves lifting the hems of their dresses, allowing them to break into a run. Still, the door at the end of the corridor remained distant.

Meredith grabbed Neridah's shoulder. "Mother, stop. We need a different approach."

Neridah complied and squatted with her dress pulled over her knees as she struggled to regain her breath. She looked at her daughter and asked, "Okay, so what would you suggest?"

Meredith bent her knees to bring herself closer to her mother's level. "The more we tried, the further away the door seemed to be. Perhaps we need to release that sense of purpose, and merely walk to the end of the corridor."

Neridah nodded. "It's worth a try."

The two women stood up, then looked at their surroundings in stunned amazement. Meredith wrapped her arms around her shoulders, steam coming from her lips with each breath. She looked up at the stars and asked her mother, "How did we end up out here?"

"Your guess is as good as mine, but I'm thinking our guest had something to do with it." She looked up the paddock to the lights shining from the windows of their home. "We'd best get back to the house."

Meredith nodded her agreement and the women started up the hill.

After a few steps, Neridah asked, "Earlier today, you looked back at me and placed a finger over your lips. I'd thought I must have been dreaming when I watched you walk through the room with me."

"Your time freeze went wrong."

"How did you know?"

"I can't tell you... not yet anyway."

"You did one too, didn't you? Only earlier... that's why mine failed."

Meredith stared at her mother but didn't reply.

They finished their walk back to the house in silence.

*

Jimmy stared out the parlour window. "Isn't that Mrs McIntyre and Mrs Corrigan approaching?"

The Reverend stood up and approached the window. "Aye, that it is."

"I thought they went upstairs to talk to their house guest?"

"You're not wrong, they did just that." He turned to Jimmy. "Perhaps they couldn't find her upstairs, so went outdoors to continue their search."

Patsy interrupted, "That's just silly."

The Reverend turned and glared at Patsy.

Jimmy's face betrayed the horror he felt at hearing Patsy speak that way. "Young lass, that's no way to speak to a man of the cloth."

"I don't care. I was in the kitchen with Cook. They would have had to go through there to end up in the garden without being seen by you."

The Reverend's words were calm but firm. "I've had a hard and trying day, and Jimmy is in distress. Under such circumstances, it's highly likely that we might miss your mother and grandmother slipping by and out the door."

Patsy's breathing was getting heavy. She knew he wasn't telling the truth.

The tension eased when Neridah and Meredith entered the room.

Meredith sat down next to Jimmy and placed a hand on his knee. "I'm sorry, Jimmy. We've searched high and low, but we didn't come across Hunter or Darcy."

Jimmy bit his lower lip as he wiped a tear from his eye. "I understand what you're saying."

Neridah looked at him and said, "Surely, you don't think—"

Jimmy cut her off. "I thought I could trust my son to be better than that." He got up from his chair. "Thank you for your care and hospitality, Mrs McIntyre." He made his way toward the door, but Patsy lunged across and blocked his path.

"It's not what you're thinking, Mr O'Sullivan. Darcy's not like that."

Jimmy gently guided Patsy out of his path. "I appreciate that you think the best of the boy, but there's things a young man can be tempted by that I don't think you're ready to understand." He turned towards the others and tipped his cap. "Ladies, Reverend, I'll be bidding you a good night and my apologies for disturbing you. There'll be hell to pay for Darcy when I see him in the morning."

"Arrgh!" Patsy couldn't contain her frustration any longer. The others knew as well as she did that Hunter had to be behind whatever had happened to Darcy. She ran past them and stormed up the stairs.

Meredith called out, "Patricia! How dare you! Come back here, now!"

The Reverend placed a firm hand on her shoulder and said, "Let her go."

As Jimmy walked out the door, Neridah turned to Meredith. "I'll go after her." She leaned across and whispered in her daughter's ear, "Perhaps you should go with Jimmy to the servant quarters and see if you can work out what's happened to his boy."

Meredith nodded and set out after the Irishman. "Hold on, I'll go with you, Jimmy. Maybe I can find a clue you may have missed."

Jimmy stood at the bottom of the veranda steps waiting for her to catch up. "That's most kind of you, Mrs McIntyre."

*

Patsy stomped up the stairs, each footfall hitting hard enough to make the whole staircase vibrate. Her grandmother called out to her, "Patsy, please. Not on your own."

Patsy paused. It was rare that her grandmother would address her in front of the others as Patsy. But it lacked sincerity. Why couldn't they see it? Weren't they aware how few friends she had living so far out of town? Darcy was the only person even remotely near her own age that Patsy got to speak to on a daily basis... and no one seemed to really care about finding what had happened to him.

No one but Patsy.

She turned away from her grandmother and continued up the stairs. She reached the top and turned to face the door at the end of the corridor. She took brisk, confident strides as she approached, throwing her arms up when she was halfway and causing the door to fly open with such force it almost came off its hinges.

The room was empty.

Patsy ran into the room and straight to the open window. She felt sure she knew where to find Hunter. As she started to climb out the window, her grandmother called out from the doorway, "It's too dangerous."

Patsy replied, "Not for me it isn't." She ducked her head to get through the window, let her feet down onto the corrugated iron, then made her way to the latticework supporting the jasmine, just like she'd done the year before.

CHAPTER 11

N eridah raced downstairs and into the parlour. "She's going to the portal. We've got to stop her!"

The Reverend grabbed her shoulders. "Who? Patricia, or Hunter?"

His question was answered by the sound of Patsy's feet scampering across the corrugated iron of the veranda roof before they saw her through the windows as she climbed down the lattice. She was illuminated by the full moon when she paused after noticing the faces in the room staring at her. She pushed her feet against the lattice and thrust herself into the night. The air around her thickened as she drew masses of atmosphere from adjacent crossworlds into their own, increasing the air's density so she was able to swim through it as she would through water.

Neridah took the Reverend's hands in hers while they watched her granddaughter labouring to pull herself along. "Alfred, we need to stop her. She can't do this on her own."

"Aye." They both closed their eyes and allowed themselves to be elsewhere. Every part of their being connected to the myriad strings of energy spreading through the Crossworlds. Their recognition of where they were allowing themselves to be shifted the energy in several nearby crossworlds to the corresponding location, causing the space they occupied in this world to snap across to the position they wished to relocate to. There was no movement as such, just a change in the location they occupied.

A moment later, when they opened their eyes, they were immediately below Patsy as she flew over the paddock. Although she was above their heads, she was still low enough that they could reach out for her. Neridah grabbed her wrist, and the Reverend caught her ankle. She kicked against the Reverend's arm as he pulled her down and she clipped her grandmother's jaw with a wild swing of her free arm.

"Let me go!" She closed her eyes and tried to be elsewhere.

The Reverend's voice was firm. "That'll not work for you while you're struggling. Particularly not while we've got hold of you... unless you believe you've enough strength to move us all."

Patsy gave up the struggle. She allowed the thickened air to return to the neighbouring crossworlds and let herself fall. The hold the others had on the girl prevented her from hitting the ground. Instead, she ended up embraced by Neridah, who wrapped an arm around Patsy's shoulders. "You can't risk this on your own. Not with Hunter. She's too powerful."

"I just want to know what she's done to Darcy."

The Reverend's voice was soft and reassuring. "Aye, and I'd like to know what's become of Bandah and Talia. But I fear that we won't learn of their fate by direct confrontation."

"She said she's leaving before sunrise! We'll never find out what's happened to them once she's gone."

"And that's why I'll be going with her."

Neridah took a step back. "No! There has to be another way."

He turned to face her. "If there is, then I'd certainly like to hear it." He looked up to the house, then at Patsy. "Seeing Hunter has obviously left the house, for now, I suggest we make our way back and get some sleep. I believe the Trilogy will need to be ready for something we've yet to learn of come the morning."

They made their way up the hill, each of them feeling tired after using the power of the Crossworlds to transport themselves.

.

Mrs Banks rushed downstairs, wearing a dressing gown and a concerned expression, when Meredith and Jimmy entered the servants' quarters. "Did you find him?"

Jimmy shook his head. "I thought I could trust him." He wiped a tear from his eye. "He's always been better than this."

Meredith asked, "Perhaps you could make a pot of tea, Mrs Banks?"

"Yes, of course."

"In the meantime, I might have a look around, if that's okay with you, Jimmy?"

He nodded his approval. "Feel free, Mrs McIntyre."

"Can I ask where you saw him last?"

"He was waiting for the girl down by the stables. I believe that's where he'd arranged to meet her."

"Thank you. I'll start there in that case."

Mrs Banks said to Jimmy, "You just go through to the kitchen and make yourself comfortable while I get the kettle on. Cook should be back from the house soon, so we'll all be able to enjoy a relaxing cuppa together. I'm sure Darcy will be back by the time we're through."

As Jimmy made his way to the kitchen, Mrs Banks followed, looking over her shoulder at Meredith. "Honestly, children today. They have no respect."

Meredith turned and headed toward the stables, her bold stride conveying a sense of purpose. Her attention was momentarily distracted by movement near the house. From this angle, she could see the back door that opened onto the kitchen. Cook had finished for the night and Ferdinand had slipped out the door with her. Cook pulled her shawl tight around her shoulders and made her way to the servants' quarters while the big tom raced around the corner and down the paddock, heading toward the portal. As Meredith focused in that direction, she noticed a dull glow behind the trees.

On reaching the stables, she felt the blue chill of the time freeze. Not on her flesh, but on the outer surface of her mind. It had colour and texture that was familiar, and an aroma of jasmine that she felt rather than smelt. It was almost identical to the echo left behind by the time freeze she'd created earlier in the library, not long after Hunter's arrival. The colour of the echo in the library had changed after the subsequent time freezes from Hunter and her mother. Three time freezes in one space within just a few hours, little wonder her mother's had gone so wrong.

She walked through the space where the freeze had occurred. The area was clearly defined. Sometimes she wondered how people without the gifts her ancestral line possessed could fail to notice such things. Even her husband, who she'd successfully taught to listen to the animals and nature, would more than likely completely miss what to her was so obvious. In that moment she wondered if Hunter had noticed the echo of her time freeze when she'd entered the library earlier. Her mother had missed it, which surprised her.

Meredith cast her eyes on the paddock below the stables. A large area of grass that had been lush and green earlier in the day was dead. She walked out and stood in the middle of the area of withered and wilted grass. She closed her eyes and waited for stray echoes from memories of what had transpired here to flow through her mind.

To her surprise, the echoes remained clear. Hunter had done little in way of cleaning up after herself. As Meredith soaked up and digested them, it became obvious. This couldn't be left until the morning. Hunter had to be dealt with now.

She closed her eyes and allowed herself to join Hunter at the portal.

·

Hunter didn't take her eyes away from the glowing centre of the portal when Meredith appeared by her side. She was holding Ferdinand in her arms and stroking him behind the ears. "I was wondering when you'd appear."

"You were careless. You left memories behind."

Hunter smiled. She still hadn't made eye contact with Meredith. "Perhaps I left only what I wanted you to find?"

"What did you do to Darcy?"

Hunter's smile grew wider. "See, you know something of what happened, but the detail you long for is missing."

"He was just a boy."

"And now, he will live for thousands of years. His life will have far greater value and meaning than it ever would have had I not intervened."

"Who are you to judge the value of a life? What gives you the right?"

"I am my father's daughter. I have the right to do as I please."

"You are Kerridwen, daughter of Albiorix. My ancestors banished your father. And we'll banish you too."

Hunter turned to face her. "And you learned this from your pretty book in the library?"

"I learned of your father's name from my grandmother. She warned me of the god-like being called Albiorix who wore a dancing garland of flowers on his head, as her grandmother had warned her. The warning has been passed through the generations since he was banished."

"But you learned my name from your book?'

"Yes."

Hunter squatted and released the cat. At first, he looked confused, then he ran up the bank and into the paddock. "The cat won't be able to speak in ways you understand now. He'll understand only your intentions but not your words."

"Why would you do such a thing?"

"The cat said he wished to join me when I leave. He's not happy. He feels that being understood only makes his life harder."

"You behave as though you're a god. But I know you're not. The mind thieves call you and your father under-gods."

Hunter laughed. "My father was worshipped as a god in this world for thousands of years."

"My ancestors banished him. He can't return."

"And in return for what they did to him, I shall banish you from this pitiful world of yours too!" Hunter drew an arm back then thrust it forward. Meredith was swept off her feet, straight toward the swirling glow of the vortex within the now active portal that lay at the pool's centre.

•

Neridah stood in the doorway to Patsy's room. Her granddaughter had changed into her nightgown and was climbing into bed. "Can I trust that you won't climb out that window during the night? You need your sleep."

Patsy rolled her eyes and looked away. "Okay, if you insist."

Neridah planted her hands on her hips. "Honestly, Patsy, I shouldn't have to ask such a thing of you. You'll send me grey before my time."

Patsy smiled and laughed to herself. It was a private joke they often shared about how a woman of Neridah's age would normally be grey by now for sure. She also liked that when they were alone like this, her grandmother often referred to her as 'Patsy' rather than 'Patricia.' She pulled up the blankets and said, "Goodnight, Nana-Neri."

Neridah entered the room and walked over to the bedside. She leaned over, kissed Patsy on the cheek, and said, "Goodnight." She turned and left the room, pulling the door shut behind her.

Patsy waited patiently until she'd heard Neridah going down the stairs. Once she felt sure it was safe, she threw back the covers, tip-toed across the room, and grabbed her dressing gown from its hook on the back of the door.

She closed her eyes and allowed herself to be at the bottom of the pathway that led to the portal. Strings of energy in multiple crossworlds moved to the location she'd visualised and, a moment later, her physical being shifted from where she had been in her room to the spot where those strings demanded she should be.

Patsy opened her eyes as Hunter threw her arms forward to send Meredith hurtling toward the open portal. Without hesitation, she thrust her right hand towards her mother, then pulled back. The gesture pushed the air between herself and her mother into an adjacent crossworld, creating a vacuum. At the same time, air from a hundred worlds filled the space immediately behind the airborne woman, creating pressure that released itself by pushing Meredith toward the shore like she'd been fired by a slingshot. She landed so hard she was winded by the impact when she hit the ground next to Patsy.

Hunter glared at Patsy with eyes that betrayed the fire burning within. "How dare you!" The daisies in her garland turned to face Patsy, each in turn seeking to break free of their constraints and snap at her... all the daisies, that is, excepting one toward the back of the garland that appeared wilted and sad.

Patsy remained calm and stood her ground. "I'm not scared of you."

Hunter stood still as the wind began building around them. Her breathing was heavy, her words slow and deliberate. "Well, you should be. I am Kerridwen, daughter of Albiorix. I am the hunter, the under-god that the Nasqa fear." The wind had built to a howling gale. Lightning flashed and a crack of thunder shook the earth. "I am the one you should fear."

"Well, I don't"

Hunter raised her right hand and thrust it towards Patsy, releasing a burst of lightning from the palm of her hand. Before it reached the space Patsy occupied, she was gone. Hunter turned and saw Patsy was now behind her. Again, she thrust out her arm, releasing another lightning bolt, and again Patsy was gone. The lightning struck a tree and caused it to explode. Hunter turned again, just in time to see the ball of energy heading towards her from Meredith's outstretched arm. Taken by surprise, the under-god was sent backward, coming down hard on the sandstone of the path. She prepared to send a reprisal Meredith's way but was knocked over by another ball of energy, this one coming from Patsy. She raised herself on her elbow and said, "Attack. Show them no mercy!"

The daisies broke away from her garland and grew. They swirled through the air in different directions as they continued to grow and develop ferocious jaws filled with razor-sharp teeth that snapped open and shut in a constant and rapid pace. Meredith and Patsy held their hands low and drew energy from across a hundred crossworlds to create glowing shields of energy around themselves.

The snapping jaws of the daisies descended on them. Each time they made contact, they tore away part of the shields, only to then be repelled by the sting of the energy produced by what remained of the very shields they were attacking.

Each time they retreated, they would regroup and descend again to take another bite.

Among all the daisies, there was one that swirled in a panicked circle, unable to resist the need to snap its jaws, but unprepared to allow itself to swoop at Meredith or Patsy.

While struggling to maintain the strength of their shields, the witches were unable to strike back. Hunter took advantage of the opportunity her snapping daisies created and began hurling bolts of lightning at the shields, reducing their size further with each blast.

Patsy had to shift her hand to avoid it coming into contact with one of the attacking daisies and Meredith was dragged backwards when a strip of fabric was torn from behind the shoulder of her dress.

A voice thundered above the chilling noise of the attack. "Enough!"

The Reverend stood at the top of the path, silhouetted by the moon.

Hunter stood up and raised both hands, gesturing with a waving motion of her fingers for the daisies to return to the garland.

Neridah stood behind the Reverend Alfred Casey, remaining at the top of the path as he descended the sandstone stairs. He spoke in a calm voice. "I'll go with you to meet your father. But we leave now, or else not at all."

With the daisies back in place within the garland, Hunter said, "Very well then, Alfred Casey." Ferdinand ran to her and let out a loud meow as she turned to face the water. She bent down and picked him up. Stroking his chin, she began walking into the swirling pool with the Reverend close behind.

At the top of the stairs, Neridah buried her head in her hands and sobbed.

CHAPTER 12

As Patsy, Meredith and Neridah began their lonely ascent up the paddock towards the house, they were brought alert by the frantic calls of Jimmy O'Sullivan running toward them. "I saw the lightning! The thunder was near deafening! But I heard voices too. One of them I'm sure was the girl." He looked around, his eyes scanning all around, expecting one of the faces to be Hunter's. "Did you see her? Have you come across Darcy?"

Neridah looked away and burst into tears. Meredith looked at the ground, unsure whether the priority was to console Jimmy or her mother. Patsy, however, showed little hesitation. She walked up to Jimmy and said, "Don't worry, Mr O'Sullivan. If Darcy isn't back tonight, he'll certainly be back tomorrow. It seems Hunter had to leave at short notice. I daresay he's travelled part of the way with her to ensure her safety."

Jimmy looked at Neridah. With his eyes transfixed on her grandmother, he asked Patsy, "Then why is it she's bursting into tears?"

Patsy put her hands on her hips and let out a deep breath as she shook her head in surprise. "Mr O'Sullivan..." Jimmy turned to face her. "In case you've forgotten, the corpse of a magistrate who came to visit today is in the larder. You know she's a sensitive woman. Is it little wonder that her concern over the panic you're feeling over Darcy's whereabouts has sent her over the edge?"

Jimmy nodded his head. "Aye, I guess you'd be right there." He turned to Neridah and said, "I'm sorry for the extra burden I've placed on you ladies this evening. As Patsy here so rightly says, Darcy will more than likely be back tomorrow... and he'll have some explaining to do." He tipped his flat cap. "I'll bid you goodnight."

Meredith replied, "You've nothing to apologise for, Jimmy. I'd be surprised and concerned if you reacted in any other manner. I'm sure Patricia is right... that Darcy will be back at some stage tonight or tomorrow." As Jimmy walked back up the hill, Meredith looked at her daughter and spoke in a soft voice to ensure Jimmy couldn't overhear. "You did well, Patricia. He may well sleep tonight after all, thanks to your quick thinking."

Patsy stared into the space in front of her as she replied, "I just hope we can find a way to get Darcy back for him before the sun rises."

·

For a second time, Sean O'Malley was woken by Captain Taylor's boot connecting with his belly. He coughed and spluttered, feeling sure the Captain had damaged some vital organ.

"Come on, gravedigger. It's time to get yourself together. We ride out within the half hour."

Sean rolled over and clutched his belly. He lay there and watched the Captain's boots as he left the room, the sound of each step reverberating through his head like a hammer hitting an anvil. This was the price he paid for allowing himself to feel the effects of the alcohol on his host. He experienced the carefree abandon, but also the repercussions the following day. His back resisted as he pushed himself up from the floor. Once he had one knee up, he felt confident to reach for the top of the table next to him. His sweaty shirt clung to his grime-covered chest as he struggled to his feet.

A loud ruckus from outside drew his attention to the window. "Oh my…" He found himself lost for words when he realised what was going on. He'd come to the barracks expecting to take a small handful of men with him to the McIntyre property. Now, as he surveyed the scene outside, there were dozens of soldiers on horseback. Seeing Captain Taylor approach a dismounting officer, he shifted himself to the side of the window, to be able to hear what was taking place without being seen.

Captain Taylor's voice boomed loud. "Lieutenant Stewart, I trust your ride from Parramatta wasn't too difficult. At least you had the light of the full moon to guide you."

Lieutenant Stewart didn't bother to look at the Captain, nor accept the hand he'd extended. "Spare me the platitudes, Taylor. Technically, you may outrank me, but make no mistake, the Governor has made it clear that the McIntyre property is to be secured as soon after daybreak as is physically possible." As he spoke, he led his horse to the water trough. "And he has placed that burden squarely on my shoulders."

The Captain's eyes darted around to see how many of Lieutenant Stewart's troops had noticed the ignored offer of a handshake before lowering his arm. "In that case, I'll have my men saddle up their horses immediately."

The Lieutenant turned to face him, the features of his round face accented by his sunken eyes, waxed moustache, and meticulously groomed hair. "Where's the gravedigger, the one who informed you of what was taking place?"

"He's eavesdropping, just behind the window back there."

"Splendid!" Lieutenant Stewart approached the window. "Come on, O'Malley, you'll be riding up front with me, as an honorary member of the Parramatta Lancers."

Sean O'Malley rolled his body against the wall until he was facing the Lieutenant. "That will indeed be an honour, sir." A warm smile emerged on his face as his eyes drifted toward the humbled vestige of Captain Taylor.

.

The Reverend Alfred Casey looked around at the unfamiliar surroundings. Never had he seen so much colour. When he brought his eyes back to the shore, he saw dozens of men and women dressed much like Kerridwen. Many wore garlands like hers as they lazed about among flowering bushes. It appeared they were enjoying a mass picnic celebration.

The Reverend turned to Kerridwen and asked, "Are their garlands all like yours?"

Before Kerridwen had a chance to reply, one of those sitting on the shore turned his head toward them and pointed. "Look, the hunter has returned!" Others turned, then stood up and watched the pair. "It's as the prophecy said. She has brought back with her a priest from another world."

The Reverend maintained his original stance, unprepared to shift till Kerridwen gave him an answer. "Answer me, girl, or I'll turn around and go back."

Kerridwen laughed as she waded through the water. Her eyes were on Ferdinand who was snuggling into her shoulder and purring as she stroked the back of his neck. "There's no turning back."

"Answer me."

She turned to the Reverend and sneered. "You dare propose to tell me what to do? You are but a worthless priest. You are mortal. I am an under-god."

"Don't treat me like a fool, woman. I don't care what you want to call yourself. You may be long-lived, but you're still mortal, I sense that. I'm here because your father needs me. And with that being the case, you'll be wanting to tell me the truth, else things won't play out well for you in the long run."

A voice boomed out from behind them. "He deserves to know the truth."

The Reverend turned to see who the voice belonged to. A man with broad shoulders, around the same height as himself, was taking giant strides above the water. As each foot came down, a hefty chunk of solid earth materialised to take his weight, dripping with violets of every hue. They flowed off the newly created earth, like a stream rippling over rocks. The footfalls echoed through the shallow valley, demanding the attention of all who were there. The imposing figure's white tunic was held tight about his waist by a leather belt with a gold buckle shaped like a garland. A red cloak with elaborate trim billowed in his wake, making his long mane of grey hair and his majestic beard stand out. On top of his head rested a garland of daisies, somewhat like Kerridwen's, but more elaborate, like a crown. In addition to the flowers, there were dozens of dark berries that grew at a rapid pace, then burst like so many bubbles. When he made eye contact with the Reverend, a huge smile lit up his face. "Alfred!" He extended his arms in greeting as he came closer. "I can't begin to tell you how pleased I am to see you."

The Reverend narrowed his eyes. "I'd be curious to know why that might be."

Having come up level with the Reverend, Albiorix reached down and extended a hand to his guest. "Come on up from the water and join me. You've no need to be wet any longer."

The Reverend accepted his hand and took a step up, a piece of earth forming at the perfect spot to create a step. When he brought up the other foot, ground formed beneath it as well.

Kerridwen looked at Albiorix, but the hint of anger that dwelt in her father's eyes told her it was not the time to ask if she could join him. He threw a thought at her. *You brought him sooner than you'd proposed. You caught me unprepared.*

I had little choice. The witches came after me.

Excuses!

The Reverend looked from one to the other, making it clear he could hear at least part of their thoughts.

Albiorix laughed and slapped him on the back. "Hah! I knew you were the right one. I should know better than to think so loudly around one such as yourself." He turned to his daughter. "Come on up and join us, Kerridwen. Let the people see their great hunter as she approaches the shore!"

As Kerridwen stepped up to walk above the water with the others, the Reverend faced his host. "So, would I be right in thinking that I'm some kind of trophy to you?"

"You are far more than that, Alfred." He reached up and took a grape-sized berry from his garland. He examined it as he continued. "You are the key to our future prosperity." He closed his eyes then placed the berry in his mouth and savoured its flavour. He swallowed then said, "You wanted to know about the garlands?"

"Aye." The Reverend stared at his host as they walked.

"The people on the shore, they aspire to be like my daughter, to have the power that she wields. But the truth is, they have spent their lives in devout service, as will continue to be their lot. They wear their garlands as a symbol of their aspirations and respect."

"You give them false hope?"

"Hah! It's so long since we've had someone come to this land worthy of being called a priest. One who has so much power yet seeks to speak for the people!" He reached up and took another berry from his garland and offered it to the Reverend. "They have everything they could hope for. They want for nothing."

The Reverend took the fruit and examined it. "You contradict yourself. A moment ago, you said they have aspirations, and now you tell me they want for nothing?" He noticed out of the corner of his eye that Kerridwen's daisies were becoming agitated, as though they were snarling at him. What surprised him most was that the cat glared at him and hissed. Kerridwen herself remained silent and ensured she was looking away from him as she smiled and waved at the gathering crowd on the shore.

Albiorix let out a hearty laugh. "Yes, yes, yes! I do that all the time." He waved a hand dismissively. "There's a feast laid out for us under the marquee on the shore. You'll get all the answers you need in good time." The Reverend looked to where Albiorix was pointing and saw a massive marquee where none had been before. They were almost at the shore now, where the growing crowd had formed into a guard of honour. "First, we must join our flock for the ceilidh and celebrate your arrival!"

.

Meredith couldn't sleep. She tried, but it was no use. The storm brewing outside didn't help. Her grandmother had warned her this day might come. She'd done what she could, but it wasn't enough. Kerridwen had achieved her goal.

The Reverend Alfred Casey was gone.

But there was always hope, a distant one that lay somewhere in the pages of the Book of Wisdom.

Colin couldn't sleep either. The day had been long and hard for him. His tossing and turning contributed to Meredith's insomnia.

In the hours before dawn, Colin dragged himself out of bed to prepare for the arduous task of taking the Magistrate's corpse to the Springwood Barracks.

Meredith pretended to sleep. She half opened an eye to watch him as he dressed. It was sad for her to see the man she knew as being so forthright and strong looking sullen and unsure of himself. Yet she felt too overwhelmed to offer him the support he needed.

In the morning, she would have to work with her mother and daughter to find a way of somehow bringing the Reverend Casey back from Kerridwen's world. If she gave in to her desire to support the man she loved now, it might drain her of the emotional energy that she'd need as the day wore on. She had little choice but to believe in Colin's strength to navigate his way through what would no doubt be a difficult day without her support.

Still, a gnawing pain remained in her stomach.

She lay in bed listening for close to an hour after Colin had left the house before she felt sure he was on his way. Then she waited a few minutes longer.

She closed her eyes as tight as she could and pulled the blankets over her head.

The thunder was getting louder as the storm came closer. Colin would be caught in it for sure.

The pain in her stomach grew stronger.

She knew its origin. Would it really have changed anything if she'd got out of bed and given her husband a simple reassuring hug before he left? The only thing preventing her from doing so was the knowledge that he wouldn't approve of what she planned to do, and her paranoia that he would've seen her intentions writ large when he looked into her eyes.

Regardless, she knew what she had to do.

When she at last felt sure it was safe, she leapt out of bed, grabbed her robe from the back of the door, put on her slippers, and made her way to the corridor.

She heard Patsy's whisper as she passed the door to her room. "Mother?"

Patsy opened her door wider and stepped into the corridor. "What are you doing?"

Meredith looked over her shoulder to where her daughter's voice came from, only able to vaguely make out Patsy's silhouette. "I'm going to consult the Book of Wisdom. I won't sleep until I know more about what we're up against."

A flash of lightning illuminated the outline of Patsy's face. "Aren't you tired?"

"Yes, but I can't sleep." Meredith sighed. "We need to find Darcy and get Alfred back. But it's worse than that. I suspect more trouble's coming. I can feel it." Her statement was punctuated by another crack of thunder. "Your father left for Springwood an hour ago, so it's just us here now. I want to be as well prepared as we can be." She reached for her daughter in the darkness and kissed her forehead. "You should get more sleep. In the morning, I'll have a plan."

Patsy's eyes looked heavy as she turned to go back to her bed. Meredith reached out and grabbed her shoulder. "If anything should happen, meet me behind the shed in the garden."

Patsy nodded then slipped back into her room.

*

Jimmy pulled down hard on the rope that secured the Magistrate's corpse to the base of the cart, allowing Colin to tie it off with ease. "To be sure, Mr McIntyre, I'm more than confident that'll be safe. If you were travelling to Parramatta or Sydney I reckon you'd be wanting to tie it down some more, but this should easily be adequate to get you to Springwood. And it's covered well enough to keep it dry when that storm hits." He straightened up and put a hand on Colin's shoulder, a very forward gesture for a stablehand to make toward his employer. "Are you sure you want to do this journey now? Would you maybe be better off waiting for the storm to pass?"

Colin appreciated Jimmy's concern. He'd come to view the Irishman as one of his closest friends. "I'm very sure. It'll be daylight before long, and the sooner this man's body is off my property, the happier I'll be." Colin tugged at the finished knot to ensure it was indeed secure then turned to the Irishman. "Thank you, Jimmy. I can't tell you how much I appreciate you getting up so early to help me out."

"Think nothing of it. I've been awake all night anyway."

Colin's look of concern presented his question without the need for spoken words.

Jimmy shook his head. "No, he hasn't. But I'll tell you what, he'll be in a world of trouble when he does show his head." He looked at the lightning in the distance. His voice softened. "I'd be a lot happier though if he was back home before that storm hits."

Colin climbed aboard the cart and into the driver's seat. "You've raised him well. I'm sure all will be fine. If he is still out, he's sensible enough that he'll seek shelter, more than likely by coming home." As Colin finished his sentence, he felt that his words came across more as platitudes than the reassurance he'd wanted them to convey.

An awkward silence followed, then Jimmy looked to the ground as Colin rode off into the night.

The full moon was falling low in the sky but was still adequate to guide Colin along the road for the hour it would take before the sun crept over the horizon. As he rode the cart away from the property, he found himself wondering for the first time how the Captain at Springwood Barracks would react to him arriving with the corpse of a magistrate who'd come to his property to discuss such a difficult matter.

He felt haunted by an unfamiliar sensation... uncertainty.

The miles rolled by as Colin rocked back and forth, struggling to see in the fading light as the moon slipped ever lower in the sky and the clouds began closing in. If the sun didn't rise soon, he'd have to stop and wait for the darkness to pass.

His head was swaying. He needed more sleep. Rain had started falling and the light was almost gone.

He had to stop.

A flash of lightning illuminated a tree under which he could achieve at least some shelter from the rain. He pulled his coat tight around himself, burying his hands beneath his shoulders for warmth. It was now so dark that he could barely tell the difference between his eyes being open or closed. A moment later, he was asleep.

He was brought back to consciousness by the sound of horses pounding the road. Lots of horses. In the dull light of the approaching dawn, he managed to make out the silhouettes of half a dozen riders moving around him through the incessant drizzle of ice-cold rain.

A voice demanded, "Who are you?"

Colin was unsure which rider had delivered the question. "I might well ask the same question."

"I am Lieutenant Neil Stewart. In the name of the Governor, I demand that you identify yourself."

"Lieutenant, this is indeed fortunate. I was on my way to Springwood—"

"Your name!"

"Colin McIntyre."

"Captain Taylor, arrest this man. Clap him in irons and take him back to the barracks. I want him tried and hung by sunset."

Colin retorted, "How can you—?" He looked from the Lieutenant to the Captain. "Since when did lieutenants order around captains?"

Lieutenant Stewart rode up, so his silhouette was immediately next to Colin, then swung his arm so the back of his hand struck him, drawing blood and almost knocking him off the cart. "Speak to me like that again and I'll have you flogged until the hide falls off your back. You'll likely beg for the hangman to end your suffering."

*

Neridah went straight to her room when they returned to the house.

Overflowing with anguish, she lay her head down on the pillow, tears streaming down her cheeks.

Why?

Why was Alfred doing this to her?

Time and again he'd rejected her love, while at the same time feeling free to let her know how deep his true feelings for her ran.

Okay, he's a priest, she understood that. She could live with that.

But no, that was wrong. She couldn't.

More to the point, how could he do what he'd done? How could he go and take those stupid vows?

And to make it worse, time and again he rubbed salt in her wounds by telling her how he'd taken his vows for *her* sake... all in the hope it would help him rescue her from Sellemae's clutches.

Mission accomplished.

He'd rescued her.

And now, he's gone.

She buried her head as deep in her pillow as possible, hoping to drown out the sound of her sorrow. "Why, Alfred, why?"

She heard the distant rumble of thunder. A storm was coming. Good, it might distract her enough that she might still get some sleep.

As the rumbling continued, she realised it wasn't thunder at all.

It was music.

The crickets, flying foxes, and frogs—all were in tune, creating a symphony unlike anything she'd ever heard.

Curious, she got out of bed, wrapped a blanket around herself, and walked to the window. She put her hands against the window, shocked by what she saw. Kerridwen had returned and was dancing in the paddock, multi-coloured violets surrounding her as she danced.

But it wasn't just Kerridwen.

There were others.

She saw Darcy spinning wildly in time to the beat... her daughter was there... her granddaughter!

There were so many others, all dancing in a circle.

The rhythm and flow were hypnotic, compelling Neridah to join in.

No!

It was too cold outside.

Kerridwen couldn't be trusted.

This was all wrong.

Then realisation hit. She wasn't just witnessing the dance; she was part of it. Somehow, she'd shifted from the warmth of her room to the chilly outdoors.

And she was dancing.

She cast aside her blanket, no longer caring about the cold. The music and the movement felt so good.

There must have been a dozen others dancing with her in the circle, some were creatures the like of which she'd never seen before.

She tried to draw Meredith and Patsy's attention, but it was no use. They were so absorbed in the dance they were unaware of her presence.

But what did that matter?

She closed her eyes and let nature's symphony carry her, spinning wild and free like she'd never done before.

When at last she opened her eyes, she was soaring above the ground with the other dancers, violets cascading off her feet as she moved through the cold night air.

She couldn't help but laugh.

This past day had been wasted in the family's resistance to their exotic guest.

To what end?

Her laughter grew louder the more she danced.

She felt Kerridwen reaching out to her. "Come with me."

"Why?" She wanted to keep dancing. "Why come with you?"

"Join me. There's no time for other choices."

"I want to dance."

The voice changed. "Nana-Neri, there's no time."

As she danced, Neridah felt hands gripping her shoulders, trying to stop her. She looked to the centre where Kerridwen had been and instead saw Patsy.

"Nana-Neri, you need to wake up. We have to go!"

*

The horses thundered through the mist as they carried the soldiers from Springwood Barracks onto the McIntyre property, Lieutenant Stewart barking orders as he rode on past the stables and headed toward the homestead, oblivious to the pouring rain that had saturated his uniform. "Secure the servants' quarters and the stables first, lest we end up watching some ill-conceived heroics play out." He turned to Sean O'Malley as the first of his troops dismounted and burst through the door of the servants' quarters. "Tell me, gravedigger, can you sense the one who called you?"

O'Malley was leaning forward in the saddle, oblivious to the rain, his arms crossed against the back of his horse's neck as he contemplated his options. "Oh, yes. But he's laying low till we secure the property. He doesn't trust the witches."

"Pathetic!" Lieutenant Stewart turned his horse and started toward the main house. "That's one Nasqa that doesn't deserve saving."

•

Jimmy O'Sullivan was waiting inside the door, holding a blacksmith's hammer. He charged at the lead soldier and let out a frantic battle cry as he swung his arm back. He didn't have the chance to bring it forward. The hammer dropped to the ground as the soldier's rifle fired and found its mark.

Mrs Banks and Cook stood further back in the corridor, just outside the kitchen door. At first, their dropped jaws emitted no sound, but their silence was replaced by screams as the soldiers stepped over Jimmy's slumped form and approached them.

•

Sean O'Malley dismounted and walked his horse to the stables. He stopped and sniffed the air when he reached the area of Hunter's time freeze, then turned his head to survey the dead patches of grass further down in the paddock where Hunter had danced. He tied his horse to a post and stared at a spot in the corner of the stable. "I'll be back for you soon." The cold moist air triggered an arthritic pain in his left ankle that made him limp as he walked over to the house to join Lieutenant Stewart.

A dozen soldiers were gathered around the Lieutenant as he strode up the stairs to the veranda. The soldiers who'd gone to the servants' quarters were dragging the still screaming Mrs Banks and Cook through the mud and rain toward the house. They went silent after a loud crack of thunder shook the ground beneath them. Lieutenant Stewart smiled at them, then turned to one of his men. "Put them in the drawing room." He kicked in the front door. "As for the rest of you, go upstairs, find whatever women and children are still here."

While half a dozen of his men raced up the stairs, Lieutenant Stewart walked toward the closed door of the library. Intuition told him there was someone in there. *No doubt protecting their precious book.* He took slow and cautious steps so as not to alert anyone behind the door of his approach. A floorboard creaked under his weight. He paused for a few seconds, then took the final steps. Once at the door, he embraced it with his body, turned the handle, and pushed.

It was locked.

He placed his ear against the door's surface and called out, "I know you're in there. I can feel it. I can feel lots of things, like the chill of the time freezes that happened here today. Those tricks won't help you now." He stepped back and raised his boot in preparation, smiling at the thought of catching one of the witches trying to protect the ancient text.

He kicked hard, causing the doorjamb to splinter as the lock broke free of its constraints. The door flew open and Lieutenant Stewart stepped into the room.

It was empty.

So was the stand that was normally home to the Book of Wisdom.

•

Meredith reached the bottom of the stairs and entered the library. She locked the door behind her before tapping the side panel on the writing desk to retrieve the key to the book's ancient lock.

She sensed that her time was limited, not so much by the impending sunrise, but by something else.

Trouble was coming, she could feel it.

As she unlocked the massive volume, she considered the risks of trying another time freeze, like the one she'd done not long after Kerridwen's arrival. She pulled out the key and placed it carefully on the desk next to the book stand. Her mother's failed try at a time freeze had ruined any possibility of attempting another. The fabric that held time together in this space had been weakened by three people freezing time in the same place within the same day. Neridah had been thrown back along her own timeline, creating a dangerous overlap. Time in this space would likely take weeks or even months to heal.

Her grandmother's words echoed through her head: *Be wary of anyone who wears a garland of dancing daisies.* When she first saw Hunter, she couldn't help but feel concerned. But even after consulting the book, she wanted to be sure before sharing her fears. It was Darcy's disappearance that confirmed her suspicions.

She found the page she'd opened the book to earlier, the page where she'd read about Kerridwen the Hunter before the time freeze had collapsed. She needed to learn more; the time freeze had been so brief.

She wanted to learn about the garland.

She struggled to decipher the words, too tired to translate the language of the book as she read it.

She had to try, despite the heaviness of her eyelids.

Then, she jumped at the sound of horses arriving outside the house. She'd been slumped across the open book. She must have fallen asleep and had no idea how long she'd been there like that.

Horses… lots of horses. They had to be one of two things: soldiers or bushrangers.

Whichever they were, Colin more than likely would have encountered them.

As far as she knew, her mother and daughter were both still upstairs.

She heard heavy boots on the veranda and one of the invaders kicking the front door open.

There was no choice. She'd have to trust that Neridah and Patricia would find a way out.

She closed the book and used all her strength to lift and hold it against her chest as she closed her eyes and allowed herself to be behind the shed near the bottom of the garden, most importantly, to be somewhere safe.

She opened her eyes and tried to adjust to her new surroundings.

.

A crack of thunder from the storm outside dispelled the last remnants of her dream. Neridah sprang upright, struggling to get a decent breath. Her nightclothes were drenched in perspiration.

After she'd taken a few deep breaths, she held a hand to her chest and looked at Patsy. "I was dreaming?"

"You were reaching out and rambling. I was starting to worry if you'd ever wake up."

Neridah glanced out the window and saw the first rays of light revealing themselves over the horizon. "What's happening?" She turned to her granddaughter. "Why did you need to wake me?"

Patsy whispered, "There are soldiers. Father left for Springwood Barracks hours ago. The soldiers have only just arrived downstairs. We need to get out while we can."

"Where's your mother?"

"She's gone to the library to consult the Book of Wisdom. These soldiers, I think they're controlled by mind thieves… I can feel it."

They heard a voice call out, "Go upstairs, find whatever women and children are still here." The pounding of boots on the stairs told Neridah and Patsy their time was limited.

Neridah grabbed Patsy's arm as she leapt out of bed. "You're right. We need to leave, now!"

CHAPTER 13

Patsy was adamant. "We need to allow ourselves to be behind the shed at the bottom of the garden. That's where Mother said we should meet her if there was a problem."

Neridah held Patsy's shoulders. "No! If you can feel the mind thieves, then they can feel you. If we move that way, they'll be able to tell exactly where we are." She looked to the window.

With the adrenaline already pumping, Patsy walked to the window and opened it, taking care not to make any loud noises on the way. She looked over her shoulder as she lifted her leg up and over the windowsill. "I know it's cold outside, but you'll need to leave your slippers behind, else you'll slip on the roof for sure."

Neridah whispered as she followed Patsy through the window, "We'll worry about frostbite later." Once they were both outside, Neridah pulled the window shut, hoping it would take time for the soldiers to realise how they'd escaped.

They heard soldiers barging into Neridah's room as they crawled along the roof, keeping as close to the wall as possible in case the soldiers looked out the window. Patsy felt her heart beat faster when she heard their voices.

"No one in here."

More footsteps, then another voice. "The bed's been slept in." There was a pause. "Check the window, they might have tried to sneak out that way."

Patsy and Neridah scrambled when they heard the window open. Once the sound of its movement stopped, they froze. A soldier's head protruded from the window. They were fortunate the shadows protected them when he looked their way.

Neridah worried the chattering of her teeth might give them away. It was, without doubt, the wrong time of year to be outdoors in the rain with inadequate clothing. They both breathed a sigh of relief when the window closed. Now was their chance to work their way to the lattice supporting the jasmine outside of the drawing room.

As they climbed down, they were mindful of what was happening in the drawing room where Mrs Banks and Cook sat huddled together, watched over by a handful of disinterested soldiers. Patsy could see from the sinister shapes their shadows threw on the wall that they were indeed controlled by mind thieves... Nasqa. Fortunately, the soldiers had little interest in what was happening outside, so missed the moments where the two witches climbing down the lattice were illuminated by the occasional lightning flash. During one such flash, Cook's eyes widened at the sight of Patsy and Neridah. Patsy put a finger to her lips and Cook nodded before turning her head away.

One of the soldiers, noticing Cook's expression, looked up at the window.

The two escapees froze as they clung to the lattice, hoping they wouldn't be given away by another lightning flash.

The soldier turned his head away and they continued their descent.

When they'd reached the bottom, they huddled in the darkness below the veranda.

Neridah whispered, "Let's wait till after the next lightning flash."

Patsy nodded.

They waited.

The rain was easing.

Patsy asked, "Should we just go?"

"No, be patient."

A near-blinding flash of light was followed by a loud thunder crack.

Neridah nudged Patsy and whispered in her ear, "Now, Patricia, run!"

As they ran, the cold ground felt like daggers cutting into their feet.

But this was life or death.

They were close to the shed when lightning again lit up the paddock. Driven by an instinct for self-preservation, Neridah and Patsy dived to the ground.

A voice called from the distance, "Did you see that?"

"What?"

"Over there, I thought I saw movement."

A moment later, a pair of wallabies hopped across the paddock, well away from where Neridah and Patsy lay in a muddy puddle.

"Keep looking. We'll spread out and work our way through the paddock."

The rain started pouring down again, even heavier than before. Neridah and Patsy weren't prepared to risk getting to their feet. Instead, they slithered through the muddy paddock hoping they'd be hidden from view by the length of the grass around them.

Neridah said to Patsy, "When we get there, we can combine our strengths and work as the Trilogy. We'll beat them easily then."

Patsy didn't respond. She continued dragging herself along.

On reaching the shed, they got up and darted around the back to meet Meredith.

They turned the corner and came to an abrupt halt.

She wasn't there.

.

Meredith looked around at the dark stone walls.

There was no door and no windows.

At the far end, there was a small stone fireplace, stoked so well the flames danced in celebration of their good fortune.

She turned back to face the other end of the room. No more than half a dozen paces from her, a small white-haired man, not much taller than the height of Meredith's knee, sat perched on a stool at a writing desk. The large feather quill he held worked its way across the large sheet of vellum on his desk. He had long pointy ears and wore a green felt hat.

The most amazing thing about the little man was that he hadn't been there when Meredith first arrived in the room just a few seconds earlier. He reminded her of a picture her grandmother had once shown her in the Book of Wisdom, the book she now held tight against her chest.

"Hello," she said, "are you a wood-elf?"

The little man kept writing with his back turned to her.

She took a tentative step closer. "Can you even hear me?"

An exasperated sigh let her know that, yes, he could. He paused from his frantic efforts to control the quill and looked up. "Do you have any idea how long I've spent trying to write down this thought while I still had it in my head?"

"Well, no… how could I?"

He turned to face her and looked over the top of his wire-framed spectacles. They sat on his nose in a manner that left Meredith surprised they hadn't fallen. "How could you indeed. That's the trouble with humans, you have so little knowledge of what other folk are doing."

"You haven't answered my question. Are you a wood-elf?"

"Come now, Meredith McIntyre." He waved a hand at her as though her question were silly. "You do remember the drawing your grandmother showed you?"

Meredith responded with an icy stare, not unlike the way her daughter was apt to do when she felt patronised.

The wood-elf put down his quill.

This was going to take longer than he'd hoped for. "Yes, I'm a wood-elf." He jumped off his stool and approached her. "My name is Krinkle-myst, and this is where I come when I want to work in peace."

"Why am I here?" She pointed to his desk and asked, "And what is your work?"

"You are here because you allowed yourself to be somewhere safe. Somewhere the Nasqa can't get to you. Somewhere that is not a part of your Crossworlds."

"What do you mean?"

"The book brought you here. It's seeking to protect itself."

"So, you had no hand in that?"

Krinkle-myst laughed. "I come here to get away from distractions. Trust me, you being here is the last thing I would've wished for."

"How do I get out of here?"

"You wait for your mother and daughter. You won't be able to leave here without the power of the Trilogy."

"How do you know so much?"

"It's my job to know."

"That leads me back to my other question, the one you've yet to answer. What is your job?"

"I write the stories that weave the fabric of morality into all that exists."

Meredith frowned. "Books are wonderful for sharing knowledge, but—"

"You underestimate the power of the written word."

"What do you mean?"

He turned and started walking back to his desk. "It's no use trying to explain. You wouldn't understand."

"I beg your pardon!" She took a step toward him. "How dare you presume such a thing!"

He replied in a disinterested voice as he climbed back onto his stool. "I suggest you put down the book and make yourself comfortable by the fire while you wait for the others to get here."

"What, just place the book on the floor?" She grappled to find words. "This is a sacred book. And where do you expect me to sit?" As she finished her question, she turned to the fire and saw a sturdy oak table and a solid chair with elaborate carvings of fairies, butterflies and flowers. It was positioned by the fire as though it had always been there. And the room—it had grown since she'd last looked toward the fire, which was now a good twenty paces away.

Her first impulse once she'd placed the book on the table was to sit in the chair and sulk, but then she decided it may be better to spend her time exploring the wisdom within the book's pages. Krinkle-myst's voice interrupted her thoughts. "What a shame you left the key in the library."

Damn!

He was right.

She glared at the wood-elf and asked, "How can you know these things?"

He turned to face her and looked over his glasses once more. "Like I said, it's my job to know things. How could I possibly hope to write moral codes people will abide by if I don't know what's going on throughout all the worlds?"

"How do you write a moral code? Isn't that something people find within themselves?"

Again, the wood-elf put down his quill. "I can see I won't get any peace until you have your answers." Meredith blinked, and then found she was sitting in the elaborate chair, with Krinkle-myst sitting in a smaller but otherwise identical furniture piece on the other side of the fire. "I write the fairy tales that guide people to find that inner truth. The sad fact is, many people can't find that truth without some form of guidance. Written words are powerful things." He pointed to the Book of Wisdom on the table. "Just imagine, where would you be without the words within that volume?"

Something deep within Meredith awoke, an awareness of how important it was to listen to what the wood-elf had to say.

*

Neridah and Patsy shivered as they huddled together behind the garden shed. The building's eaves had provided some welcome respite from the driving rain. But their drenched nightclothes clung to them and their hair was so saturated that water from it ran down their backs, making them colder by the moment. Despite the sound of the rain belting down on the shed's roof, they could hear the chatter of the soldiers searching the paddock.

Neridah whispered to Patsy, "We need to make our way to the trees and hope we lose the soldiers in the darkness of the forest."

A flash of lightning, the brightest they'd seen since climbing out the window, illuminated the paddock, revealing a path neither had noticed before. The accompanying thunder crack was immediate and deafening.

They got up and raced for the trees, mud splashing over them as they went. It was at least fifty paces to the forest, and despite her legs moving faster than Patsy could remember, their destination seemed to remain ever more distant with each painful stride.

A soldier's voice called from the distance, "Someone's making a run for the trees!"

"There's two of them!"

"Stop them!"

They heard a loud blast like thunder, only different. It was followed by another, and then several more in quick succession.

Gunshots!

Patsy's chest hurt from the strain of breathing as they continued struggling to reach safety.

The sounds of the pursuit faded into the distance the moment they entered the forest.

The storm no longer persisted and, instead of running through the darkness of the morning downpour, their way was lit by beams of sunlight streaming through the trees.

Neridah grabbed Patsy's arm. "We need to stop for a moment."

Happy to oblige, Patsy stopped. She looked around. None of the trees looked familiar. "Nana-Neri, did you ever come across this path?" Before Neridah had a chance to reply, Patsy continued, "I thought I'd explored every inch of Father's property, but this looks totally unfamiliar to me."

"The trees are all wrong." Neridah turned and faced where they'd come from. "We've only run a short distance into the forest, but the house seems so far away." She turned back to Patsy. "And the storm… where'd that go?"

Before she had a chance to respond, Patsy noticed a small cloud of sparkles sweep past. She looked up at her grandmother and asked, "What's that?"

Neridah smiled, "It's pixie-dust!"

"Pixie-dust? What's that?"

"For us, a guiding light." She took Patsy's hand. "Come on, let's go after it."

The pixie-dust paused, as though waiting for them, then continued its merry dance through the trees. They ran on and on for close to an hour before the pixie-dust dispersed without warning and they found themselves staring at a small stone cabin with a roof of slate shingles.

The whole thing appeared from the outside to be too small for an adult to stand upright on the inside. There was a chimney at one end delivering a liberal quantity of white smoke that rose high before dissipating into the forest air.

Patsy asked, "Do you notice something strange about this?"

Neridah replied, "That's it's too small, and that it shouldn't be here?"

Patsy walked around to the other side. "There's no doors or windows." She looked across the roof at Neridah. "I want to see what's inside."

In the next instant, they found themselves sucked in toward the little cabin, then realised they were within the structure's walls. Patsy looked around in wide-eyed wonder when she saw how much bigger it was inside.

Meredith rose from her chair and raced across the now massive hall to embrace her mother and daughter. "Thank God, you made it!"

Patsy threw her arms around her mother.

Neridah joined them in a group hug, holding her daughter and granddaughter tight, then eased back when she noticed the small figure sitting by the fire. A goblet appeared in his hand that hadn't been there when Neridah had first noticed him.

Krinkle-myst remained in his chair. He took a sip from a goblet of spiced mead, savouring its soothing flavour. He turned to face Neridah and cut her off before she'd begun to ask a question. "In regard to your first question, the building is only ever as big as it needs to be. It has different needs outside and inside. And its internal needs change depending on how many people it's playing host to."

Patsy said, "The world doesn't work that way." She looked unconvinced and miserable as she stood shivering and dripping water on the stone floor.

The wood-elf got up from his chair and walked toward them. "Ah, Patricia McIntyre, or would you prefer I call you Patsy?"

Patsy's lips trembled as she asked, "How did you know that?"

Krinkle-myst ignored the question. "You are destined to be the most legendary of all the Witches of the Crossworlds. But what you need to understand is that, for all the vastness of the crossworlds you are destined to visit, there is still far more that exists beyond those realms." He sighed. "But we'll have to discuss that another time. You have more pressing concerns to deal with today. You and your grandmother need to warm yourselves by the fire. You won't be solving any problems if you catch a cold."

As if on cue, Patsy sneezed. She looked up and saw she had shifted from the far end of the room to be standing by the fire. Her legs collapsed under her and she fell into a chair that appeared at just the right time to catch her… a chair that she somehow knew would be there. She looked around and saw they were all seated by the fire and the room was smaller and cozier. The warmth of the flames was a welcome respite from what Patsy and Neridah had endured. Patsy extended her hands toward the flames. "We need to find out what Kerridwen did to Darcy."

Neridah was quick to respond, "We need to get Alfred back first."

Meredith followed up, "I want to ensure Colin's safe. He must surely have encountered the soldiers after he left for Springwood. And the servants, we need to protect them."

Neridah looked at her daughter and said, "You and Patsy should try to drive out the soldiers while I go through the portal and go after Alfred."

Krinkle-myst laughed. "And break up the Trilogy? You have many problems that require solving. And each one requires that you work together. The first thing you need to do is fetch the key for the Book of Wisdom. You won't solve your other problems without help from what's been written within its pages."

Patsy asked, "How can you know that?" She looked across at the wood-elf's writing desk that seemed closer now the room had shrunk. "The page you're working on… it's vellum, like in the Book—"

Krinkle-myst replied, "I've contributed to many books."

Patsy stared at him, enthralled. "You wrote the—"

"Parts of it, yes. As you have done, and many thousands of others."

"But I—"

"There is much that you have written in the future. Your contribution is greater than most have made."

Neridah said, "I don't understand."

Krinkle-myst turned to her. "And that's why your contribution is so small compared to that of your granddaughter. Despite all you've been through, you have so little understanding of how time works. It's small wonder you made such a mess of your time freeze." He stood up. "But I digress. There are many constraints of time that matter right now." He addressed Meredith, "Before the sun's last light today, you will need to place faith in someone who's intentions you distrust if your husband is to have any hope of being rescued from the gallows."

Meredith grasped her chest as her mouth hung open.

"If you attempt his rescue yourself, all hope of saving him, or bringing back Alfred or Darcy, will be lost."

Krinkle-myst turned to Neridah. "You will indeed travel to the world of Albiorix, but not on your own. Albiorix and his daughter are strong. Only the Trilogy of Crossworld Witches has a chance of defeating them in their own world. He has ways to influence Alfred to join his crusade. You will need to consult the Book of Wisdom and learn the power of written words to succeed. Your love for him is strong, and that is your greatest strength."

Neridah protested, "But what of his love for me? What power is there in my love if his is not equal?"

"Learn to look past your dreams and hopes and you'll see how deep his love for you truly is. You must trust in this, or else you'll surely fail." The wood-elf turned to Patsy. "And you, young lady, if you wish to see your friend Darcy again, must learn to think before you call on the science of magic."

Patsy crossed her arms in defiance. "My power is at its greatest when I'm angry."

"That's only because you don't understand the science of the magic."

Patsy's face contorted and her breaths grew shorter

Krinkle-myst stuck his arm out and dropped his now empty goblet. "See how that just fell to the floor? Was that not magic?"

Patsy's response was quick. "That's not magic, it's gravity. I've learned all about gravity. It's part of the science called physics."

Krinkle-myst smiled as he pointed his finger in the air. "Exactly! Yet the fact that you understand the science behind it doesn't reduce the magic of how something almost always falls when you drop it. All magic is driven by science, just not so much of it is well known or understood, even by some of its most accomplished practitioners. It's through gaining this understanding that you will reach your fullest potential."

He took a step back and addressed them all. "Now, it is time for you to retrieve the key and bring it back so you can learn what you must to defeat Albiorix and Kerridwen."

Her breathing having returned to normal, Patsy asked, "But how will we find our way?"

Krinkle-myst stepped toward the fire, reached in, and grabbed a handful of flame. He threw it in the air, and it became a dancing cloud of sparkling pixie-dust like the one Neridah and Patsy had followed through the forest. "Follow the dust. It will guide you there and back again whenever there is the need."

Neridah asked, "Will you be here when we return?"

"No, but the book will remain here till it is safe for it to return to your home. I've no doubt that we will meet again sometime soon." As soon as he'd finished his sentence, the wood-elf and his writing desk were gone.

*

Sean O'Malley stepped over Jimmy O'Sullivan's slumped body and made his way to the servants' kitchen. Sure enough, there was a bottle of rum on the sideboard. He pulled out the stopper with his few remaining teeth and spat it out as he made his way back down the corridor. This time, when he stepped over Jimmy's slumped form, he heard a moan escape the dying man's lips. Sean paused and splashed some rum over Jimmy's head. "You can have a drink on me." Satisfied with himself for what he saw as a noble gesture, he made his way out the door and ambled back to the stables.

On the other side of the bounds between reality and the void, Bandah, Talia, Mrs Smith and their Nasqa companion waited in anticipation, hoping that Sean O'Malley would be able to release them. The Nasqa turned its shadowy head to the others. *Ak-ney boe-jas pisa bo-opi bo-nassie-elphie gamoo. Bo-numma ja-dista ak-prac-nestwee ol-lie koop-boost-ast sess.*

Mrs Smith looked at Bandah. "Well?"

"He says we need to wait near where a time freeze has happened, that the bonds between worlds are weakened by a time freeze."

Sean O'Malley made it back to the stables, knelt down, and took a long swig from his stolen bottle of rum. He tossed the bottle aside. "Let's see what we've got here." He held his hands together and pushed them into the air in front of him before pulling them apart in a slow, deliberate action, then pushed his head into the gap and looked around. He smiled at the sight of Mrs Smith. "You're a funny looking fairy if ever I saw one."

"I was held captive in human form for just forty short years and this is what I'm stuck with now."

He looked toward Bandah and Talia. "Hmmph. Pixies! Well, *you* won't be leaving the void any time soon."

Bandah stepped forward to protest, but Talia held him back. "Don't bother, darling. Look at his eyes. You'll never get past hate like that."

Bandah looked at their shadowy friend. "But we—"

Again, Talia pulled him up and whispered in his ear. "At least if the fairy gets out, she may be able to get us help from elsewhere."

O'Malley said to the Nasqa, "Come on through. There's probably just enough of you there to take over my horse. It's a good healthy runner that one."

Without hesitation, the shadowy figure slipped through the hole O'Malley held open and was gone. O'Malley looked at the fairy and said, "Come on then, I'm not going to hold this open forever." He glanced at the pixies. "As for you, pixie vermin, you can rot forever in there for all I care." Mrs Smith flew out of the gap and was out of sight within seconds. Sean O'Malley released his grip on the hole into the void and let it snap shut. He picked up his bottle of rum, mounted his newly possessed horse, and rode off into the night.

Bandah squatted and buried his head in his hands. "I just can't believe it. I thought we could trust him."

Talia sat on the ground next to him. "Don't worry. Help will still come for us."

"Oh yeah? The options for where that might come from seem to be running out."

Talia stood slowly. "Honey, you need to see this."

Bandah turned to see what she was looking at. In all his years, he'd never seen something that surprised him quite so much. It was Mrs Smith, standing right where Sean O'Malley had been a minute earlier. She looked into the space around them. "I can't see you, but I trust you're still there. I'm going to get help. I'm going to find the witches and we'll get you out of there."

*

Colin groaned when Captain Taylor's boot connected with his belly. "You've caused me a good deal of anguish, McIntyre. I've a good mind to save the hangman the effort and finish you off myself before you face justice." He swung his boot again, pushing Colin up against the wall of his cell. "The only reason you'll live till sunset is because you killed a magistrate, so the Legislative Council will insist that justice is meted out in accordance with the law. If it were up to the Governor and myself, you'd be dead already."

Colin groaned. "I didn't kill anyone."

Another kick to the belly. "Liar!" The Captain departed the cell. He walked a few steps then turned and walked back. "By the way, the Justice of the Peace will be here in an hour for your trial. Try to make sure you're cleaned up and presentable by then." He grinned. "We do want you to look your best when you swing from the gallows."

·

The Reverend Alfred Casey sat next to Albiorix at the main table of the feast. There was an amazing variety of fruits, vegetables and breads. Alfred held up a yellow fruit with purple spikes protruding from its top. Albiorix leaned across and said, "That's an obellie. Tastes like an orange but has the texture of an apple. You need to peel it as you would a banana." He waved a hand across the table. "You'll not see any meat within this spread, Alfred. It's not that I've got anything against how many of the people on your world eat meat. Goodness no! I quite happily ate meat there, and while I travelled through many other worlds. But here, we have such an abundance of fruits and vegetables to choose from, there's no need to end another creature's life for the sake of simple sustenance.

You know what, Alfred? During the centuries that I roamed your world, being treated as a god, your people would sacrifice all sorts of animals to me… even other people on occasion. It was all just part of their need to worship, and I took it as such. But I must stress, I never encouraged such behaviour. That was all due to the priests of the day. And that's what I like about you, Alfred! You're unique on your world! A priest who understands!"

A priest who understands? The Reverend was struggling to understand why Albiorix was so keen on him being there. He slowly peeled the fruit, almost oblivious to his host while he surveyed the scene around them.

All eyes were on him.

There were two dozen men and women who sat on the ground close by. Each of them reached out at some point to try to touch him. He turned to the closest and asked, "What's your name, boy?"

He came forward and knelt before the priest. "I've had many names over the centuries. Right now, I'm known as Felibrey the Humble. I've had the honour of serving in the garlands of both Kerridwen and Albiorix, and now I'm hoping you'll allow me to serve in yours."

"And how old would you be, Felibrey?" The Reverend took a bite of the obellie fruit as he waited for Felibrey's answer.

"I am past twenty thousand rounds of the seasons."

The Reverend turned his attention to Albiorix. "The boy, Felibrey, referred to serving in the garlands. What exactly does he mean by that?"

Albiorix slapped his hand on the table and laughed. "Hah! I was wondering when you'd ask about that." He gestured toward the crowd of devotees. "All of these beautiful men and women have served in the garlands. It's the ultimate training. They enter service as mere mortals, and they leave after a thousand years' service as immortals." He nudged the Reverend's shoulder and made a show of whispering in his ear. "And now, Alfred, they all long to serve you… to worship and protect you. As long as you are the bearer of a garland, you too will be immortal."

"And their garlands?"

"Some are merely floral decorations. Others are hosts for novices from a thousand worlds. They all aspire to live in what many on your world would refer to as heaven."

"Do these souls all enter service willingly?"

Albiorix spread his arms wide. "Look around you. Why wouldn't they? All of them have the opportunity to explore their full potential as artisans, as poets, philosophers, whatever their hearts desire."

The Reverend looked into the smiling faces of those who would be his disciples. "Be that as it may, I see little in the way of individualism among them." He turned back to Albiorix. "You still haven't told me the truth of why I was brought here."

Albiorix took on a more serious tone. "I've been unable to travel to your world for the past five thousand of your years. I very much miss the devotion and love of your world."

"What prevents you from travelling there? Why do you send your daughter in your place?"

"I am burdened by my own success as one who is worshipped. When so many look on you as a god, it becomes more difficult to travel through the portals. For thousands of years now, I have relied on priests of different faiths on your world to maintain the people's devotion. But, with time, the priests corrupted the faith of my followers to suit their own needs and desires."

"So, do you see yourself as a god?"

"No, not at all. I am a channel, a conduit for their worship to reach its intended destination. People see me as a god, as their god. But the truth is, gods are elusive. They rarely make their presence known or felt. Often, devotion that is meant for them becomes lost. Gods require devotion for strength, and I ensure they receive that devotion."

"But a part of it is withheld for your own gain?"

"A small percentage. It's a symbiotic relationship that all involved win from. I am an under-god. My service assists countless gods throughout what you would call the Crossworlds." He put his arm around Alfred's shoulder. "I know that your god insists his followers see him as the one true god, but can I tell you how many gods make the same claim? I have never shown favour to one god over another, but if you wish to continue to do so, that's fine with me. Just say you'll join me in my quest for all the gods to receive the devotion they deserve… that you'll become the under-god you were born to be, one who lives to focus the devotion of those who worship on your world."

CHAPTER 14

A s the three witches struggled to keep up with the ball of pixie-dust, Patsy asked, "So, why haven't I heard about pixie-dust before?"

Meredith said, "It's the first I've heard of it as well."

Neridah smiled and looked over her shoulder toward the others. "It's one of my favourite memories from childhood. Mother used to ask me where I'd most like to go on the property, then she'd reach into the fire, throw a ball of pixie-dust, and I'd follow it."

Meredith frowned as she countered, "Well, that's something that was missing from my childhood." She couldn't help but feel disappointed. *Why did grandmother do that for my mother, but not for me?*

Patsy asked, "Why is it called pixie-dust?"

Neridah replied, "The pixies were the first to draw our attention to it." They ran on a bit further, then, between breaths, she added, "Ironically, it has nothing to do with the pixies. In fact, they rarely use it themselves."

The ball of pixie-dust came to an abrupt halt.

Taken by surprise, Meredith stumbled into her daughter, who'd been the only one to anticipate the stop. As they fell, Patsy threw an arm forward to cushion the impact, catching her grandmother's ankle in the process and causing her to also tumble to the ground. The three of them made for an interesting sight as they tried to disentangle themselves. Neridah and Patsy's nightclothes were already filthy and torn because of their earlier escape from the soldiers. Meredith, on the other hand, had transported herself to Krinkle-myst's cabin, so had mostly avoided exposure to the elements... until now. She landed face first in a generous mud puddle.

Meredith looked up and said, "It's raining." She pushed herself up, the front of her nightgown now covered in mud. "And it's freezing!"

Neridah, having also found her face in a puddle, pulled a strand of muddy hair from her mouth. "I noticed."

Patsy looked at the paddock and the house that stood in the distance then glanced over her shoulder to where they'd come from. The pixie-dust was gone, but the pathway they'd travelled along remained, with dappled sunlight sprinkled across the forest floor. "It's a portal." She got to her feet and took a step back onto the path, passing from the cold wet of Blackheath into the warmth of the other world. When she looked over her shoulder, she could barely even see the world she'd just stepped back from. It seemed somehow distant. "Can you hear me?"

Neridah and Meredith gave each other a puzzled look then Meredith said, "Of course we can. You're only a few paces away."

She walked backwards along the path. "I only need to take a few steps back and you disappear. I can't see you at all." She walked forward to what appeared to be a never-ending forest. The paddock, along with

Meredith and Neridah, reappeared, becoming clearer the closer Patsy got to them. She reached out and felt raindrops on her arm then took a tentative step from the sunlit forest into the rain-soaked paddock, rejoining her mother and grandmother.

Neridah looked toward the house. "We'd best keep quiet and stay out of sight. We can consider ourselves lucky we weren't seen." She glanced across at the garden shed. "If we stay low, we can make it to the shed without being seen. Then we can consider the best course of action from there."

Patsy was about to make a suggestion when she was distracted by something she saw out of the corner of her eye. She pointed to the low-flying fairy approaching them. "Look, it's Mrs Smith."

·

The Reverend took another bite of the obellie. He had to admit that it was probably the most delicious flavour he'd ever experienced. Kerridwen looked across at him. She picked up what looked like a green mandarin and began peeling it. "If you like the flavour of the obellie, then you'll likely love this even more." As the skin of the fruit fell away, she broke apart the segments of the red inner flesh and, leaning across her father, held one out for the Reverend. "It's called a phelare." Albiorix leaned back to make it easier for Kerridwen to reach across. The daisies in her garland turned toward the Reverend in expectation.

He looked at her smile and couldn't help but wonder about the wisdom of accepting anything the girl had to offer. The thoughts of one of those who would be a disciple ran through his head. *Oh, the phelare! You've never tasted it? I wish you wore a garland and I were in it now, so I could experience this with you.* He glanced around at the smiling faces that surrounded him. They looked full of innocence and awe, making it easy to ignore that these souls had lived for many thousands of years.

Albiorix's voice sounded distant. "Do you not trust my daughter?"

The Reverend looked back to Kerridwen. Where there had been a smile there was now a look of wistful sorrow, like that of a puppy seeking the affection of its master. Even the daisies within her garland seemed to wilt a little. Her smile returned when the Reverend reached across to take the fruit and said, "Thank you." Kerridwen's face glowed as her eyes followed the piece of fruit.

The Reverend felt the quiet expectation of all those around him. He took a bite from the small segment of fruit. The moment his teeth pierced its skin, the flavour began running through his mouth. It reminded him of a tender roasted lamb, but with the sweetness of fresh honey. The texture was like a runny jam. Tiny seeds rolled through his mouth and popped open, releasing small bursts of a subtle chilli-like bite that was immediately soothed by an aftertaste reminiscent of vanilla. When he swallowed, his mouth felt fresh, like it would after eating some mint leaves. He looked toward Kerridwen and said, "Delicious." Keen to savour more of the flavour, he took the rest of the segment into his mouth.

Kerridwen's eyes sparkled as she took a segment of the fruit for herself then offered the rest to the Reverend. She somehow looked older now that they were in her domain, more like a mature woman than the adolescent she'd appeared to be at the McIntyre property. He reached out and accepted the fruit, reminding himself that such perceptions were misleading when dealing with someone who'd lived for so long. He turned to Albiorix. "I can see why you wouldn't feel the need for meat when you have fruits with such abundant flavours."

Albiorix slapped him on the back, as he seemed so fond of doing. He plucked a berry from his garland and popped it into his mouth. "Hah! Wait until you try the fruits that will one day grow from your garland. The tastes you most enjoy, extracted from across a thousand worlds, their raw essence packaged in bubbles of strength."

"I've no desire to wear such a thing."

"Of course not! I wouldn't expect you to when you've just arrived. It wouldn't be in your nature."

The Reverend asked, "Why is it that yours is the only garland I see that bears fruit?"

Albiorix extended his hands by his side in a gesture that showed surprise, as though the answer should be obvious to all. "It is one of the privileges of an under-god."

The Reverend broke away another segment of the phelare then gestured toward Kerridwen. "Is not your daughter an under-god?"

Albiorix put his enormous arm around Kerridwen's shoulders and pulled her close to him as proud fathers are wont to do with their children when boasting of their achievements. Kerridwen wore a wry smile and looked away. Her father held his right hand over his heart. "Ah yes, but she is also a hunter! While she has the right to bear fruit as an under-god, such a thing would be a distraction from the importance of her role and could place her success in jeopardy."

The Reverend asked, "And what would that role be?"

"That, my friend, shall become clearer with time." He released his grip on Kerridwen's shoulder and placed a hand on the back of the Reverend's neck. "I want you to relax, Alfred. Your muscles are all tight and twisted... I can feel it." He glanced toward those who would be disciples. "The man needs a massage, across his shoulders and down his back." He clapped his hands. "Help the poor man relax. He's had little sleep and requires the attention of those who would serve him." He looked back to the Reverend. "Trust me, Alfred, you'll feel much better for it."

Before the Reverend had a chance to raise an objection, half a dozen hands had begun working at the knots in the muscles of his back and shoulders. He had to admit it felt good, and it seemed to protest would be seen by his host as provocation. He took another segment of the phelare fruit into his mouth. He hadn't even realised that he'd closed his eyes until Albiorix's voice snapped him back to reality.

The under-god held aloft a polished stone goblet encrusted with sparkling gems of every hue imaginable. A ring of blue stones, like gigantic sapphires, stood out just below the rim. "Some wine?" The offer made Alfred aware of his thirst. He took the goblet and drained it in one draught. He could hear the thoughts of his masseurs. *It's such joy to bring you relief... I look so forward to learning from you, the priest the hunter had promised to bring back for so long... We will be envied by all when we are in your service... The hunter was wise to choose you.*

The Reverend wondered about the last thought. *The hunter was wise to choose you.* Again, he realised only on opening them that he'd let his eyes fall shut. Kerridwen was now seated next to him, filling the goblet with more wine. She held it to his lips and said, "Drink of the wine, Alfred Casey, and let it help you rest as you prepare for your destiny."

He wanted to resist, but he found himself taking hold of the goblet and draining it once more. He moved back and forth, then became aware he was lying on a bed under the bough of a tree with sunlight streaming through. He felt his muscles relax more than they had in a long time. A dozen hands continued working on his back, legs and shoulders.

The hunter was wise to choose you.

What did it mean?

The last thing he saw before drifting off into a deep sleep was

Kerridwen's face as she leaned forward and whispered in his ear, "Sleep well and prepare."

*

Mrs Smith was frantic. "It's a good thing you're back. The pixies, they're trapped in the void between worlds... I was stuck there with them but was freed by a mind-thief-possessed gravedigger. He reached in and opened a hole in the membrane separating the void from existence. And Jimmy... he's barely clinging to life after a gunshot wound to his chest. The poor fellow's slumped in the hallway, just inside the door to the servants' quarters." She burst into tears. "I can't begin to tell you what a relief it is to see you three."

Neridah turned to the others. "We'll need to get to Jimmy before we worry about anything else."

Patsy added, "Going through the stables is probably the safest way for us to get to the servants' quarters. While we're there, we might as well try and rescue the pixies on our way."

Neridah replied, "And what do you suggest? Are we going to try to just reach in and open a hole like the mind thief?"

Meredith cut in, "Why not? If a mind thief could do it, then why can't we?"

Neridah screwed up her face and threw her hands in the air. "What are you thinking? We can't even consult the book for how to approach such a thing!"

Patsy said, "If the Nasqa could do it so easily, then maybe it's simple, like when we swim through the air or let ourselves be elsewhere. Maybe it's not a matter of trying, but of letting it happen."

Meredith looked at her mother and said, "It's worth a try."

Neridah asked, "What about soldiers? They're bound to have someone on guard."

Mrs Smith said, "I can round up the fairies from down near the creek and create a diversion."

Neridah felt the weight of Meredith and Patsy's expectation. She threw her hands in the air once more, looked to the sky, and said, "Okay, I give up. It's obvious you won't let up on this, so we might as well give it a try."

*

Bandah stared into space.

Talia ran a hand across the back of his shoulders. "Don't worry, baby, we'll get out of here sooner or later."

"I know that, but when? Will it be all too late by then?" He rubbed a hand against his forehead. "I can feel that Alfred's in trouble... big trouble." He looked up at Talia. "He's my grundai, and I've let him down."

"Oh, Alfred's in trouble! And we're not?"

"Are you even listening? There's a point to the commitment. Humans don't live for long. The ones who can make a difference deserve to be protected." Bandah looked to the ground. "I should have done better. He shouldn't be in the danger he's in."

Talia felt the blood pulsing through her temples. "An under-god flicked a finger and you were thrown into the void. How is that letting him down? And while we're at it, if you want to talk about promises and commitments, I'm your wife. Do you even remember the promises and commitments you made to me way back when?"

"And I've stuck to them."

She stood back and put her hands on her hips. "I beg your pardon!"

"What do you mean?"

"How many years has it been since you even bothered to contact me?"

"That's not a fair comparison you're making."

"It is from where I sit."

"I love you, surely you know that."

"It helps to get a reminder sometimes."

Bandah's attention seemed to stray.

"Hello?"

He pointed toward the trees. "Look, there. It's Mrs Smith." He turned to face his wife with a huge grin on his face. "She's been true to her word."

Talia's anger dissipated. "She must have found the witches!"

Mrs Smith said, "I don't know if you can hear me, but we've got a plan. Whatever you do, stay close to here. I promise you, I'll be back soon."

*

Vincent Donaldson pulled his coat tight. The rain was getting heavier. Today was Cook's day off, and he'd promised to take her into town for lunch. With luck, the rain would soon ease enough that they could still follow through on their plan. If not, he'd just have to settle for spending some time sitting with her by the fire at the McIntyres'.

He reached the turnoff that led to the property and noticed the road had been carved up by heavy traffic.

That could only mean one thing.

Soldiers.

He brought his sulky to a stop and ran his fingers along his waxed moustache, as he was wont to do when he was thinking. *I don't like this. I don't like it at all.*

He'd had dealings with Captain Taylor from the Springwood barracks before. And the last time he'd met up with Cook, she'd told of how Colin was feeling stressed because of attempts being made by a Sydney based magistrate to take over the property. If soldiers really were there, it more than likely had something to do with the magistrate she'd spoken of.

Vincent leaned back and opened the gun box that sat behind the driver's seat. He looked at the rifle and the loaded revolver, feeling glad that he'd followed his gut instincts and brought them with him today. His original concern regarded bushrangers. But with the reputation Captain Taylor's soldiers had built for themselves, he felt this was a far greater concern.

He closed the case and continued on his way.

*

The Reverend looked around as he rose from the bed. It was night, and the sky seemed unfamiliar. What had been a crowded and fertile landscape was now barren and dry.

The hunter was wise to choose you.

The thought continued to run through his head.

He moved toward the dry lakebed, then walked through an ancient market that appeared the moment his foot touched the cracked clay. The people wore long woollen robes and elaborate headdresses adorned with colourful feathers. Their skin was covered in dense fur, so short that it appeared like velvet. The faces had a feline quality, particularly around the nose and eyes. One of them was holding a decorated pot, inspecting the story illustrated on its surface. His fingers were longer than one would expect and, instead of fingernails, he had short claws. In the distance, a stepped pyramid towered over the landscape. At first, the Reverend couldn't make out what the people in the market were saying to one another, but it didn't take long before the language moulded into his own.

"Will you be going to the offering at sundown?"

"I wouldn't miss it. It'll be my son's first sacrifice."

"You must feel proud."

He walked on further and heard another conversation.

"That's a lot to pay for such small fruit."

"What do you expect? It's been almost a year since the last sacrifice."

"You blame the gods for a poorly tended crop?"

"Hey, there was no sacrifice last year. What do you expect? The gods punished us. They made us wait for the rains."

"We went almost a year without a sacrifice the season before, but there was plenty of rain."

"Don't expect me to know what the gods are thinking. That's the job of a priest, not a merchant."

He walked on but was pushed to the side as warriors came through, forcing a pathway through the crowd.

"Look, here he comes!"

"It's the priest!"

A muscular figure with a long dark mane of hair and a stern expression walked through the newly created passage. As he walked, the Reverend noticed the man's shadow reaching out and making threatening gestures to the crowd.

The Reverend turned at the sound of Kerridwen's voice. She was behind him, but unseen. "He's betrayed us! He's allowed himself to be taken by Nasqa! How could you let this happen?"

Albiorix's voice responded, "Don't worry, this will not go unpunished." As he spoke, the people disappeared. Within seconds, the city became desolate and overgrown by weeds.

The images dissolved away and a thick fog descended. The Reverend sensed a sentience within it as a deep voice echoed through the mist, "What do you have to offer?"

The response came from behind him. "The devotion of billions who would not know of you without my guidance." It was Albiorix, his voice carrying a humility that was unfamiliar to the Reverend.

The god's voice came not from a specific point, but from everywhere. "So, he who would be under a god, what would you seek in return?"

"Nothing more than to be the conduit for your devotion."

"I have dealt with your kind before. While it's true that without regular devotion, a god cannot exist, your kind are parasites. But you are a parasite that a god needs to survive in these times of change."

"All times are times of change."

There was a brief pause. "How many other gods do you now work under?"

"Not more than one hundred and fifty-two at last count."

"And how many of those would be darker gods?"

Albiorix stuttered for a moment then went quiet.

"Don't test my patience, Albiorix, or you may regret it."

There was an uncomfortable silence before Albiorix replied. "There had been some among those I served who were darker than I had imagined."

"There is dark or there is light."

Albiorix's voice betrayed a great pain underlying his words. "It is not always that clear when one works under a god."

"How can I be expected to trust one who is so uncertain?"

"I am certain now that I will serve only those where the light is clear."

"And what led you to this wiser path?" There was a long pause. "ANSWER ME!"

Albiorix whispered, "They… they took my wife."

The fog cleared to reveal a star-filled sky. The Reverend was surrounded by a ring of roughly cut stones set up to form a circle.

"Alfred!" It was Kerridwen's voice, coming from behind him.

He turned and saw her silhouette approaching. "Where are we?"

"A place that will be known as the Drombeg stone circle. My father had the people of your world construct this circle of standing stones not long before your ancestors banished him. He had them build many stone circles over thousands of years. They were built around portals, like the one on the McIntyre property. Whenever the portal shifted, he had a new circle built around the new location. They helped to channel the devotion to where my father and the druid priests directed it."

"My ancestors?"

"Your ancestors, and Neridah's ancestors. Did you not know? You come from the same bloodline. That's why you were able to absorb her father's power. You were born to be a druid priest."

Alfred was speechless.

Kerridwen came up to him and placed a hand on his shoulder. The Reverend could feel the warmth of her breath as mist rose from her lips before dissipating into the cold night air. "We need you. Your god needs you. All the gods that the people of your world worship need you. Without someone to channel their devotion, many of their prayers go unheard. We, the under-gods, are the brokers who ensure the prayers get heard by the gods they were intended for. People will follow you. Accept what we offer, and you will be a leader on your world. You'll bring change. You'll make your world a better place."

The Reverend looked around. The darkness had been replaced by the paddock outside his church. It was filled with a vast crowd, all eyes looking to the Reverend and Kerridwen. There must have been tens of thousands of people. They were all bowing toward him and chanting: "The hunter was wise to choose you."

"Together, Alfred, we will bring the people of your world to a spiritual enlightenment. It is not so much which god they worship, but that they must worship. It will make them stronger and more resilient, as it will the gods their devotion is channelled to."

An image rose up in the back of the Reverend's mind. It distracted him. It was a memory of a thought... of an emotion... of love.

Neridah.

Kerridwen grabbed hold of his shoulders and turned him to face her. "Don't let outside thoughts distract you and destroy the potential of our mission and what we can build together." The crowd was gone, as was his church. "The future of a thousand worlds relies on you."

The Reverend's eyes narrowed.

Kerridwen stamped her foot and clenched her fists. "You need to restore the balance." As Kerridwen's anger rose, the daisies of her garland began to lurch out and snap at the Reverend, never moving more than a hand's width from Kerridwen's head, but still enough to be intimidating. "The balance that was lost when the ancestors of those witches you're so fond of banished my father at Drombeg." She looked deep into his eyes. "We need you to help us right the wrongs."

The Reverend could feel movement around his scalp. He reached up and confirmed his suspicion. There were flowers coming together in a garland. The thoughts of his would-be disciples echoed through his head... a dozen voices all repeating the same thought. *The hunter was wise to choose you. The hunter...*

"Listen to them."

The Reverend stared at her as he tore the garland from his head and examined it, searching for signs of the personalities within.

Kerridwen fell to her knees, tears streaming down her cheeks. She buried her head in her hands.

The Reverend turned his gaze back to her, his eyes cold with brewing rage.

She looked up and said, "Do you have any concept of what it's like for an under-god to be banished? The humiliation?" Her own daisies had withdrawn and appeared to be wilting. "He didn't just lose the gods he worked under for your world. When news of his humiliation at the hands of a few human witches spread, other gods lost faith in his ability to hold the devotion of their followers. He had no choice." She looked up into the Reverend's unmoving eyes. "He took on work for darker gods. They took my mother, Alfred. And it was all because of three pathetic little witches."

The Reverend looked at the garland then tossed it aside. "This is just a dream." He turned and walked off into the darkness. "I'll not be drawn in by such mind games."

He walked on.

Again, he found himself approaching Drombeg.

There were three women in flowing white robes. The moon was full, its light making their flesh glow. They were talking to a small elf-like creature. As the Reverend approached, the women seemed unaware of him. They concluded their discussion with the wood-elf then started to dance around the circle.

As the wood-elf approached, the Reverend squatted low to look him in the eye. "I've not seen a creature like yourself before. Would you have a name, or a title, that you go by?"

"The name's Krinkle-myst. And I must say, Alfred, it's a pleasure to meet you." The wood-elf extended a hand.

The Reverend looked at the little hand, but instead of extending his own, he asked, "Would you be in league with the under-god and his hunter?"

Krinkle-myst laughed. "Heaven forbid! Goodness, no. I've far more important things to deal with than helping the likes of them." He raised a finger to emphasise the point he was preparing to make. "And I can assure you. They won't know you and I have had discussions." He turned and watched the witches dance. "They move beautifully, don't you think?"

The Reverend watched in awe. Their movements were fluid and graceful. As their pace quickened, a small fire flickered into life at the circle's centre. It was a fire that burned without fuel. The flames grew higher with each footfall of the witches' dance, with each pirouette, each turn or leap. The fire seemed to be in sync with them.

"This is the ritual to banish Albiorix, just as it happened," Krinkle-myst explained.

"Are the under-gods aware I'm witnessing this?" the Reverend asked, as he continued watching the dance.

"Oh yes, they intended that you would."

The witches picked up torches and lit them from the central flame, making that part of the ritual appear as a natural component of their performance.

The Reverend took a small step forward as the torches illuminated the dancers' faces.

Each one was familiar.

Krinkle-myst looked up at the Reverend's shocked expression. "This is what they wanted you to see. They want you to associate the witches you know with those who banished Albiorix."

"Did he deserve it?"

"He was playing favourites… taking devotion meant for one god, and sending it to another, all for the sake of his own gain."

"So, you intervened?"

"No, that's not my job. But I did let those who could intervene know what was happening. I also helped them find the pages in the Book of Wisdom that would help them do what they had to do." He turned from watching the dance to face the Reverend. "Misdirected devotion is a dangerous thing. It tears at the moral fabric that holds all of everything together. And that makes my job so much harder." He sighed. "And it also makes Mrs Krinkle-myst unhappy. She'd much prefer that I spend time with her, helping untangle people's sad thoughts and turning them into happy ones."

"What would you have me do?"

"Trust in the one who loves you." As he spoke the words, Krinkle-myst began fading away.

"Alfred!" There was a hand shaking his shoulder. "You need to wake up." There was an urgency in Kerridwen's voice.

The Reverend opened his eyes and saw those who would be his disciples gathered around as he lay on the bed with Kerridwen standing over him. Her smile triggered an identical reaction from the Reverend's devotees.

Alfred rubbed his eyes and said, "As far as dreams go, that was one of the more memorable." He looked at Kerridwen. "The visions in my dream, they were your doing?"

Kerridwen threw her head back and laughed. "Oh, my poor Alfred." She leaned in close, ran a finger down his cheek, and whispered. "This is all about helping you find your destiny."

He grabbed hold of her hand and pushed it away. "Then why was the need to wake me so urgent?"

Kerridwen's expression softened. She almost looked sad. "There was a moment where I lost sight of you. You were hidden from me like there was someone else steering you away from your purpose." She took on a serious tone. "You cannot do this without my guidance."

He felt himself drifting back to sleep as the would-be disciples began chanting: "The hunter was wise to choose you."

CHAPTER 15

"**Y**ou must be crazy," said Elpheen. The fairy's iridescent emerald eyes glared at Mrs Smith. "Why would we want to help you?" Waves of blonde hair flowed over her shoulders and down to her waist. A frown was etched into her face as she hovered in front of Mrs Smith.

Mrs Smith replied, "I'm still one of you. And it's not me you'd be helping. This is about the witches."

"Hah! You don't even go by a fairy name anymore. You gave that up years ago." Her eyes narrowed, "And you can never change that."

Another fairy, Eldah, flew forward. "Of course we'll help." She turned to the others gathered by the creek, well upstream from where the Nasqa-possessed soldiers were patrolling. "What do you say?"

One by one, they flew forward.

"You can count me in."

"How could we not?"

"I think it goes without saying."

"We'll never forget what they did."

Elpheen protested, "You are joking, aren't you? They went in there to rescue one of their own!"

Mrs Smith turned to her and said, "And they could have left you there. They could have left me there. They could have left us all behind."

Elpheen glared at the others. "I guess I don't have much choice in the matter." She sarcastically threw her hands in the air. "I was so obviously wrong."

Mrs Smith took to the air. "Come on then, let's work some fairy magic on them."

As they flew off, Elpheen trailed behind the others. *How dare that freak make a fool of me*, she thought to herself. *One day I'll make her pay for this. She'll end up wishing she'd stayed in human form.*

*

Within the Reverend's dream, Kerridwen's voice was distant but forceful. "It's time to choose the disciples that will make up your garland."

A hundred voices echoed through his head.

The hunter was wise to choose you.

"You'd have me choose from these voices running through my head?"

He could see her now, standing before him, the would-be disciples standing behind her. "Every one of them would die for you."

He watched the movement of the daisies in her garland. "I'll not wear one of those things around my head."

"You don't need to. And I wouldn't want you to... at least, not while in your world. Once they are chosen, they will follow you. They'll be your garland whether they be flowers you wear as a crown or whether they be followers who walk with you. There have been many under-gods who have walked through your world with garlands of twelve disciples. Some have even been mistaken for gods or prophets." She looked at the anger in the Reverend's eyes. "Oh, don't worry, true gods and prophets have also had garlands of twelve, but only when they chose to walk through a world in mortal form. It's part of the natural order. We just use ours more proactively than they tend to."

"Why twelve?"

She shrugged her shoulders. "No one really knows. Some things just have to be accepted for what they are, as part of the natural order."

He turned away and shook his head. "I've no wish to do this. I'll not be seen to have disciples."

"Just do it, Alfred. The longer you put this off, the harder it becomes for everyone concerned."

The hunter was wise to choose you.

The Reverend looked around at the faces. "Why do they say that?"

"Perhaps, it's because they believe in you. And I do too, despite your persistent recalcitrance."

The hunter was wise to choose you.

They were getting louder. He stared at the ground near his feet.

"It's time for you to choose, Alfred." She placed a hand on his shoulder and lifted his chin with her other hand, forcing him to look her in the eye. "Time for you to make wise choices."

He tried to hold on to his memories of those he loved, but they were slipping away, leaving a dark void that he felt in the depths of his soul.

There was one person in particular, but her name eluded him.

The darkness was replaced by images from his future. Huge crowds gathered to listen to him preach. Kerridwen and his disciples by his side.

He walked through streets with throngs of people reaching out to touch him, their faces glowing with adulation.

It felt like years had passed when he heard Kerridwen's voice work its way into the dream he was having within his dream. "Choose, Alfred." She softened her tone. "They won't leave you to sleep in peace until you do."

The hunter was wise to choose you.

He looked around once more at the souls who would be his disciples. "My first choice is Felibrey the Humble."

.

The fairies flew up through the rain. They approached the stables from the high end of the paddock. When they felt they were close enough to be heard by the soldiers inside, they began singing.

> *Est nar-deh ace lief eft-lei bre kay,*
> *Eft-lei kay maelief est ses-deh teal.*

The words loosely translated as, "You don't know where we'll all be, we'll be somewhere you can't see." They sang in counterpoint harmonies that contrasted against the sound of the ongoing downpour. Despite the sweetness of the melody, the rain thundered so loudly that the handful of soldiers stationed in the stables were barely able to hear the fairies' voices.

The soldier closest to the upper end of the stables asked, "Did you hear that?"

His nearest colleague raised an eyebrow as he focused on the song. He looked up and said, "Fairies!" He turned to the other soldiers in the stables who were gathered around an upturned wheelbarrow they were using as a card table.

One of them looked up and asked, "Should we check it out?"

"Aye," replied the first soldier.

They picked up their rifles. Some made their way to the lower end while the rest went in the opposite direction, with the idea that they'd be able to surround the fairies behind the stables.

The first soldier to look around the corner of the building pointed. "There they are." The group of fairies flew away from the building toward the top of the paddock. Without a second thought, the soldiers ran after them.

Once the fairies had led the soldiers over the crest of the hill, the mud-soaked witches moved out from the cover of the trees. As they dragged themselves forward, it would have been hard to distinguish them from the dull background.

Unknown to the witches, there was one soldier who had stayed behind. They had almost reached the stables when he looked their way.

"Halt! Who goes there?"

Neridah and Meredith came to a stop, but Patsy was undeterred. Breaking into a run, she continued moving forward. Meredith reached out to grab her, but it was too late.

Patsy thought to herself, *If Kerridwen can rip out a mind thief. Why can't I?*

The soldier lowered his rifle so its bayonet was directed at her.

Patsy's momentum was carrying her toward it. There was no way she could stop in time to save herself.

"Hey! You should be ashamed of yourself, pointing that thing at a child." The voice next to his ear took the soldier by surprise. He turned his rifle toward the source of the sound as Mrs Smith disappeared into the darkness.

Patsy crashed into the soldier and did as she'd seen Kerridwen do before.

Don't think about it. It's like everything else. Let it happen.

She reached into his chest with ease and pulled out the Nasqa, throwing it as far away as she could.

The soldier fell to the ground.

She grabbed hold of his shoulders. "What's your name?"

He blinked, then said, "William Daniels." He looked at her, surprised by the young girl's confidence. "Who are you?"

"Listen to me, William. You need to shut your mind, and you need to shut it now! You need to make sure that thing can't re-enter you."

Neridah came up from behind. She grabbed Patsy's shoulder and swung her around to face her. "How could you be so foolish?"

Patsy frowned. "What do you mean? I just saved him."

"And probably ruined any chance we had of surviving this."

The soldier asked, "Who are you people?"

A distant voice called out from the front veranda of the main house, "They're at the stables!"

Neridah struggled to contain her anger. "You ripped it out without a thought of what it might do afterward."

Meredith stood in the spot where she could feel the time freeze had happened. "But we're here now. Can't we at least try to get Bandah and Talia out of the void."

"There's no time, we need to go."

Patsy ignored her grandmother. She went down on her knees next to her mother and did exactly as Mrs Smith had described the gravedigger doing. When she pulled her hands apart the two pixies flew out of the void before she'd even had a chance to see them.

Talia landed on her shoulder and hugged her around the neck. "Thank you."

Bandah was already flying toward the servants' quarters. "Let's save the gratitude for later. These three ladies need to make a run for cover while we tend to Jimmy."

Talia lifted into the air. "He's right. They won't even notice us while they're going after you. This is the best chance there's going to be to save him." She was already flying after Bandah. "His wounds are easy enough to heal, but there's little time."

Neridah said. "This isn't good. We need that key." She glared at Patsy. "That was supposed to be why we're here."

"And what key would that be?" They all turned to see a soldier approaching with his rifle fixed on them. "Get on the ground, with your hands behind your head. You too, Daniels."

The soldier felt the coldness of gunmetal on the back of his neck. "I'd drop that rifle if I were you." It was Vincent Donaldson with his revolver.

The soldier let his rifle fall.

Patsy casually stood up and walked toward him.

Neridah called after her, "Patricia, we don't have time for this!"

Meredith grabbed her mother's arm and said, "Let her do it, Mother. We need all the allies we can get."

Neridah looked toward the soldiers approaching from the house. "We don't have time."

Patsy ignored them both. She reached forward, but the soldier slumped to the ground before she'd even touched him. The mind thief, or Nasqa, had preferred to flee the host of its own accord than suffer the humiliation of being torn out by a young girl.

Vincent raised an eyebrow as he watched Patsy reach down to help her fallen adversary.

A gunshot rang out.

William helped Patsy raise his comrade to his feet. "Come on, we need to go."

Vincent stood his ground and returned fire, sending off three shots in quick succession before he turned and joined the others in their dash for the trees.

•

The Reverend groaned, tossing and turning in his induced sleep.

"You've chosen one." Kerridwen stood over him, both inside and outside of his dream. "Now, who will be the next?"

The Reverend's head was buried in his hands. "I don't know them."

Felibrey sat next to him. "If it's your wish, I'm happy to help you. I've known them all for a long time. I can tell you of their strengths and weaknesses."

"That's interesting, lad. You call yourself humble, yet you offer judgement on others?"

Kerridwen was fed up with taking the gentle approach. She looked up and shook her head in exasperation. "Can we *please* just get on with it?" She glared at the Reverend while gesturing to Felibrey. "He absolutely reeks of humility. Can you just go with his offer? Otherwise, we'll be here forever while you procrastinate over your choices."

The Reverend lifted his head and surveyed the dreamscape. Within this phase of his dream, the disciples looked as they were to born to be, as opposed to the masking of reality within Albiorix's celebration. There were lifeforms that defied description and those that seemed familiar.

He looked across at a soul far off in the distance who seemed more concerned with reading his scroll than what was happening around him. He had pale blue flesh and deep black eyes. "You, the lad with the scroll, what's your name?"

Kerridwen interjected, "No, you can't choose him. He is not one who would choose to be your disciple. He is here as an observer. His interest lies only in learning rather than service." She stared at the creature who continued reading from his scroll, oblivious to the unwanted attention he was garnering.

"Nevertheless, he interests me."

Feeling the intensity of the Reverend's eyes on him, the creature glanced up from his scroll. "They call me Bordauex the Learned." He turned back to his scroll and continued reading.

Felibrey whispered into the Reverend's ear. "He is from a world where learning is not valued. Since his arrival here two thousand years ago, he has rejected the quick path to knowledge and the grace that comes from service in the garlands, preferring to spend his days buried in the slow learning that comes from reading books and scrolls."

"I like those who seek knowledge in the pages of books." He looked across at Bordauex. "You are welcome to join me, Bordauex the Learned."

Kerridwen's knuckles whitened as she clenched her fists. "Alfred, you need to choose from those who would follow you. Urgh, you can be so frustrating."

Bordauex looked up from his scrolls. "Are books and learning valued in your world?"

"Aye. I have learned much from books, and those who I care to spend time with have done the same."

Bordauex stood up from his desk and said, "Very well then. I shall join with the others in their desire to follow you and say that the hunter was wise to choose you."

Kerridwen said, "Alfred, these choices are supposed to be about building your power, about making you stronger."

The Reverend's voice was calm. "Your understanding of power is obviously very different to my own."

●

"We need to do it."

Meredith put a hand on Patsy's shoulder. "No, it's far too big a risk."

Neridah said, "Patricia's right. I have to agree with her on this one."

Meredith sighed and shook her head. "I'm not happy about it."

"What are you talking about?" asked Vincent as he continued watching the paddock.

"I need to ask something of you, Vincent," said Meredith. "I need you to trust that Patricia, my mother, and myself are able to secure Cook's safety."

He stared at her for a few seconds without responding before turning his attention back to the soldiers. "I'm listening."

"But there's more than that." She paused to compose herself. "Captain Taylor has taken Colin to Springwood, with the intention of taking him to the gallows before day's end." She looked at the two soldiers who had joined them, then back to Vincent. "You and these two soldiers are his only hope."

"I'm not leaving this property till I know that Cook's out of harm's way."

Patsy said, "Don't worry, Mister Donaldson, we'll make sure she's safe."

"All these soldiers, against two women and a child? No." He was looking at Patsy, then turned to Meredith. "Don't get me wrong, I care about your husband as though he was a brother. But my first concern has to be Cook."

Daniel Williams stepped forward. "Forgive me if I'm speaking out of turn, but I really think you should listen to them." He looked at Patsy then back to Vincent. "I swear to you; your friend is safe in their hands. And they're right. If Mister McIntyre is to be saved from the gallows, he'll need the three of us to leave now to ride into Springwood and do what we can to intervene."

Neridah approached Vincent. He looked perplexed as she placed a hand on the side of his head and said, "You need to remember." She closed her eyes and began whispering, "Nelkar cane phay-tamullah ma-bel dae predae." She opened her eyes and pulled her hand away.

Memories of extraordinary events that had taken place the year before flooded through Vincent's head. He lowered his rifle and looked at the witches, studying each of them. When his gaze reached Patsy he said, "Are you sure of this?"

"I promise, Mr Donaldson, Cook will be safe when you get back. Just please, can you promise me you'll bring Father back with you?"

He bent over, placing a firm hand on Patsy's shoulder. "I can't make any promises. We'll be greatly outnumbered, and I've no idea how many soldiers we'll be up against."

Williams said, "Most of the soldiers still at the barracks aren't possessed as yet by these things that take over the mind. Those that are won't want to have the truth revealed. They'll need to take him before a Justice of the Peace for a sentence to be passed before they can lead him to the gallows. He's accused of the murder of a magistrate, and Captain Taylor will claim that he's too dangerous to risk transporting him to Sydney for a proper trial."

Vincent replied, "But surely if the crime is that serious, there's no choice but to take him to Sydney."

Williams shook his head, "The Governor himself is possessed by one of these things, and he is desperate to take control of this property. There will be tremendous pressure on the Justice to pass sentence swiftly. And if he does declare that Mr McIntyre should be tried in Sydney, Captain Taylor will ensure he dies en route. One way or the other, without our intervention, he'll be dead by sundown."

Meredith took both of Vincent's hands in hers. "Please, bring him back to me."

Vincent looked down at her hands, then brought his gaze up to meet her eyes. "I'll do what I can."

She threw her arms around him, burying her face in his shoulder. "Thank you."

Vincent returned the embrace then turned to the soldiers. "Do you two have horses up there in the stables?"

William replied, "We'd never get them out of there without getting caught."

Patsy said, "I've got an idea."

They all turned to hear what she had to say, but in that instant, she was gone.

*

Lieutenant Neil Stewart didn't appear surprised when Patsy materialised in the library. "I was wondering when you'd turn up." He held up the key as he leaned back in the leather-lined chair and put his feet up on Colin's desk. "Are you looking for this?" She watched the hideous shape of his shadow through the matted hair that draped over her eyes. Its talon-like fingers dangled a silhouette of the key near the muddy puddle at her feet.

"Oh, yes," said Patsy. "And I'll be taking it with me when I leave here."

"You really should be more careful of the situations you transport yourself into."

Hearing boots on the floorboards behind her, Patsy turned around and saw three soldiers just inside the door to the library pointing guns at her. Another walked toward her with a rope.

"Oh, and you'll have fun trying to reach into our souls with your hands tied behind your back."

Patsy closed her eyes, preparing to let herself be elsewhere.

The Lieutenant laughed, "Hah!" He took his feet off the desk and pointed her way. The soldier with the rope was tying Patsy's hands as the Lieutenant continued, "I knew you'd try that. But all those little time freezes that were happening in here today... oh my, how they play havoc with how the fabric between crossworlds reacts." He put the key down next to the inkwell and made a show of holding his hands out then brought them closer together as he walked around to the front of the desk. "The space around where the freeze happened slowly closes in, making it easy to pop in... but when you try to pop out? Why, it's a bit like having your feet stuck in a bucket of molasses. When your mother managed to get out with the book, the ability to leave that way from here pretty much snapped shut behind her." He leaned back against the desk and crossed his arms. "Now, I wonder how long it'll take before your mother and grandmother make the same mistake as you."

CHAPTER 16

"Oh, Patricia." Meredith beat a hand against her brow. "Why? Why can't she be more patient?"

Neridah said, "Probably because she didn't believe we'd let her do it."

Meredith looked up. "And for good reason."

Neridah looked out at the paddock. "Maybe not. Look, the soldiers, some of them are heading up to the house." She turned to Vincent and the soldiers. "This could be your chance to get the extra horses you need from the stables."

Vincent shook his head. "There's still more of them out there looking for you."

"That's just it, they're looking for us. They'll be assuming that you and the soldiers made a run for it as soon as they were set free."

"I think my mother might be right," said Meredith.

Vincent wasn't convinced. "They know I'm trying to help you."

Neridah said, "Think about it, Vincent. Think about what happened last year. They know how powerful we are together. If they think the three of us are in the house together, they'll want every mind thief they can muster up there. We just need to keep them distracted long enough for you to get to the stables undetected."

"And you'll be able to get Cook out of there?"

"Not yet, there's too many of them for us to defeat them straight away. We need to get a few things from inside and get out of there while we put our plan together."

Meredith said, "She's right, Vincent. They can feel where we go to when we travel the way Patricia did just now. They'll follow us."

Vincent looked at a group of soldiers who were heading toward the bushes they were hiding in. "Then, doesn't that mean they can tell where she came from as well?"

There was no answer. He turned around and both women had vanished.

.

Neridah appeared in the room Alfred was using as his temporary accommodation. The box he'd retrieved from his house when it burnt down was on the bedside table. She picked it up, then allowed herself to be in her own room. She went straight to the wardrobe and grabbed some clean clothes and shoes, then heard soldiers running up the stairs as she allowed herself to be in Meredith's room. Meredith appeared just after her, holding a bundle of clothes from Patsy's room. She dropped them on her bed then grabbed a suitcase from the top of the wardrobe. The soldiers had reached the top of the stairs.

Neridah whispered, "I grabbed enough for both of us."

Meredith nodded. Once she'd opened the suitcase, they threw the clothing and the Reverend's box in.

Neridah said, "We need to send it to the shed."

"Can we do that without going there ourselves?"

"We have to try."

Meredith slammed the case shut, closed her eyes, and thought of the garden shed, allowing the suitcase to be there. She opened her eyes as the soldiers kicked the door open.

The suitcase was still there.

A soldier raised his rifle and said, "Put your hands up."

Neridah grabbed the suitcase and said, "My room."

A shot rang out as the witches disappeared.

When they materialised in Neridah's room she said, "We need to see it. Look, through the window." They both closed their eyes, visualised the suitcase in the shed, and allowed it to be there. They opened their eyes as the soldiers kicked the door in. The suitcase was gone. Neridah looked at Meredith and said, "Library." The next instant, they were gone.

*

Vincent let out a breath he'd held for over a minute when the soldiers turned away. He said to his companions, "That was close." They looked across the paddock. The witches were right in their assumptions. All the soldiers were making their way up to the house. Once they were more than halfway, Vincent said, "We won't have much time. Let's go."

The rain eased as they worked their way up the hill toward the stables. They froze at the sound of a kookaburra bursting into laughter in a tree not far from them. When it was clear the soldiers had ignored the bird, they continued walking.

Having reached the back of the stables, they clung to its walls and shimmied around to the lower entrance then, one by one, slipped inside. Williams remained silent as he pointed out the saddled horses not controlled by mind thieves.

There were just two of them.

Vincent was fine with that. He knew his own horse well enough that he felt comfortable with the idea of unhitching it from the sulky and riding it bareback if he had to.

"Hey, what are you up to?"

They turned around to see a soldier raising his rifle at them. Vincent pulled out his hunting knife and threw it as the soldier prepared to pull the trigger. The soldier let out a dull scream when the knife lodged in his shoulder. As he fell to the ground, he fired his rifle into the air, drawing the attention of other soldiers nearby.

Vincent said, "Now or never." They ran for the horses, Vincent leaping into the saddle of one while Williams jumped onto the other. Vincent lifted the other soldier to join him on the back of his mount then kicked his heels into the beast, causing it to rear up before it hit the ground running for the road.

"Stop them!"

They rode away from the stables, surrounded by the sound of gunfire. They were on the road out of the property when Vincent heard a bullet whiz past his ear then felt a jolt from behind. The soldier he was carrying had taken a bullet in the back. His arms fell away, then he fell off the back of the horse. Williams looked over his shoulder and called out, "We can't go back for him." Vincent turned his head and saw that Williams was right. The soldier was already dead.

He caught up to Williams and said, "I don't see anyone riding after us."

"No, the Lieutenant wants to keep everyone he has left there to fight against the witches. He'll likely send word somehow to the Barracks about us. We'd best keep our heads low. That soldier they shot as we were leaving will be blamed on us. We'll be wanted for his murder now."

*

Meredith and her mother appeared in the library on either side of Patsy.

Lieutenant Stewart smiled while he picked at his fingernails. "Well, that took a while. I was starting to wonder whether you even care about the girl."

Patsy looked at her mother and said, "The key. It's on the desk."

Neridah reached toward the desk and pulled back. The key flew toward her as though they were connected by a rubber-band. As her hand snapped shut around it, she said, "The shed."

Patsy looked up at her grandmother. "I tried it before. It doesn't work now. The time freezes have left us stuck here."

Meredith said, "Don't underestimate the power of the Trilogy."

The Lieutenant addressed his troops. "Shoot them."

The three witches closed their eyes as the gunshots rang out. They opened them a moment later in the shed, staring straight into the face of the Lieutenant. He grinned. "Well, that was a fun ride. I must say, I am impressed by what you three can achieve together." He took a step toward them. "But it won't help you now."

Neridah leaped forward and reached for his chest, as she'd seen Patsy do earlier.

Lieutenant Stewart laughed as he swung his arm across, the back of his hand connecting with Neridah's cheek and sending her to the floor.

Meredith looked around and saw the suitcase she'd transported to the shed before and stretched out to place a hand on it. She turned to her mother and said, "The pathway."

They closed their eyes and could feel the rain on their backs before they'd even opened their eyes.

Once again, they saw the Lieutenant's sardonic smirk. "We can play this game all day. Wherever you go, I will follow."

Meredith's jaw dropped when she looked past the Lieutenant. Where before there had been dense bushes, a pathway had revealed itself, a potential portal to safety via an altogether different world. Golden sunshine beamed through the trees. There was no doubt in her mind. It was the pathway to Krinkle-myst's cabin, where the Book of Wisdom was waiting for them to return. It had to be.

Meredith looked at the beckoning pathway behind the Lieutenant. "Maybe not." She lifted the suitcase and swung it by the handle so it connected with the Lieutenant's head, sending him to his knees. She turned to Patsy and Neridah, "Run!"

The path was just a few strides away.

Patsy wanted to take her grandmother's hand, but her own were still bound behind her back. As she followed her mother across the threshold between worlds, she looked over her shoulder and called out, "Come on, Nana-Neri."

Neridah was almost across the threshold herself when she felt a hand grip onto her ankle, pulling her to the ground. She turned just in time to see the humour had drained from Lieutenant Stewart's face.

"Where are they? How could they just vanish like that without me feeling where they'd gone?"

Beyond the threshold, Patsy said, "He can't see us!" She turned to her mother. "Cut me free, so we can help her."

"No time." Meredith stepped back through the threshold and into the rain. She pulled her hand back and drew power from across a hundred worlds.

Lieutenant Stewart looked up at the woman with the matted hair and mud-covered nightclothes. His expression betrayed his fear. He let go of Neridah and started to back away.

Meredith threw her hand forward, releasing the energy burst. Lieutenant Stewart was lifted off the ground by the impact, landing on his back several paces away.

The strain of drawing up energy from the Crossworlds after so many transportations left Meredith drained. She swayed back and forth and watched the world around her fall out of focus as she collapsed.

Neridah grabbed her daughter under the shoulders and began dragging her the short distance to the threshold between worlds. She looked toward the Lieutenant just in time to see him aim his pistol toward them, ready to fire.

*

The Reverend sat up and rubbed his eyes. He was on a bed in the middle of a grand garden. Creatures he'd not seen until experiencing the visions in his dreams wandered about enjoying casual conversation.

A male with feline characteristics, like he'd seen in his first vision, approached him. He wore a Roman-style toga with red trim. When the Reverend glanced down at himself, he noticed he was now wearing the same. The feline-like creature extended his arms. "Ah, the Reverend Alfred Casey. At last, we can speak on a more honest level." The voice sounded oddly familiar.

"What do you mean?"

"Do you not recognise me?"

The Reverend shook his head. "No, I don't believe we've met."

"Perhaps my name will help you. I am known as Ferdinand, Seeker of Knowledge."

"Ferdinand? You're the McIntyres' cat?"

"Oh please, must you insult me by inferring I was their property? Did you never see the absurdity of it? It's one thing to hear the gossip of the cicadas, but didn't the idea of having philosophical conversations with a cat ever strike you as being somewhat strange? I was sent to your world by my mistress."

Kerridwen walked up behind Ferdinand and stroked his neck. "Isn't he a lovely pussy cat?"

"You sent him to the McIntyres' property to spy on them?"

"I'd say it was more of a fact-finding mission. He is the Seeker of Knowledge." She extended her hand to Alfred. "Come. It's time you join us for breakfast. There is much you must do today. Father is eager to plan his return to your world."

Alfred rose and took Kerridwen's hand. "I'm struggling to remember much about the McIntyres'. The memories seem so distant, like they're fading away. Names and faces, they are all gone."

Kerridwen put her arm through his as they walked through the golden, dappled sunlight streaming through the trees, Alfred's chosen twelve just a few steps behind. "That's of no great surprise. It was quite an ordeal for you to choose your garland."

"Aye, it took a good deal of consideration."

Kerridwen smiled. "I was frustrated at how long you took, and I questioned your early choices. But now, when I look at your garland holistically, I see the wisdom in your selection. They are not who I would have chosen, but I'm a hunter, not a priest."

"Aye, that's true."

She looked up at him as they continued their walk. "Is there anything you feel you're missing from your world?"

He looked at her as he replied, "Aye, I feel a sense of loss, but what that sense relates to eludes me."

She leaned in close to him. "Don't worry, Alfred. That will pass."

*

"Nana-Neri!" Patsy yelled as loud as she could, hoping that somehow her voice may stop the bullet from reaching its intended target.

Neridah watched in horror as fire flared out from the barrel of the pistol that pointed her way. She could see the aim was accurate.

The sound of the gunshot thundered in her ears.

Instinctively, she went to her knees and released her grip on Meredith, then felt around her chest for where the bullet should have found its mark. She looked down but couldn't see any signs of a wound.

Lieutenant Stewart stood up and looked around, his gun dangling by his side. "Where are you, witch?" He screamed, "SHOW YOURSELF!"

Patsy went down on her knees next to Neridah. "You made it!"

Neridah struggled to get a decent breath as her heart raced. She stared through the portal at the Lieutenant. "He can't see or hear us."

Lieutenant Stewart walked along the tree line, yelling at the troops running down the hill. "Find them! They must be here somewhere. Reach out through the Crossworlds. Do whatever it takes! Just find those damned witches!"

Neridah turned Patsy's shoulders so she could untie her granddaughter's hands. "We'll get you free, and then see about waking your mother."

Meredith stirred and began to moan. "What happened? Did we make it?"

Neridah breathed a sigh of relief then hugged her daughter. "Yes, thanks to you. You were amazing." She took a breath before continuing, "We still need to get to the wood-elf's cabin."

Meredith replied, "Do you know the way?"

Neridah finished untying the knots in Patsy's bonds then shook her head. "We walked for an hour last time. I can't remember how we got there."

Patsy smiled. "The pixie-dust! Krinkle-myst told us it would lead us there whenever we needed it to."

Neridah put a hand on Patsy's shoulder. "I wouldn't be so quick to place my faith in promises made by a wood-elf if I were you." The moment she finished speaking a ball of pixie-dust sprang up behind her. There was a moment's silence while Neridah looked at the stunned expressions on Patsy and Meredith's faces. "It's behind me, isn't it?'

Patsy and Meredith nodded.

Neridah slowly turned around, then allowed herself to smile when she saw the dancing ball of pixie-dust.

•

"Alfred!" Albiorix threw his arms around the Reverend as Kerridwen took her seat. "I'm so pleased you've chosen your twelve."

"Aye. But tell me, why was it that I had to choose while in a dream? Are not sober choices in a wakeful state more valid?"

"You would question the validity of your choices? Trust me, my friend, you should never underestimate the power of decisions made within dreams."

The Reverend thought about his conversation with Ferdinand. He was struggling now to remember where he knew the feline from. There was a name, McIntyre, but he couldn't associate it with faces or places. He swayed back and forth and had to grab the back of a chair to steady himself before he took a step back and asked, "Why? Why am I here? What is this really about? Tell me, Albiorix, what do you want of me?"

Kerridwen looked up with a stern expression. "Alfred, I thought we'd been over this."

"Aye, but that was in a dream."

Albiorix looked to the sky, rocking his head from side to side. "Why, why, why?" He turned back to the Reverend and, for the first time, looked angry. "You dare to ask me why? I'll tell you why. Because the ancestors of your beloved witches banished me. They were jealous of the devotion I channelled to the gods and they shut me out." He moved closer to the Reverend, so much so that their noses almost touched. "Did it make your world a better place? Do people feel that their gods hear them better now? Too many prayers go unheard without an under-god to channel them. Or, do you feel that everyone's prayers in your world are answered?" He leaned back and gestured toward the multitude of creatures calmly going about their business. "Look at them, Alfred. Are the people on your world this content?"

Witches? Alfred remembered the witches in his dream, dancing among the standing stones at Drombeg. They were familiar, but he couldn't remember why. Again, he felt unsteady. He sat down in his chair and looked at the scene before him. "A small moment like this is barely adequate to determine the full extent of anyone's happiness." A thought rose up in the back of the Reverend's mind. *The hunter was wise to choose you.* "Tell me, if you will, why does this singular thought keep invading my mind? You surely know the one I mean."

"Hah!" The Reverend grimaced when Albiorix slapped him on the back as he too took his place at the table. It was a habit he was growing weary of. "This is just the beginning, Alfred. This is how you will learn to channel devotion. They who would follow you love and adore you. They have been trained in how to focus that devotion, so it opens the pathways within your own mind to accept devotion of any kind, no matter where it be directed. You have chosen twelve, and they will keep your mind open to devotion, wherever you may go."

A plate of fruit was placed in front of the Reverend. Despite his hunger, he resisted the temptation. His thirst and hunger were blurring his vision and his mind as he whispered, "I'll not be your puppet."

Albiorix threw an arm around the Reverend's shoulder. "Oh, Alfred. Tell me, do you think you really have a choice? You are going through changes. As this day progresses, your resistance will falter. You have chosen your twelve. Later today you will be ready to cross back to your world. You will meet your destiny and you will pave the way."

Kerridwen grabbed her father's arm. "It's too early for this discussion."

Albiorix pulled his arm away from his daughter. "Nonsense!"

The Reverend lowered his head, hoping it may help to stop his head spinning. "What would you have me pave the way for?"

Albiorix stood up and threw his arms out wide. "For my triumphant return."

The Reverend looked at the goblet set before him on the table. "I thirst."

Kerridwen smiled as she poured him a wine. "Don't worry, Alfred. Once you've eaten your fill and sated your thirst, you'll see things in a different light."

*

Bandah and Talia stood on Jimmy O'Sullivan's chest. They pulled their wings fully closed, turning them into heavy shields on their backs and making them resemble cockroaches. Talia looked at Jimmy's wound. "It's a nasty one. He's lost a lot of blood."

Bandah followed Talia into the wound. "Yes, but he's still alive. If we can pinch the damage together, he should be able to recover after a few days of induced sleep." They continued through the bloody mess created by the gunshot. "We'll have to get the bullet out first."

"What fun that'll be." Talia turned to Bandah. "He's lucky it didn't lodge somewhere worse." She wrapped an arm around the lead ball and tried to dislodge it. "Can you lend me a bit of muscle, Big Boy?"

"Maybe we can save ourselves some trouble if we push it into the void, rather than trying to drag it out."

"I like the way you think." She allowed herself a smile. "I knew there was a good reason why I'd married you."

Bandah worked his way in behind the bullet and readied himself to push. "We just need to make sure we don't slip across with it."

Talia squeezed in next to him, leaning against Jimmy's heart. "We can use his heartbeat to help us push. On the count of three." She made sure her count was in time with the beats and closed her eyes. "One... two... three!"

They pushed forward, creating a momentary break in the membrane that separates this world from the void. The lead pellet slipped through. Then Talia fell forward, starting to slip through with it. Bandah held her tight around the waist with one arm while hooking the other around Jimmy's aorta. The membrane closed tight around her, trying to suck her through, but Bandah's grip persisted. The membrane felt like icy water cutting through her as it slid along her body, leaving behind a trail of gooey mucus as it sought to close itself. Once it had passed over her fingertips and snapped shut, she fell back against Bandah and gasped for breath. She wiped the goo away from her eyes before daring to open them. "That stuff is disgusting."

CHAPTER 17

Within minutes of arriving at Krinkle-myst's cabin, the witches had changed into dry clothes and were seated by the fire.

"It's so good to be warm and dry again." Patsy turned to her mother. "Thank you."

Meredith put an arm around her daughter's shoulder. "I'm the one who should be thanking you. I'm so sorry, Patricia."

"What for?"

"For decisions being forced on you that a girl your age shouldn't have to make."

Patsy embraced her mother in a warm hug.

Neridah walked over to the table where the Book of Wisdom lay defiantly shut. "Cosy as it may be sitting by the fire, we have urgent matters to attend to."

Meredith stood up and said. "Of course." She held up the key. "What's the main word we should focus on?"

"Kerridwen," said Patsy.

"Albiorix," said Neridah.

Meredith opened the book and said, "Under-gods."

The book opened to the page that best met their combined needs. There were drawings of Albiorix, Kerridwen, and a close-up image of a daisy baring its teeth. It took a few seconds for the witches to be able to decipher the language of the text and read it as they would English.

As they worked their way through, Meredith said, "This is worse than I thought."

Patsy said, "Going by what it says here, Darcy's trapped in her garland."

Neridah said, "Albiorix was banished by our ancestors. They sent him back to his own world, Dellakaran. Kerridwen, her coming here and taking Alfred back with her, it's all about him trying to come back."

Meredith continued reading for a while then looked at her mother, "You're right. They're going to manipulate Alfred to end the banishment by creating a new following. They want to make Alfred an under-god and have him channel devotion directly to Albiorix."

Neridah looked at her daughter. "Albiorix wants to become a god?"

Patsy asked, "How can he do that? I thought gods always were what they are."

Meredith shook her head, "No, most gods are created by people's belief in them. You should never underestimate the power of belief. If he is seen to be a god by enough people, then he'll be able to return. He was banished as an under-god, but if he comes back as a god, then no banishment will likely stop him."

Patsy said, "I'm a little confused. Doesn't it say that he was worshipped as a god while he was here before?"

Neridah replied, "Yes, but he was here acting as an under-god, channelling the devotion to others who were elsewhere. It's when power is channelled to those who are unseen that it is most powerful. To become a god, one has to be unseen."

"So, why would he want to come back? If he intends to use the Reverend that way, wouldn't he be better off staying in Dellakaran?"

Neridah put a hand on Patsy's shoulder. "He wants revenge, and he wants to take his revenge out on us."

Meredith said, "From what it says here, once Alfred has selected twelve disciples to make up his garland, the pathway is inevitable. His followers will be chosen from those who have served Albiorix, and they will likely control him more than he controls them."

Patsy turned the page, keen to learn more about Dellakaran. "It says here that Dellakaran isn't even real. It's an artificial world created by Albiorix and his garland." She looked up. "If we can destroy his garland, it will destroy his world." She turned to her mother and grandmother. "All the souls there would be sucked back through the Crossworlds to where they originated from."

Neridah said, "We need to go there, now. We need to bring Alfred and Darcy back. We need to let Albiorix and his daughter know we won't be beaten."

"I agree," said Meredith.

Patsy said, "Wait. Before we go, I want to look up a spell." She closed her eyes and turned to another page. "We need to be ready to banish Kerridwen, in case she tries to follow us back through the portal once we've rescued Alfred."

*

Talia and Bandah worked their way backwards as they pulled together torn tissue and fused it like they were pushing pieces of playdough together. Where they could see signs of potential infection, they tore out the offending pieces of flesh and put them in a sack they'd made from some damaged tissue.

It was difficult and tedious.

After several minutes working together in silence fixing the unfixable wound, Talia asked, "Have you missed me?"

"Yes."

"Then why did you leave?"

Bandah replied, "I needed to remember how it feels to miss you."

"We've been married for thousands of years. Don't you think we could have talked about it instead?"

Silence

"Hello?"

"We'd become so accustomed to it," said Bandah

"So accustomed to what?"

"To talking about it. We both knew what to say to every question, every thought or reaction."

A tear formed in Talia's eye. "I like to think that we respected each other enough that we were always honest in our responses."

"I wanted to think that too, but it felt like we became so close that we were losing what brought us together… that desire to want to know each other better…"

"So, you thought leaving me without saying a word would help?"

Bandah looked away from her. "You don't understand."

"No, I don't."

They continued patching Jimmy O'Sullivan back together in silence.

•

Kerridwen refilled the Reverend's wine as she spoke. "When we get there, they'll be so pleased to see you."

The Reverend ate a piece of a phelare then picked up the replenished goblet. "Who is it that you're talking about?"

Kerridwen said, "The witches who tried to stop you coming here."

Albiorix threw an arm around the Reverend's shoulders. "You need to jog your memory, Alfred. They were like family to you."

"Be that as it may, I don't remember them."

Kerridwen reached across in front of her father and placed a reassuring hand on the Reverend's wrist. "It's okay, Alfred. It's normal to lose memories when preparing for a garland. I'm just glad that you're past the mood swings and the anger. You had me worried."

The hunter was wise to choose you.

"The voices of my disciples, they seem to help dispel the confusion. I just wish I could remember more."

Kerridwen's voice was soothing. "Do you remember the witches dancing in the circle of stones in your dream?"

"Aye."

"The witches who would betray you, who tried to keep you from coming here, they appear the same as their ancestors. You will recognise them from your dream. It's crucial, Alfred. You cannot trust them, especially not the one who calls herself Neridah. You need to prepare to protect yourself from their deceptions."

Albiorix held up his goblet, spilling wine across the table as he raised it to the sky. "But first, we will feast! Soon, you and my daughter will return to your world, and that is as good a reason as any I've known to celebrate!"

The Reverend ate hungrily from the fresh bowl of fruit placed before him to replace the one he'd already finished.

Kerridwen whispered in her father's ear, "I'm not sure now that I want this."

Albiorix raised an eyebrow as he turned to his daughter.

"Oh, Father! Why do you never understand me? You may like his world, but I hate it. Now, I have to go back there with someone I absolutely detest and pretend to care about both him and the people of his loathsome world?" She looked across to make sure the Reverend wasn't aware of their discussion. The juice of the phelare was doing its job, reducing the Reverend's anxiety and rendering him unaware of most of what was taking place around him. Meanwhile, his chosen twelve worked through his mind, shielding his consciousness from memories that might create conflict with the desired outcome of their true masters. There was spite in Kerridwen's words as she whispered, "This is all because of your petty vendetta against that pitiful bunch of witches."

Albiorix whispered back, "You forget our purpose. Aren't you fed up with having to kowtow to the whims of the gods we serve? Don't you want to see your own father become a god, and maybe even become one yourself?"

"Why can't I just go back and kill off those stupid witches before we send the priest back? With them out of the way, we could rely on the garland to guide him, and I could stay here, where life is more civilised."

"No, I want the witches kept alive till I return, so I can have the joy of banishing them to a place where I know they'll suffer for eternity." Albiorix placed a hand on his daughter's knee. "As for the priest, don't worry, my little dove. Once his role is fulfilled, you can discard him any way you wish."

*

Neridah held the Reverend's box and wondered what special treasure was concealed by its puzzle lock. Although she had no idea what it contained, she felt sure that it was important that they take it with them if they were to have any hope of bringing Alfred back.

"Nana-Neri, are you ready?"

"Yes, of course."

Patsy reached into the fire and, in one sweeping action, grabbed a handful of flame and threw it into the air. They watched the pixie-dust dance about the room for a few seconds then Patsy said, "I've got an idea. Let's close our eyes and allow ourselves to follow the dust this time. Maybe it'll be quicker."

Meredith said, "That's an interesting idea. I'm happy to give it a try." She looked across at her mother.

Neridah tucked the box under her arm and nodded agreement. The three witches held hands and closed their eyes. A moment later, they could feel the wind against their faces. They opened their eyes and watched the trees rushing past as they flew through the air behind the ball of pixie-dust, tumbling and turning as they went.

"Woo-hoo!" An enormous grin spread across Patsy's face. "This is so much easier than swimming through the air."

Meredith spread her arms out, imagining how a bird might feel. "We'll have to learn more about pixie-dust the next time we consult the Book of Wisdom."

Neridah pointed ahead. "Look, we're almost there." They could see a few soldiers gathered near the entrance to the pathway. "Let's walk the rest of the way."

Their momentum made them roll and tumble as they dropped to the ground and the pixie-dust vanished. Neridah pulled her hair back from her eyes. "So much for the clean clothes."

Meredith got up and brushed herself off. "At least they're still dry."

Patsy walked to the edge of the pathway. The rain beyond the portal to the paddock had eased to a fine drizzle. "The soldiers, they can't hear or see us." She turned to the others. "Do you think we might be able to sneak down to the portal without them seeing us once we've left the pathway?"

Neridah said, "It's worth a try. If we can keep ourselves mostly concealed by the tree line, we might pull it off."

Meredith put a hand on her daughter's shoulder. "I'm relieved you're not wanting to go out there and face them head-on."

Patsy looked up at her mother. "We need to save our energy. We're going to need it when we get to Dellakaran."

"I'm proud of you, you're learning."

Neridah looked up toward the house. "Oh, oh. This isn't good."

Lieutenant Stewart was leading Cook down the paddock with a gun pointed at her temple. He was halfway to the bottom when he yelled out, "HEY! WITCHES! I don't know where you are, but I'm sure you can hear me." His voice echoed through the valley. "You have one hour to show yourselves, or the servant dies, and it'll be on your conscience, not mine. Do you hear me, witches? I SAID, DO YOU HEAR ME! ONE HOUR!" Cook stood trembling with her hands on her head.

Neridah turned to the others. "We have to go, now!"

The three of them lifted the hems of their skirts and started toward the creek. Patsy asked her mother, "Do you think we can do this in an hour?"

Meredith replied, "We don't have a choice, we'll just have to."

"But, shouldn't we do something to rescue Cook before we cross over? We promised Mr Donaldson."

Neridah said, "Not while there's someone holding a gun at her head in the middle of the paddock."

Patsy came to a stop. "No. I'm not running." She disappeared, then, a moment later, reappeared a few paces behind the Lieutenant. She reached forward then pulled back, ripping the pistol out of the Lieutenant's hands.

He turned to face Patsy. "Do you think you've saved her?" He sneered. "You've just sealed her fate."

"I don't think so." She closed her eyes and reached into the Crossworlds with both hands to draw power. Glowing balls of energy grew around them.

She was ready to unleash the energy when she was knocked to the ground. She looked up and saw the Lieutenant. "Did you seriously expect that I'd sit there and just wait idly by while you drew up the energy to kill me? You really are quite stupid." He pulled back his fist then felt Meredith and Neridah shift.

"Not as stupid as some." Meredith's arm went forward, hurling a ball of energy at the Lieutenant, closely followed by one from her mother. He managed to evade the first but was hit square in the chest by the second. It pushed him onto his back. As he lay there winded, Patsy sprang up and lurched across his chest, ripping out the Nasqa in one smooth motion. She threw it aside and called to her mother, "Time freeze!"

Meredith lifted her arms and pointed them toward where Patsy had hurled the Nasqa. "Ka dae marsie karn, com-ba swa-ba keb vog." She turned to her daughter. "That won't hold it for long."

"But it'll give us a chance to make a start."

Neridah helped Lieutenant Stewart to his feet. He rubbed his eyes. "None of this could possibly be happening. The past year of my life…

it's a nightmare."

Neridah helped him down the paddock to where Patsy and Meredith were gathering around Cook. "Trust me, it's all real. And the time freeze my daughter captured that thing in will last a minute at most. We need to get you out of here, or it'll try to take you back. If it follows you when you leave here, you must shut it out. Do you understand?"

He nodded. "What would you have me do now?"

Meredith said, "You need to get Cook to safety, then do what you can to help the others who are already riding to Springwood to try and stop my husband being sent to the gallows."

"Yes, of course. What of the other servant, the one still held in the drawing room?"

"We'll look after her."

Patsy looked at her mother. "Mr Donaldson, he left his sulky at the side of the road near the entrance to the property. Maybe it's still there."

Neridah said, "Good thinking." She looked over her shoulder and saw the shadow within the time freeze was starting to show subtle signs of movement returning. "We need to go, now."

The three witches created a circle around Cook and the Lieutenant. They held hands, closed their eyes, and allowed themselves to be at the sulky.

*

The Nasqa that had possessed Lieutenant Stewart slipped out of the time freeze. It was too late to go after the witches, and it was powerless without a host body to control. It drifted up to the homestead in search of a possible new vessel.

Mrs Banks shivered as the cold shadow swirled around her. She was so petrified that her mind had erected barriers, leaving nowhere for the Nasqa to enter. Anyhow, the thought of inhabiting the body of someone who was so emotionally frail held little appeal. The Nasqa struggled to see how the troops would respect it if it spoke from within such a body. But then what choice did it have? Would it have to lower itself to inhabiting an animal?

The Nasqa drifted about the property, searching every room in the hope there was something it had missed.

It made its way to the servants' quarters. There, in the hallway, it came across the unconscious body of Jimmy O'Sullivan, with the pixies still working their way out of his chest wound.

The Nasqa watched as the pixies pulled the flesh of the stablehand's chest together. The moment the last of the wound was sealed, it flew into Jimmy's head, snapping him out of his induced coma and slapping the Irishman's hand to his chest.

Bandah and Talia were caught by surprise, the big hand leaving them breathless as it squeezed down on them. They looked up at the sinister grin spreading across Jimmy's face.

"Hah, I always wanted to catch me a pixie or two."

Bandah struggled to get air as he protested. "You can't do this to him. It's too soon. His body needs time to heal properly."

Talia followed up with a desperate plea. "You'll kill him."

Jimmy shrugged his shoulders. "What do I care? It'll do for now." Jimmy got to his feet. "Now, where would I find a nice, big jar, I wonder?"

*

Lieutenant Neil Stewart helped Cook into the sulky then turned to the three witches. "Thank you, for everything. I wish you luck."

Meredith spoke for the three of them. "And we wish you luck as well. You'll need every bit you can get."

"I'll see to it that Cook is comfortable at Mr Donaldson's property and then I'll ride with haste to Springwood."

A tear ran down Meredith's cheek as she threw her arms around the Lieutenant and said, "Thank you."

Patsy looked up at him as her mother stepped back. "Please, please bring Father back safely."

He put a reassuring hand on her shoulder. "I'll do everything I possibly can to see justice is served."

The witches held hands and allowed themselves to be at the pool that housed the portal.

*

The Justice Callum Sessions dismounted his horse and tied it to the hitching post outside the Captain's office. He took a handkerchief from his pocket and blew his nose as he stared at the gallows. The wood looked weathered, as though the structure had been there a long time, but the rope was new.

Captain Taylor opened the door to his office and stepped out into the light as the sun struggled to break through the clouds. "Ah, Justice Sessions. I'm so glad you could make it at such short notice."

"It would seem to me from the readiness of the gallows that you've already made up your mind how I'll be ruling in this case."

"The evidence is overwhelming, and the murderer is a dangerous man. Ordinarily, I would have transported him to Sydney for trial, but the risk of him escaping and causing further deaths was too great to ignore."

"I'll be the judge of whether he should be referred to as a murderer."

"Yes, of course." The Captain gestured toward his office. "You must be thirsty after your ride. Can I offer you a brandy?"

The Justice looked the Captain up and down, as though insulted by his very presence. "I never touch the stuff." He surveyed the barracks and asked, "Where will we be holding court?"

Captain Taylor pointed to a stone building across the courtyard. "Over there, in the mess hall."

"And the victim's body?"

"On its way to Sydney for burial."

"Good God, man. How do you expect me to conduct a fair trial if I can't inspect the body?"

"We have the testimony of several soldiers from the Parramatta Lancers who were with me when I took the accused's confession."

The Justice fanned himself with his handkerchief before returning it to his pocket. "Very well then, let's get on with it."

*

When the witches appeared at the pool housing the portal, a dozen soldiers raised their rifles. One of them said, "We've been waiting for you."

Elpheen rose up behind him and covered his eyes. "So have we." The soldier reached up, grabbed the fairy, and tossed her aside.

There were several fairies for every soldier, each of them focused on creating a distraction.

Patsy reached toward a soldier's gun and pulled back, causing it to go hurtling into the pool. Neridah and Meredith followed suit. One weapon after another was made useless as they hit the water. Mrs Smith flew up to Patsy. "You should go and do what you have to. We can't hold them back forever. Elpheen's wings are broken now, and the same will happen to the others. More soldiers will likely come down from the house."

Meredith said, "She's right." She looked up at Mrs Smith. "Thank you."

The three witches joined hands and started chanting as they walked toward the water while the fairies continued to distract their assailants.

Emblae ka pista lu Dellakaran,
Emblae ka pista lu Dellakaran...

The water pushed away from them as they approached, as though each drop was in a hurry to crawl over the others to get away from the approaching witches. A glowing ball of energy formed around them, and their eyes flared in an electric blue dance of raw power.

The soldiers who still held guns fired in desperation but were unable to aim as they were kept blinded by the persistent fairies.

Injured fairies started to pile up on the bank of the creek. Some had broken wings, others broken limbs.

The witches were nearing the centre of the pool. The water had become a swirling vortex around them.

But the soldiers now outnumbered the fairies as they continued throwing them aside. The first one to feel free of them lowered his rifle and took careful aim for the centre of the vortex that now hid the witches. As he squeezed the trigger, Mrs Smith threw herself at his face and bit down hard on the tip of his nose.

Patsy felt the wind from the bullet whistle past her ear before a blinding flash indicated their transition from one world to another.

CHAPTER 18

Neither Cook nor Lieutenant Stewart said a word until they reached the turn-off leading to Vincent Donaldson's property.

Cook pointed to the turn-off and said, "You'll be needing to head up there."

The Lieutenant turned the sulky and chewed on his lower lip as he weighed up what he wanted to say. He had crystal clear memories of what he'd done to Cook while possessed by the Nasqa. After a long and uncomfortable silence, he said, "I'm sorry."

Cook waited as she collected her own thoughts. For the past year, she'd managed to shut out the memories of what had happened before, but it had all come flooding back the moment Lieutenant Stewart and his soldiers arrived. She turned to face him and saw his humanity in the tear that was running down his cheek. "Don't worry yourself... it wasn't you."

Ten minutes later, they arrived at Vincent's property. His stablehand greeted them as they neared the homestead. "Hello, Cook." He looked at the Lieutenant then shifted his gaze back to Cook.

"Don't worry yourself too much, Toby. Mr Donaldson's heading into Springwood on some urgent business. There's trouble at the McIntyres' and Lieutenant Stewart has been good enough to escort me here so that Mr Donaldson can know I'm safe. He is just dropping me here now, for my safety, and will be back with Mr Donaldson either tonight or in the morning."

Toby nodded in acknowledgment, then helped Cook out of the sulky.

The Lieutenant thought that he saw something strange in the movement of Toby's shadow.

*

Albiorix turned when he heard the waters erupt at the centre of the lake. Large waves formed as space was made for the Witches of the Crossworlds to enter Dellakaran. They walked forward with their protective cocoon of energy, the waters parting before them, causing a tidal surge at the shore that pushed water right up to where Albiorix, Kerridwen and Alfred were sharing in their morning feast. The three witches continued walking, unblinking as they fixed their electric blue gazes on the Reverend.

Kerridwen rose to her feet, the daisies from her garland snapping violently in their desperation to break free and deal with the intruders.

Albiorix reached across to restrain her. "No! This is for Alfred to deal with. He is an under-god now, one of us. Let him prove his worth."

Kerridwen's eyes narrowed as she turned to the Reverend who was staring at the table and mumbling incoherently. She nudged his shoulder with her elbow. "Alfred, don't disappoint me."

The Reverend raised his head as though waking from a deep sleep. As the witches approached, he noticed an oddly familiar silky oak box tucked under the arm of one of the women. He looked around at his disciples who were bunched in close to him.

The waters receded as the witches neared the table. The Reverend asked, "Why have you come here?"

The ball of energy around the witches dissipated when they released each other's hands. Neridah stepped forward, extending her arms to present the Reverend with his box. "I bring you a gift. A token of my devotion. It is our hope that in return you will see it in your wisdom to assist us in our search for our friend, Darcy O'Sullivan, that he may join us when we leave Dellakaran."

"I know nothing of your friend, but I must say, this box… it appears familiar."

Kerridwen sneered. "Don't trust her, or anything she has to offer. This is the one they call Neridah, the most deceitful of them all."

Albiorix grabbed his daughter's shoulder. "This is for Alfred to deal with."

Felibrey the Humble stepped in front of the table to stand between the witches and the Reverend. "Be warned, she who has cheated age, I may be but a humble servant to a newly born under-god, but I will defend him to my death, as will the others of his garland. Be aware, we have all lived more than a hundred times longer than yourselves. We have spent our time learning to be strong for those we serve."

Neridah was unmoved. "Be that as it may, I have a gift that symbolises my devotion to the one you would call an under-god. Is it not fitting that I should be the first to present him with such a token?"

The Reverend asked, "Why? Why is it fitting?"

"Perhaps, when you inspect the gift, you will find out."

Kerridwen snapped, "Alfred! This is ridiculous!"

The Reverend turned to her. There was something in her spite toward this woman that made him angry. "Quiet, woman! As your father said, this is my business to deal with." He took a moment to compose himself, then addressed Felibrey. "Step aside, that the witch can come forward and present me with her supposed gift of devotion."

Felibrey looked to the other disciples. They moved away from the Reverend and walked down to create a semi-circle around the witches to block their retreat. Felibrey stepped back to join the others and bowed as he said, "As you wish, oh Chosen One."

Neridah stepped up to the table and handed the puzzle-box to the Reverend.

He stared deep into her eyes as he accepted the gift. There was a sensation he felt in his stomach that defied description when their hands briefly touched. She stepped back, looked to the ground, and burst into tears.

The Reverend was oblivious to her as he turned the box over in his hands. There were scorch marks on its surface, exactly where he expected them to be. He pushed back on the right-hand panel, down on the back, then slid the top to the left. The lid lifted slightly of its own accord. He glanced down at Neridah, who had now fallen to her knees as she continued crying. Meredith and Patsy had gathered around and embraced her to try to console the woman's anguish. The Reverend felt anxiety wash over him as he looked down at the box and lifted the lid.

•

Mrs Smith groaned in agony as she was tossed onto the sandstone rock with the other fairies. The exploding pain in her ankle told her it must be broken. She had no feeling at all in her wings or left arm. Elpheen glanced across at her. "We should never have given up our wands when we came here."

"What wands? You didn't have wands when you came here. Surely, you'd remember that? It was Sellemae who took them from you, not the McIntyres."

Elpheen had a minor convulsion, coughing and spluttering bile down the side of her mouth.

Mrs Smith asked, "How badly are you hurt?"

"I can't feel anything from the neck down."

Mrs Smith found herself thinking how insignificant her own injuries were.

"Hey, Smith. Do you think we've repaid our debt to the humans now?"

"Aye, I think we have."

"Good." Again, Elpheen found herself convulsing. Once she'd settled, she said, "The way I see it, they owe us now."

"Well, that's good to hear." It was Jimmy O'Sullivan's voice. He leaned down so he was at eye level with the wounded fairies. "I think I can help you get back some of what they owe you." He placed a jar on the rock. Bandah and Talia held their hands against the glass as they looked out at the fairies. Jimmy smiled. "And, I think I can help you with mending your wounds."

On the other side of the creek, Eldah, the one fairy to avoid injury and capture, watched through the bushes. "Please, Elpheen, please don't sell us out," she whispered.

Elpheen coughed and spluttered some more, then took a few deep breaths. She turned her eyes up toward Jimmy. "If you can help us, we'll help you."

Mrs Smith looked at Elpheen. "That's not what I meant when I agreed our debt was paid."

Elpheen coughed again before replying, "Hey, I can't move, and I can barely breathe. This is about survival."

Mrs Smith frowned at her. "Then tell me, what was this for?"

"To free us from the burden of our debt."

*

The Reverend Alfred Casey looked down into the box, the one thing he'd felt the need to rescue from the charred remains of his house at Pulpit's Hill.

There were letters.

Dozens of letters, all carefully stored in the envelopes they were delivered in.

Each one treated as an individual treasure.

He pulled one from the stack at random.

> *Dearest Alfred,*
>
> *This is, without doubt, the most difficult letter I have ever written, and probably ever will.*
>
> *My father has found a suitor whom he believes is appropriate for me to marry. I do not love him. I don't even care for him. But, I am with child, and as such, I must be wed before it becomes obvious and brings shame on the family.*
>
> *I wish with all my heart there was another way. But it is not my choice to make.*
>
> *Maybe, in a future time, people who love each other will be free to make their own choices.*

It still grieves me that Father banished you from my life. You are, and forever will be, the only man I've loved.

I just pray that you will one day meet someone and find the happiness you deserve.

I will forever carry you in my heart,

Neridah.

Tears welled up in his eyes, blurring his vision. He wiped them away before looking over the top of the letter and down at Neridah. She pushed Patsy and Meredith away as she rose to her feet and moved forward, toward the man she loved. The Reverend gazed into her eyes. "How is it that I'd somehow let the madness of this world steal away the memories of all in this life that has ever mattered to me?" He put down the letter. "You will always be the most powerful magic in my life."

Kerridwen slammed her fists on the table. "NO!" She glared at Neridah. Her daisies were breaking away from her garland and snapping in Neridah's direction before withdrawing. They were anxious to be set free to attack those who would invade Dellakaran.

Albiorix turned to the Reverend. "See the power of devotion, Alfred?" He gestured toward Neridah. "This woman has travelled across worlds because of her devotion. And that is where the true power she gives you comes from."

The Reverend replied, "These analyses you make are nothing but an illusion. You twist everything that you or others experience to suit your purposes. You and your daughter delude yourselves when you suggest you have a mastery of magical powers. You are merely masters of the deception of others... and of yourselves."

Albiorix rose to his feet, sending the table, and all that was on it, flying forward. The witches were forced to duck, lest they be hit by flying trays, platters, and foodstuffs. "How dare you!" Albiorix appeared to be three times the Reverend's height. "You will do as I command!"

The Reverend looked up at the towering figure. The daisies in Albiorix's garland were now as agitated as those in Kerridwen's. The Reverend's reply was soft and filled with humility. "No, I won't." He turned back to Neridah.

Kerridwen sneered at him. "Then, you will watch as your pitiful witches die!" She turned to Alfred's disciples. "Don't let any of them flee." She glared at Patsy. "We'll start with this irritable little pest."

Patsy's eyes narrowed as she prepared to defend herself. She reached back and drew power from across a hundred worlds.

Burning with resentment at the memory of Patsy humiliating her by the creek, Kerridwen threw her right arm forward. "I owe you this one." A bolt of lightning flew out from her hand. It hit Patsy square in her chest and sent her flying back at least twenty paces. Kerridwen prepared to follow through with her other arm.

Seeing what Kerridwen was doing, Meredith lunged forward in a reflex to protect her daughter. She hurled a ball of energy at the hunter. Its impact was minimal, but still enough to break Kerridwen's momentum. Kerridwen turned her attention to Meredith and screamed at the daisies in her garland, "Attack them, my pets! Show no mercy! Tear them apart and scatter their remains through the void."

The daisies broke free from Kerridwen's garland, growing in size as their razor-sharp teeth snapped again and again. It was as though the snapping motion was how they propelled, or rather dragged, themselves through the air.

The Reverend reached up at the nearest daisy, grabbing it from behind and pulling it from the air. He threw it to the ground, brought his foot down hard, and crushed it. A shrill scream rang out that drew

Albiorix's ire. "You could have one day been a god! Now I will crush you as you have crushed my daughter's disciple. Then my garland's souls will devour your remains."

"You talk too much." The Reverend pushed his hand toward Albiorix's face, hitting him in the jaw with a burst of energy. The under-god stumbled backward while the Reverend swung his other arm around, releasing another burst that hit Albiorix square in the back. The Reverend called out, "Hah," mimicking Albiorix. The under-god fell forward and landed face first among the scattered paraphernalia from the breakfast table. One of Kerridwen's daisies closed in on the Reverend. It was about to snap down on his shoulder when it was snatched from behind. Bordauex the Learned pulled it back and tore the creature in two, causing another scream to ring out.

He turned to the Reverend. "I chose to follow you to the end. The only wise thing the hunter has done was to choose you."

Kerridwen looked at the Reverend's disciple and said, "You idiot." She pushed a hand forward, sending a bolt of energy toward Bordauex that knocked him to the ground. She pulled her arm back to prepare for another attack but felt a hand grip it tight. She turned and saw Felibrey.

The disciple turned to the Reverend. "Leave now." He grabbed hold of Kerridwen's other arm. "We'll distract them as long as we can."

"What of your own well-being?" replied the Reverend.

Kerridwen was struggling to break free. But Felibrey's grip was strong. "We swore an oath to protect you to the death. The hunter was wise to choose you."

Kerridwen vanished.

Felibrey continued, "And you were wise to choose us."

Albiorix rose to his feet. His voice roared across the landscape. "Disciples of Dellakaran, I call on you all to defend our realm." Disciples wearing garlands began appearing around Albiorix.

Kerridwen reappeared behind Felibrey. He looked at the Reverend and said, "You need to go."

Kerridwen struck Felibrey in the back, causing him to lurch forward in pain. The Reverend thrust a hand toward Kerridwen and again she disappeared.

Meredith called out, "Patricia!"

The Reverend turned and saw a daisy preparing to bite down on Patsy's face as she struggled to sit up. It was too close for the Reverend to stop it, but he drew his arm back anyway. The daisy's jaws were open wide as it positioned itself. Then a shrill scream rang out as it was bitten from behind by another of the daisies.

"Darcy?" the Reverend whispered.

The battle intensified.

Meredith saw Albiorix prepare to thrust his hand toward her. She reached for a gleaming silver tray that had come from the upturned table and held it in front of her as a protective shield. The power unleashed when Albiorix extended his arm pushed her to the ground, but the bulk of it was reflected by the tray's shining surface. It scattered in several directions and knocked down one of Albiorix's followers who'd been racing toward her with a knife.

Kerridwen was walking slowly toward Patsy, drawing her arm back. Her hand glowed with the lightning that danced around it. She addressed her remaining daisies, "Leave the girl to me and don't fret about your wayward brother, Darcy. I'll replace him with a more worthy follower when we're through."

Neridah swung a wine jug and smashed it into a daisy that was descending upon her, sending it flying as it squealed in pain. She thrust her arm forward and hit another that was approaching Meredith.

The Reverend's disciples were doing their best to distract the other daisies, hurling whatever items they could find at them. The Reverend ran to Patsy's aid but was stopped by one of Albiorix's minions who appeared next to him and tackled him to the ground. He quickly rose to his feet again, drew back his arm, and summoned power, but was brought down again by another minion who'd appeared from nowhere.

Neridah watched from the distance as Kerridwen prepared to unleash the crackling energy she'd called up. There was no other choice. She closed her eyes and allowed herself to be between Kerridwen and Patsy, taking the full force of the blinding surge of power unleashed when Kerridwen's arm went forward.

The world stood still for the Reverend as he watched Neridah fall. The blood pulsing through his temples seemed deafening as he cried out, "No!"

Patsy sat bolt upright. "Nana-Neri!"

Meredith turned her attention from a ring of attackers that had her surrounded. "Mother!"

Patsy was brought back to the reality of the battle when Kerridwen laughed at her. "Your precious Nana-Neri is finished, as will you be soon." Again, Kerridwen drew her arm back with dancing lightning building around her hand.

Patsy rose to her feet wearing an expression of grim determination. She held her hands in front of her, burning energy coalescing between them and building a dazzling ball of light in the centre that blazed as bright as a sun. "You really shouldn't make me angry," she said.

Kerridwen shielded her eyes with her left hand as she thrust forward with her right. Patsy pushed both hands forward to release her miniature sun. A deafening crack of thunder drew the attention of everyone as the two energy sources collided. Patsy's sun had the greater momentum.

It flared so bright that all who watched were forced to cover their eyes. Kerridwen began backing away as it approached. She threw her arms forward again, releasing more lightning bolts, but they did little to hinder the burning ball of light's progression toward her.

Albiorix thrust an arm at the miniature sun, sending forth a power surge that caused the ball to explode. Everyone, Albiorix included, was knocked off their feet and sent backwards.

Everyone except Patsy.

She maintained the stance that she'd struck when defiantly bracing herself against the power of the blast. She called to her mother, "The garland!" She pointed to Albiorix. "We need to attack his garland."

Albiorix rose to his feet. "How dare you! You should be grovelling at my feet, begging forgiveness."

Patsy said, "I think not." She disappeared and reappeared a few paces behind Albiorix. She was about to thrust her arm forward when Kerridwen appeared in front of her, thrusting out her hand and hitting Patsy with a bolt of lightning from her outstretched hand.

Patsy flew back and hit the ground. Kerridwen looked down on her and prepared to make another strike when Meredith appeared between them, pushing her tray forward to intercept the blast. The tray reflected the lightning back at the hunter, forcing her to stumble and almost knocking her to the ground.

The Reverend reached the spot where Neridah lay. He felt for a pulse, but there was nothing. He turned and extended his arm toward Albiorix, hitting him in the shoulder. The under-god looked at where he'd been hit and laughed. "You'll have to do better than that, Alfred." He leaped up and started running through the air toward the Reverend, large blocks of earth appearing under each footfall. Again and again, the Reverend thrust forward, each blast of energy hitting its mark but making little if any impact on the approaching figure.

The Reverend's disciples continued to battle the daisies of Kerridwen's garland, but almost all were now surrounded by the under-god's followers.

Patsy said to her mother. "We need to stop Albiorix."

In the split second that Meredith was distracted by her daughter, Kerridwen unleashed a bolt of energy that knocked her to the ground. She turned to face Patsy again, but the girl was gone.

Patsy struggled to balance when she appeared on Albiorix's shoulders. She lost her footing and slipped down his back. Hooking an arm around his neck, she tilted her head back as far as she could to avoid his snapping daisies.

Albiorix grabbed the arm she'd placed around him and pulled her up. He held her high, ready to hurl her to the ground. "You dare to touch me? Foolish—"

His mouth hung open in disbelief. With her free hand, Patsy had ripped the garland from his head. The daisies were attacking her hand and wrist, but she held tight, grimacing in pain with each snap from the daisies' jaws. Unlike Kerridwen's garland, none of the daisies had been prepared to leave the all-important garland that held Dellakaran together. Patsy swung her arm and hurled it as far as she could. It landed just where she'd intended it to... at the Reverend's feet. He looked at the fear in Albiorix's eyes as he stomped down hard on one of the daisies. The most ear-piercing screech any of them had heard rang out, and the ground beneath them began to rumble. Shocked by what he was witnessing, Albiorix let go of Patsy's arm. Her ankle twisted when she hit the ground. When she tried to get up, it collapsed beneath her.

Kerridwen stared in shock at her father, distressed that he seemed to have given up.

She failed to notice Meredith had disappeared, reappearing the next instant next to Patsy. They held hands then both closed their eyes and allowed themselves to be next to the Reverend.

Felibrey ran up to the Reverend as he stomped on another of the daisies. "You and your witches really must go now. Go to the lake, and you'll get safely back to your world as this illusion decays." As a second screech rang out, rocks and trees exploded.

"Aye, it's time we go." The Reverend carefully picked up Neridah's limp form. Meredith had an arm around Patsy's shoulder as the girl supported herself on one foot. They were about to allow themselves to be in the middle of the lake when Patsy was distracted by an urgent meowing and the feel of a cat rubbing against her shins.

"Ferdinand!" She reached down with her free arm and picked up the cat. "We can't leave you behind."

The Reverend glared at the cat. "You don't want to be taking that thing back with you."

The cat snuggled into Patsy's shoulder as she held it tight. "Nonsense. He deserves to be safe as much as the rest of us." The ground was shaking, and huge chunks were exploding into dust.

Albiorix dropped to his knees.

Kerridwen screamed at him as she struggled to balance on the shaking ground. "Father! Do something!" When he ignored her, she called out to her remaining daisies. "Come back to me, my pets!"

Meredith said, "We need to go, now!"

Patsy said, "No, wait." There was a daisy circling around them, trying to resist being pulled back to Kerridwen. "It's Darcy! I just know it is! We need to save him!"

Meredith saw that, unlike the other daisies, this one wasn't snapping. She reached out to snatch it from the air.

Then Kerridwen appeared between them.

The Reverend stamped on another of Albiorix's daisies. Kerridwen covered her ears at the sound it emitted as the creature imprisoned within the flower perished.

The ground beneath them slipped away.

Kerridwen lost her balance and fell backwards.

Meredith reached again for the daisy. Her fingers wrapped around it and she said, "Now."

They closed their eyes and were gone.

CHAPTER 19

Colin's face was covered in bruises. His left eye was blackened and almost fully closed. His jaw was so swollen it was barely possible for him to talk. He shuffled across the courtyard in his handcuffs and leg irons, trying to ignore the presence of the gallows to his right.

Once he'd reached the mess hall, the Justice looked him up and down. "For God's sake, will someone give this poor wretch some water?" The Captain nodded to one of the soldiers who dutifully left the room. "Colin McIntyre, do you understand the charges that have been brought against you today?"

A dry whisper cracked through Colin's parched and swollen lips. "I'm innocent, Your Honour."

"Hmmph! I've heard that before."

The soldier returned with a cup of water he'd filled at the horses' trough. Despite the foul taste, Colin drank thirstily.

The Justice looked over his spectacles toward Captain Taylor. "What evidence do you have?"

"As I told you before, there are several of my men who witnessed his confession."

The Justice looked at Colin then back to the Captain. "We're talking about a man's life here, a man you'd have swinging from those gallows out there before sunset. You'll have to do better than that."

Captain Taylor stepped forward. "Your Honour, this is a man who killed a stipendiary magistrate in cold blood. The Magistrate was acting on orders from the Governor to take possession of Mr McIntyre's land after he'd been found to have defrauded the crown. There is evidence, motive, and guilt."

"In my court, I will decide who is innocent or guilty."

A soldier entered through the back of the room and whispered in the Captain's ear. "Sir, the gravedigger's back. He says he wants to give testimony."

The Captain nodded his approval then turned to the Justice. "Your Honour, it seems another witness has just arrived. The local gravedigger in the area where the accused resides, one Sean O'Malley, a fine and respected member of the community."

"Very well then, have him come in."

Sean O'Malley sauntered into the room. He reeked of every foul smell imaginable, causing each soldier he passed to gag as they tried to hold their breath till he'd passed them by. He smirked when he made eye contact with the Captain. He turned to the Justice and rubbed a hand across his belly, still tender from the impact of the Captain's boot. Well, he was about to kick the Captain back, inflicting an even greater pain. "McIntyre's innocent. The Magistrate died of a heart attack."

Captain Taylor was outraged. "How dare you come in here and—"

The justice banged his wooden gable. "Order! Let the man continue."

O'Malley smiled at the Captain then turned back to face the Justice. "The Captain had the body sent to Sydney knowing that if it were left here while the trial took place, you'd want the body examined and that any doctor worth a pinch of salt would tell it was a heart attack that killed him."

The Justice looked at Colin. "Do you know this man?"

Colin said, "No, I've never seen him before. But he speaks the truth."

"So, Captain Taylor, you say O'Malley's a well-respected member of the community, yet this long-time resident, the defendant, says he's never met the man."

"They're both liars."

"Hogwash! It's my opinion that you are somewhat overzealous in your desire to see this man swing from the gallows."

"The Governor himself considers this man guilty."

"What? While he sits behind his desk in Sydney? If your intent with such comments is to intimidate me, then, may I remind you, I answer to the Legislative Council, not your precious Governor."

"He represents Her Majesty, Queen Victoria!"

"That has no bearing on this man's guilt or innocence under the law." He banged his gable on the table. "Court is adjourned. I shall have a cup of tea while you see if you can provide some decent evidence of this man's guilt."

*

The centre of the lake became a swirling vortex. The witches and the Reverend had no choice but to let themselves be swept along as they slipped down the spiralling funnel of water.

Patsy felt Ferdinand's claws dig into the back of her shoulder as he clung tight.

Meredith couldn't maintain her grip on Patsy but managed to continue holding the daisy they hoped was Darcy.

The Reverend clung to Neridah's limp form. He made sure to keep a hand behind her neck and her head above water, often having his own head submerge for extended periods as a result.

The sky erupted in an explosion of thunder and lightning, the clouds rolling and tumbling as though they too were attempting to escape the dying world of Dellakaran.

The walls of the vortex steepened, creating a turbulent tunnel to darkness.

The Reverend and the witches fell, wind rushing past as they continued to plummet.

Patsy strained to look over her shoulder at where they'd come from and saw only darkness. When she turned her head back to face the wind, she saw the same.

They continued falling. The roar of the water swirling around them made it pointless to attempt communicating with one another.

Then Patsy saw dull, watery light ahead, like being underwater and looking up at the surface, only more distant.

They hit the water and Patsy felt its cold embrace as their momentum pulled them deep below the surface.

*

Justice Callum Sessions was walking back to the mess hall when two horses rode into the barracks. The horses carried a soldier and an older gentleman wearing a full-length coat and broad-rimmed hat, sporting a waxed moustache. Because he was accompanied by a soldier, he rode past the guards at the gate without being questioned.

Vincent looked at the noose swinging in the breeze as it dangled from the gallows.

Once they'd dismounted, Daniel Williams approached the Justice. "Gunner Daniel Williams, at your service, Your Honour."

The Justice looked at the young soldier then across to Captain Taylor. He turned back to Daniel and asked, "Why would you be reporting to me and not your superior officer?"

"Because he's corrupt and would see you condemn an innocent man to be hanged."

Captain Taylor looked at a pair of soldiers he knew were possessed by Nasqa, and thus loyal to him. "Arrest this soldier and clap him in irons. He was under strict orders to remain with Lieutenant Stewart." He looked at Daniel. "You'll be court-martialled for this."

Vincent glared at the Captain with an intensity that was hard to look away from. He put out a hand to stop one of the arresting soldiers from grabbing Daniel. "Now you hold on for just one minute. There's a bigger story to this, and I think you boys know it."

Captain Taylor smiled. Something in his gut told him he held an advantage over this man, that he had a lot more to lose than the Captain this day. "He deserted his post. He'll have ample opportunity to explain why at his court-martial."

Vincent turned to the Justice. "Are you going to just let this happen?"

The Justice shrugged. "It's a military matter. There's nothing I can do in that regard."

"An innocent man's life is at stake."

"Then we'd best get to the mess hall and resume the court proceedings, so you can testify to his innocence."

·

Jimmy wore a cheeky grin as he peered into the jar at Bandah and Talia. "What a shame for you two that pixies have to be on the move to jump between the Crossworlds." He laughed. "I've always wanted to have a pixie as a pet. Now I've got two of you!"

Bandah sat at the bottom of the jar with his head slumped between his knees. Talia stood and started to let fly, telling Jimmy what she thought.

Again, he laughed. "Oh, I'm so sorry. Can't hear you through the glass. Maybe that's because I forgot to put the air holes in. Might be wise to calm down and conserve your air. I've got things to attend to. Don't run away now, will you?"

He stood up and walked away from where the glass sat next to the injured fairies on the large rock downstream from the pool. The soldiers were sitting around, relaxing and soaking up the sun that had broken through the clouds not long before. A couple of them stood by the water's edge skipping stones. "Hey! Snap to it. We don't know when the witches are going to come back through that portal. When they do, we need to be ready."

One of the soldiers turned and asked, "Should we even pay attention to what you've got to say now you're in a civilian body?"

Jimmy walked up to the man and swung his fist, sending him flying onto his back in the pool's shallows with a broken nose. "You can get the pixies to fix that for you after we're done here." He turned and faced the others. "Any more questions or suggestions?"

They shook their heads, grabbed their rifles, and got to their feet.

Then the cicadas started. Jimmy looked around the trees. "Cicadas, at this time of year?" The birds joined in: magpies, bellbirds, whipbirds, and kookaburras.

The soldiers could barely hear Jimmy over the cacophony. "They must be coming."

The cicadas grew louder, starting to sound more like words as the deafening noise reverberated in the soldiers' ears. *They are coming, they are coming...*

With Jimmy and the soldiers focusing their rifles on the centre of the pool, Eldar took the opportunity to come out of hiding, flying across the creek and landing by the jar. She wrapped her knees around the base, to keep it steady, with her arms around the lid. Satisfied that she had a good grip, she tensed the muscles in her arms and shoulders, putting everything she had into trying to twist the lid. It was no good. She relaxed, took a breath, then clenched her teeth as she tried again. Still no good. She looked at her broken and injured sisters lying on the rock. If she was going to have any chance of getting them to safety, she'd just have to get the pixies out first.

Inside the jar, the pixies watched. Talia said, "She'll never do it. She doesn't have the strength."

Bandah got to his feet. "I've got an idea. What if she pushes the jar off the rock, letting it break when it falls. If we huddle together in a ball, we can use our wings as shields to protect us when the glass breaks."

Talia smiled. "And again, I like your thinking." She tapped on the glass to get Eldar's attention, then they started gesturing with their hands, as though playing charades, to communicate their idea.

Eldar smiled once she understood what they were suggesting. She braced herself behind the jar and rocked it back and forth while indicating with her fingers that she would do it three times then push it all the way. Bandah and Talia embraced each other and covered themselves as much as they could with their wings. They felt a moment of free-fall when the jar toppled over, then had the wind knocked out of them when it hit the ground and shattered.

In the instant before the jar hit the ground, the cicadas and the birds stopped. Jimmy and his soldiers turned as one at the sound of the jar shattering. He raised his rifle and aimed at Eldar.

His finger was about to squeeze the trigger when the water at the pool's centre erupted. An impossible wall of water, holding more than what the whole pool contained, rushed from the pool's centre to the shoreline. The soldiers turned to flee, some of them casting their guns aside in panic. It was to no avail. The wave crashed over them, knocking them to ground and sending them tumbling against rocks and trees.

The surging water left the centre of the pool dry, revealing the Reverend, the witches, Ferdinand and Darcy. Having broken away from Kerridwen's influence when crossing between worlds, Darcy O'Sullivan had reverted to human form.

They were all hunched over and coughing up water when they heard Jimmy's voice. "Who's first?" He stood in a knee-high muddy torrent that was rushing back down the hill. Still holding his rifle, Jimmy once more prepared to fire.

"Dad!" yelled Darcy as he started toward the shore.

The possessed Jimmy O'Sullivan smiled. He looked at the boy and said, "You'll do," as he squeezed the trigger.

Nothing happened.

The flintlock rifle was waterlogged.

Meredith reached out then pulled back, ripping the gun from his hands. She held her hand low to draw power from the Crossworlds.

"No!" yelled Patsy. She got up and ran toward Jimmy, blood still pouring out from the torn flesh of her left hand. The water running back to the pool knocked her from her feet. With grim determination, she got up and continued.

Jimmy yelled at his soldiers, "Get them." He pointed at Patsy. "She's the danger, stop her!"

Those who didn't have broken bones from the crushing of the wave stood up and ignored him. They'd had enough.

As Patsy approached, two of the soldiers turned to each other and nodded in agreement.

It was time to bring this madness to an end, time to cut their losses.

The only way to do that was to stop the Nasqa possessing Jimmy O'Sullivan… to force him to face his reckoning with the young witch.

They grabbed him and held his arms back.

"No, this is treachery!" Jimmy struggled to break free as Patsy approached. He looked into her eyes and saw emotionless determination.

Throughout the ages, the Nasqa had always feared the under-gods, but never witches or wizards.

But this girl was different.

She was someone to fear.

Patsy stood before him and for a moment did nothing. Then she reached inside and tore the Nasqa from Jimmy's body.

Instead of flinging it into the void or another crossworld, she held it high and addressed the remaining soldiers. "If you agree to leave now, I will let you go back to your own world rather than cast you into the void. But hear this…" She climbed onto a rock so all could see her. "It is on the understanding that you will all vow never to come back and that you will spread the word. For countless centuries my family's bloodline has fulfilled the sacred task of protecting this world from that which would come across worlds to do us harm. We have defeated Sellemae and now, we have defeated the under-gods. Take us on at your peril."

She opened her hand, releasing her grip on the Nasqa. It slipped away, grateful to be still in one piece and not trapped in the void.

The soldiers holding Jimmy's slumped form eased him to the ground while the last of the water ran down the hill, then they collapsed as the Nasqa controlling them departed. The same happened with the other soldiers gathered by the creek.

Darcy O'Sullivan ran up the bank and threw himself to his knees next to his father's unconscious body. He turned to Patsy and asked through his tears, "Will he be alright?"

A small voice behind him said, "He'll be fine. He just needs a day or two to sleep and recover."

Darcy turned. "Who, or should I say what, are you?"

Patsy said, "May I introduce you to Bandah? He's a pixie… and he does a wonderful impersonation of a cockroach when he wants to."

Bandah wanted to respond, but his eyes were drawn to the pain etched across his grundai's face as the Reverend carried Neridah's limp form from the pool, Meredith walking alongside him with her head bowed in sorrow.

The Reverend carried Neridah up the path until he reached a dry section where he could lower her to the ground. Bandah sought to console him while Talia inspected her body. She ran a finger along the side of Neridah's neck then looked up and declared, "There's still life!"

The Reverend raised his eyebrows as hope returned.

Talia reached into Neridah's chest and began massaging her heart, coaxing it to beat again. She looked up at the Reverend. "She needs your heart to help hers."

"How would I do that?"

"Sing to her," said Talia. "Sing from your heart to hers."

"What should I sing?"

"Whatever is deep within you. It doesn't need to be words, and it doesn't need to be heard. Her heart needs to feel yours. She needs to feel your love."

The Reverend took hold of Neridah's hand. He took solace from the lingering feeling of life's warmth in her soft fingers. Looking down at her closed eyes, he marvelled at the simplicity of a beauty that couldn't hide behind scratches, bruises, or any of the other evidence of the battle she'd been through these past hours... a battle she'd fought because of her love for him. If his heart had limbs, he felt it would reach out from within and embrace her.

He let his face hover over hers, inspecting every detail of the face he knew so well.

The only woman he'd ever loved.

He heard a gentle sound that soothed his anguish. It took several seconds before the truth dawned on him. The melody was his own voice, a tune that unfolded of its own volition as he explored the depth of his feelings. It was only then that he realised something had changed. Neridah's hand was gripping his as he was hers. The next instant, Neridah's eyes sprang open. Her chest heaved violently, sending Talia flying back. She sat bolt upright and coughed up copious amounts of water.

Once the coughing subsided, she turned to the Reverend and buried her face in the warmth of his chest, wrapping her arms around him and holding him tight. "You made it. You came back."

"Aye. And it's your doing more than anyone else's. I don't know that anything other than those letters would have been able to break me out of the bewitching spell Kerridwen and Albiorix had me under." He stroked her hair, tilting her head back slightly so she was looking in his eyes. "How did you know the box contained those letters?"

"I didn't. I just trusted that if the box meant enough to you that it was all you had bothered to save from your house, then it must somehow relate to us." She smiled. "I placed my hope in trusting that your love for me was equal to my love for you."

·

"So, Vincent Donaldson, you claim this man to be innocent on the basis of his good character and the assurances of a soldier who is now awaiting court-martial?"

Vincent looked the Justice in the eye. "Absolutely, Your Honour. And I believe the soldier to be innocent as well. The guilty parties here are Captain Taylor and his lackey, Lieutenant Stewart, who he sent to terrorise Mr McIntyre's family."

"Hmmph." The justice looked at the witness, then to the defendant who stood with his head bowed as he struggled to remain standing in his chains, then to the Captain with his bushy sideburns, medals of honour, and full ceremonial uniform. "Captain Taylor, while I see the possibility of the truth in your accusations against this poor soul, you have yet to convince me of his guilt."

A soldier rushed in through the back of the mess hall and approached the Captain. Everyone watched in anticipation when the soldier whispered in the captain's ear. The Captain smiled as he looked up to the Justice. "Your Honour, I have just received word that Lieutenant Stewart has arrived and wishes to give evidence."

The Justice leaned back in his chair. "By all means, send him in."

As soon as Lieutenant Stewart entered the room, Captain Taylor sensed something was wrong. His smile disappeared as the impeccably groomed Lieutenant approached the bench.

The Justice looked at him. "Lieutenant Stewart, do you swear to tell the truth, the whole truth, and nothing but the truth, so help you God?"

"I do, Your Honour."

The Justice gestured toward Colin. "Do you know this man?"

"I have met him only once, Your Honour. Captain Taylor and I encountered him on our way to his property. He was on the road himself, setting out to bring the body of a magistrate, the Justice Albert Johnson, to the barracks, here, at Springwood. He told us the man had died from what he believed to be a heart attack the day before during a meeting at his property. He wanted to be sure that the truth of his death was known and that he could be examined by a doctor to determine the true cause of his death. He was setting out to carry out his duty as all good citizens should."

"Do you believe him innocent?"

"Yes, Your Honour, I do."

The Justice turned to face Captain Taylor. "It would seem to me that the only case you have against this man is your own personal vendetta." He banged his gable. "I declare Colin McIntyre to be innocent of all charges."

Captain Taylor's eyes bulged as he protested. "Your Honour, we were heading to his property for a reason, under the orders of the Governor himself!"

"You will shut your mouth, Captain, or I will hold you in contempt of court. If the Governor has a problem with my release of Mr McIntyre, then he can follow due process under the laws of New South Wales. Case dismissed." He got up from the table and prepared to leave, then stopped and looked at the Captain. "I'll be sending a report of this trial to the Legislative Council and, I can assure you, it will not be favourable to you personally. I would suggest you keep your head low." He turned to Colin. "I believe you to be a good man. The injuries I see upon your body tell me more about the Captain than about you." He then cast his gaze on the Lieutenant. "Will you see that this man reaches his home in safety?"

The Lieutenant nodded. "Absolutely, Your Honour."

The Justice walked to the door then paused in the doorway. He looked over his shoulder. "One more thing, Captain. If I hear of any harm coming to the gravedigger or that soldier you intend to court-martial, I'll personally see to it that you're tried on charges of perjury. Good day, sir."

·

Patsy was sitting on a rock with Bandah inspecting her wounds. Ferdinand sat on her lap purring while Patsy stroked him under the chin with her good hand. Meredith sat next to her and put an arm around her shoulder. "I was so proud of you when you made that speech. You're learning."

Patsy allowed herself a half smile. "I'm still angry with myself about Kerridwen. I trusted her."

"And it's good that you did."

"You didn't. But you pretended you did."

"Yes, but I'd been warned as a child by my grandmother about the under-gods. Despite that, I wanted to be sure before I cast judgment and influenced the opinion of others."

"She played with our minds. She had me convinced... and Father too." Patsy looked down at the cat. "The Reverend says that I shouldn't trust Ferdinand."

"Well, that's your decision to make."

Bandah looked up and asked, "Can I offer an opinion?"

Patsy and her mother looked at each other, then Meredith replied, "Maybe later. With everything else we're dealing with, the last thing I want to worry about is whether or not to trust a cat."

Bandah went back to tending Patsy's wound. He'd never liked the cat.

Meredith looked around at the soldiers. Some were on their feet, but many of them had injuries that prevented them from moving. Their moaning made it feel as though they were in the aftermath of some great military campaign. She looked downstream to the rock where Eldar was doing her best to comfort the wounded fairies. Then, she allowed herself to wonder about Colin's fate. She wanted to believe those who had gone to his rescue had been successful, but it was hard while surrounded by such suffering.

She'd become lost in her thoughts about Colin when her attention was drawn to a soldier coming down the hill with his hands in the air. He was waving a white handkerchief and was followed by another three holding their hands in the air. "We surrender, your surviving servant is free... as we are free from the creatures that stole our minds."

Patsy and Meredith smiled, then hugged each other. Maybe they'd be able to relax now.

Patsy lifted her head from her mother's shoulder. "Did you hear that?"

The cicadas.

Meredith said, "This isn't good."

She is here, she is here...

Neridah walked across to join them, drawing the Reverend behind her by the hand. She looked at Patsy. "I'm glad now that you looked up the spell."

Patsy and Meredith stood up and the three witches held hands in preparation.

The noise of the cicadas rose to a deafening roar, then the pool exploded, every drop within it flying into the surrounding trees. Standing in the centre, shrouded in an electric dance of energy, stood Kerridwen. Her youthful appearance was gone. Rotting flesh dripped from her bones like wax dripping from a candle.

The Reverend leaned in toward the witches and whispered, "Whatever she does, whatever she throws at you, don't fight back."

Kerridwen sneered, "Why would that be, Alfred?" She thrust an arm at one of the injured soldiers, causing him to scream out in pain.

The Reverend continued, "If you attack her, she'll use what's left of her garland to absorb the power. She's weak, too weak to fight you head on."

Kerridwen glared at the Reverend. "How dare you accuse me of weakness." She threw an arm forward, sending a bolt of lightning at him. He flew back ten paces, landing on his back unconscious.

Neridah put her hands to her lips and screamed, "Alfred!"

Kerridwen turned her attention back to the witches. "Come on, take me on."

Patsy said, "The Reverend was right. She needs us to fight. She knows she can't beat us unless she draws from our power."

Kerridwen locked her gaze on Patsy. "You recalcitrant pest! Kneel before me or taste my wrath."

Patsy said, "No."

Kerridwen disappeared and reappeared directly in front of Patsy, then physically pushed back against her with her hand engulfed in the dancing lightning.

Patsy hit the ground laughing. "That didn't even hurt. You used the last of your real power trying to scare us when you hit the Reverend."

She got to her feet. "You probably can't even go back to where you came from now without our help." She smiled. "Which we're more than happy to give." She started chanting. *Kerridwen le cana dis-tarah...*

Kerridwen said, "No, don't... there's nothing left for me there. We can work together. I can give you power beyond your dreams."

"And that's what you don't understand about me. I don't dream of power."

The three witches picked up the chant together: *Kerridwen le cana dis-tarah, Kerridwen le cana dis-tarah...*

It was hard to distinguish between the moment Kerridwen was there, and when she was gone. The witches didn't care one way or the other. All that mattered was that Kerridwen was gone... banished from their world forever.

CHAPTER 20

Neridah couldn't believe it. "You're doing this to me again?"

The Reverend continued packing his saddle bags. "I have a house to rebuild and a church that is my responsibility. It doesn't mean I love you any less."

"How so? You can actually recant your vows, you know. Other priests have done it."

"I believe we've had this discussion before."

"I don't see how you can call it a discussion when you avoid giving a decent answer every time."

The Reverend took a deep breath and looked to the ground as he composed his thoughts. "I followed the path I chose so as to find the strength to rescue you from Sellemae's lair. Without having done that, we wouldn't be sharing this discussion now." He looked into her eyes. "I love you more than I imagine it's possible for any man to love a woman. But I did take those vows, so we have little choice but to content ourselves with sharing what we can of our lives. In all honesty, Neridah, my life would be meaningless without you."

She started crying. "You just don't get it, do you?" She turned away and ran back to the house.

The Reverend looked up as she disappeared inside. He'd have to make a point of coming by to visit more often than he had in the past year. He secured the last of the saddlebags, then mounted Elsa and rode away.

*

The Reverend Alfred Casey could feel a presence as he rode up to his church and the burnt out remains of his home. He dismounted and walked Elsa to her stall in the stables.

A pair of wallabies watched him walk from the stables and up the paddock to the steps of his church.

There was something in there, he could feel it. Something that tried to reach into his mind. The wooden steps creaked under his weight. He put his ear to the door and wrapped his fingers around the handle. He couldn't hear a thing inside.

A magpie warbled in the distance as he pulled down on the handle. He leaned in, the door creaking on rusty hinges as it opened.

His foot echoed through the church as he stepped inside. The silhouettes of twelve heads sat motionless in the front pews.

He walked up to the end of the aisle then turned to face the one who sat closest. "Felibrey?"

Felibrey stood up and held out the Reverend's silky oak box. "We brought this for you. We have seen the power it gives you."

The Reverend took the box. "Thank you." He surveyed the faces of the twelve he'd chosen while his mind was held captive in Dellakaran. "Why are you here?"

Felibrey spoke for them all. "Because the hunter was wise to choose you. We feel privileged to have sworn an oath to serve you."

"But, with the collapse of Dellakaran, would you not have been free to return to your own worlds?"

"We have served in the garlands for many thousands of years. Those we knew in our own worlds have long since passed away. Our worlds have changed, and so have we. They are no longer our homes. In serving you, we found a purpose. You have a wisdom that the under-god did not."

The Reverend felt humbled. "It is I who feels that I should be learning from you."

Bordauex the Learned stood up. "No, we are not teachers. Short though your life has been, you have used it well. We have all learned much from you already. We will follow you, that we may learn more."

Destellie the Devout stood up next to Bordauex. "And we will help you rebuild your home."

The Reverend placed a hand on her shoulder. "Well then, we may need to add a few rooms."

*

Patsy walked down the stairs and heard her parents talking to someone in the sitting room. As Patsy tentatively looked through the door, her mother gestured to her and said, "Patricia, this is Miss Jenkins. She'll be your new tutor as of next week."

Miss Jenkins turned and looked at Patsy. "I'm so looking forward to spending time with you. Are there any subjects that you like more than others?"

Patsy smiled as she took a tentative step into the room. "Do you know much about science?"

"It's my favourite subject… especially when it comes to what's being learned today about physics."

Patsy clapped her hands, giggled, then raced out of the room and down the passage to the kitchen. "Cook, you simply must meet the new tutor. She likes science."

Cook leaned back and looked Patsy up and down. "And what would you be wanting to learn about science for?" She placed a bowl of porridge on the kitchen table where Patsy had taken a seat and continued talking before Patsy had a chance to answer. "A young girl like you should be focused on learning about manners and needlework—things that will help you find a good husband." Patsy smiled, she knew Cook meant well and that there was no point trying to convince her the world was changing, that men and women would one day be seen as equals.

She ate her breakfast then said, "I'm going for a walk in the paddock."

"Okay then. Just make sure you're back in time for lunch."

The pathway to Krinkle-myst's cabin appeared as Patsy approached the bottom of the paddock. As soon as she saw the ball of pixie-dust she closed her eyes and allowed herself to travel the winding pathway through the forest in its sparkling wake. A minute later, she was in the stone cabin. The Book of Wisdom still sat on a table by the fire. Krinkle-myst was sitting in his corner writing on sheets of vellum.

"Hello, Mr Krinkle-myst."

The wood-elf turned and looked at Patsy over the top of his glasses. "Hello, you've had quite an adventure."

"Would you like me to tell you about it?"

"Oh, there's no need for that. I've just about finished writing your story, that others might know of your recent exploits."

"Who would want to know about that?"

"Lots of people, like the one who's reading about our discussion right now."

Patsy looked around. "Can I see them?"

"No, but they can see you."

"How can that be?"

"Never underestimate the power of words and the imagination. Think of all the times you've seen something in your mind's eye that has turned out to be real."

The wood-elf turned back to his manuscript.

Patsy walked over to the fire and warmed her hands. She looked at the Book of Wisdom and asked, "Is it safe for the Book of Wisdom to return to the library now?"

Krinkle-myst sat back and turned to face her with an expression that suggested the answer was obvious. "Of course it is."

"Then, why is it still here?"

"Because it's been waiting."

"For what?"

"Open the book and you might find out."

Patsy turned the key to unlock the book, then opened it to a page in the middle. She turned to face Krinkle-myst. "The page... it's blank!"

Krinkle-myst opened the drawer of his writing desk. He pulled out a bottle of ink and a quill then walked over to Patsy. "Well, I guess the book must be waiting for you to share the wisdom you've learned during your latest escapade."

THE END

www.ingramcontent.com/pod-product-compliance
Lightning Source LLC
Chambersburg PA
CBHW020354120726
47904CB00002B/561